BADLANDS

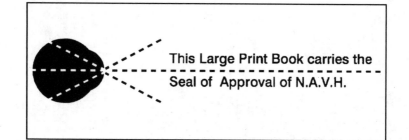

This Large Print Book carries the
Seal of Approval of N.A.V.H.

BADLANDS

C. J. BOX

LARGE PRINT PRESS
A part of Gale, Cengage Learning

GALE
CENGAGE Learning·

Farmington Hills, Mich • San Francisco • New York • Waterville, Maine
Meriden, Conn • Mason, Ohio • Chicago

GALE
CENGAGE Learning®

LIBRARY OF CONGRESS CATALOGING-IN-PUBLICATION DATA

Box, C. J.
    Badlands / C.J. Box. — Large print edition.
      pages cm. — (Wheeler Publishing large print hardcover)
     ISBN 978-1-4104-7744-6 (hardback) — ISBN 1-4104-7744-4 (hardcover)
    1. Policewomen—North Dakota—Fiction. 2. Drug traffic—North Dakota—Fiction. 3. City and town life—North Dakota—Fiction. 4. Large type books.
I. Title.
    PS3552.O87658B335 2015b
    813'.54—dc23   2015022517

ISBN 13: 978-1-4328-3421-0 (pbk.)
ISBN 10: 1-4328-3421-5 (pbk.)

Published in 2016 by arrangement with St. Martin's Press, LLC

Printed in the United States of America
1 2 3 4 5 6 7 20 19 18 17 16

For the good people — old and new —
of North Dakota
. . . and Laurie, always

After nightfall the face of the country seems to alter marvelously, and the clear moonlight only intensifies the change. The river gleams like running quicksilver, and the moonbeams play over the grassy stretches of the plateaus. . . . The Bad Lands seem to be stranger and wilder than ever. . . .

— THEODORE ROOSEVELT,
Hunting Trips of a Ranchman

■ ■ ■ ■

PART ONE:
DAY ONE

2014

■ ■ ■ ■

CHAPTER ONE

Grimstad, North Dakota

Twelve-year-old Kyle Westergaard was halfway through his route delivering the *Grimstad Tribune* when he heard the high whine of car engines out on the highway in the dark. He eased his bike to a stop — never easy with the bulging canvas newspaper panniers hanging down on either side of the front wheel — and squinted south across the dark prairie. There were a lot of hot cars around town these days, and these particular cars were *screaming.* Kyle wanted to see them before they had to slow down to enter the town of Grimstad.

He liked this view from the chalky bluff and he looked forward to it every morning. It was the only thing on his route he looked forward to. His newspaper route was the worst one in town and the farthest one from the *Tribune* dock. It was assigned to him because he was the newest carrier. His mom

11

had said she'd drive him when he signed up for the job and he handed over his signing bonus of $250, but after his first day on the job two weeks ago she'd never been able to get up on time. Instead he pedaled his bike to the *Tribune* and got in line behind the other carriers, most of whom were older and had cars. His route included all the new houses they were building on the south side of town and the homes that got the newspaper were few and far between. Kyle spent a lot of time and effort riding his bike around mounds of dirt, fresh concrete curbs, and piles of lumber and building materials to locate the subscribers. Most of the people who lived in the new part of town were from somewhere else and couldn't care less about local news so they didn't subscribe to the paper yet. At least that's what Alf Pedersen, the old gnome in charge of deliveries, told Kyle at the newspaper building.

Although he had no trouble locating the houses for subscribers — he was good with street numbers and numbers in general — he was still having trouble keeping track of all the special requests. Some people wanted their paper placed inside the storm door, some wanted it on their front porch, and one lady wanted it in her mailbox. He got confused over who wanted what, and he heard about it when the angry customers called Alf to complain about him. Too many had called, Alf said. Kyle's job was on thin ice.

He paused and listened as the car engines got louder. He still couldn't see them. It was unusual to be able to hear them. On most days there was an endless stream of heavy trucks on the highway to Watson City, and the usual traffic noise would have drowned out the sound and impeded the car race.

It was another cold morning in the town of Grimstad in western North Dakota. Condensation billowed around his face and his lungs stung from the cold. Frost clung to the metal frame of his bike and the seat felt like a block of ice. His feet and hands were cold because he'd outgrown his boots over the summer and he couldn't find his gloves that morning. Kyle liked to V his fingers and draw them to his mouth as if holding a cigarette, then exhale breath that looked like smoke. He did it now while he waited. It made him feel sophisticated.

The prairie, as far as he could see, was punctuated by natural gas flares next to oil pumper units. The pumpers had heads like

13

grasshoppers and they bobbed up and down. The flares made what was once grassland look like a big city, although Kyle chose to think of those flames out there as Indian campfires. He liked that idea — that the prairie looked the same as it had when the Sioux and Cheyenne were around.

Between where Kyle was on the bluff and the flares out on the prairie was the Missouri Breaks. The iced-over river steamed in the cold. Kyle had a plan and it involved that big river.

Two sets of headlights blasted out of the darkness to the south on the highway from Watson City. At first, they looked joined together — nose to tail. Then the second car swung alongside the first car and they were neck and neck. The headlights of the outside car were bright white halogens. Kyle thought, It *is* a race!

The two hot cars stayed like that for a quarter of a mile, their engines wrapped up. There was a bang and squeal of tires and the inside car suddenly veered off the road. Kyle could hear the crashing of glass and metal, and the headlights made circle after circle. Something small and white shot through the beam of the rotating headlights and vanished. The car stopped rolling and

Kyle couldn't tell if it was on its wheels or on its roof.

He realized he'd been holding his breath the whole time and exhaled with a *puh* sound.

The driver of the second car on the road below hit the brakes. Kyle saw the car fishtail on the highway before it came to a stop. After a few seconds, it reversed to where the first car had gone off the road.

Kyle turned his front wheel toward the lip of the bluff and pushed off. There was a trail there that would take him to the basin where the crash had occurred. He knew about the trail because he took it home when his route was complete. He didn't even think about what he was doing.

The wrecked car was upside down. Its motor was no longer running but the headlights were still on. Dust swirled through the beams.

Kyle was about fifty yards away from the wreck when he looked up toward the highway and saw that the second car had come back and was now pulled to the near shoulder of the road. The driver's and passenger doors opened at the same time and the dome light came on inside. Two bulky men stepped out. One was bald and the other wore a stocking cap. Kyle was too far away to see their faces, but by the way they moved they looked determined to do something. Kyle heard a shout and couldn't make out the words except for the word "fuck" several times. Something about that word just cut through the air.

He slowed his bike on the trail, not sure whether to proceed to the wreck or wait for the men to hike down to it from the road. Crashed cars always blew up on TV, and Kyle had no idea if that happened in real life. He could smell gasoline fumes from the wreck, and green smoke was now rolling skyward from the undercarriage.

Kyle thought there was someone in that wrecked car who might be hurt or dead. Maybe even more than one person. There was no light from inside the car so he couldn't tell.

He walked his bike back a few feet so he could hide behind a tall, skeletal, Russian olive bush. From there he could see the well-illuminated scene in front of him but he doubted he could be seen himself. As he backed up, his rear tire thumped against something in the trail that stopped his progress. He assumed it was a rock at first but when he pulled on his handlebars for leverage the rear wheel didn't climb over it.

It wasn't a rock because it had some give to it.

Kyle twisted around and looked behind him. He remembered he'd seen something small and white eject from the rolling car. It was bigger than he'd thought, though: a thick bundle of something.

He wasn't sure what to do. Leave it there behind the bush? Or take it?

While he was trying to make up his mind, he looked up and saw the two big men start to walk down toward the wreck. One of them had a flashlight. The beam illuminated the wrecked car and Kyle could see inside briefly for the first time. A man — Kyle guessed it was a man — was partially extended out the driver's side window clawing desperately at the ground like a dog digging a hole. But the poor guy couldn't get out of the wreck because the lower half of his body was pinned between the frame of the car and the crushed roof. The man glistened because the light reflected off the blood and the pieces of glass embedded in his face and hair.

There was a roar of an oncoming vehicle and a sweep of headlights and the flashlight in the field went off. Kyle turned his head toward town and saw a big SUV speeding up the road. The car was coming fast but it would still be several minutes before it got here. Kyle guessed the driver of the SUV had seen the wreck happen and was coming to help whoever was in the rolled car.

He heard that word again from the two men, who had turned on their heels and were climbing back up the ditch toward their car. It took less than a minute for the two men to throw themselves inside, do a three-point turn, and roar back the way they'd come.

Kyle wondered if the driver of the SUV would pursue the fleeing vehicle or stop at the crash. His question was answered when the SUV slowed at the place in the road where the car started rolling. It was easy to find because the earth was churned up.

He winced when bright spotlights bathed the wreck in white. Kyle could see that the driver of the wrecked car was still and was no longer trying to claw his way out. The driver had either passed out or died. Kyle knew the image of that man trying to crawl out of the car would stay in his mind for a long time, like when that Nazi's face melted off in *Raiders of the Lost Ark.* He still had dreams about that. Kyle was sickened by what he'd seen but fascinated at the same time.

A second SUV had now joined the parked

one and suddenly the dark prairie was psychedelic with multicolored lights from the roof of the second SUV. Kyle could now see that both vehicles belonged to cops. Both had Bakken County decals on their doors.

He didn't know what to do so he stayed there on his bike and pushed back a foot or two around the bundle. Watching. Not moving.

Two sheriff's deputies approached the crash with their flashlights. The first one to arrive rounded the rear bumper of the upside-down wreck and shined his light on the driver. The deputy was a big man with a big gut and a handlebar mustache. He limped when he walked.

"Oh man, he's gutted."

"Should we call the ambulance?" the other deputy asked.

"Maybe two — one for each half." The man laughed harshly.

"Anyone else inside?"

"Not that I can see. But I haven't checked around yet to see if anyone was ejected."

"Do you know who he is?"

The flashlight choked down and illuminated the bloody head of the driver. Kyle could see jet-black hair, blood, and winking glass in his scalp.

"Don't know him, but he looks like a Mex. Got a bunch of unattractive neck tattoos."

The second deputy shined his light on the back bumper. "Arizona plates."

" 'Land of Enchantment,' " the first deputy said and he dropped to all fours and shined his light inside the vehicle.

"That's New Mexico. Arizona is 'The Grand Canyon State.' "

"Oh. My mistake." Kyle thought the deputy seemed to be looking for something inside. "I would have guessed he was an Idahole. Either that or a Utard or Washingturd."

"Did you see anything? You seemed to be all over this."

"Yeah," the first deputy said. "I had a speed trap set up on Everett Street so I was watching the highway. Then I saw this guy driving his car like his hair was on fire when he went off the road. I hit the gas and I was the first on the scene. How did *you* get here so fast?" The tone was accusatory.

"I just punched out and was heading home when I saw you peel out. I'm surprised you didn't hit your lights, but I thought I'd head over here to see if you needed a hand."

"Yeah, I appreciate that. I guess I was just so surprised to see the wreck I didn't think about my siren or lights. Don't tell anyone."

The second deputy laughed, and said, "I won't."

The first deputy said, "One car rollover at five thirty in the morning. Want to lay odds on what this guy has in his system?"

Kyle thought, One car? Had the deputy not seen the race with the second car?

"No bet," the second deputy said. He turned away from the first deputy and spoke into a microphone attached to his left shoulder. "This is BCS thirty-two requesting an ambulance for a deceased subject and an evidence tech for a one-car rollover on highway . . ."

While he made the call, the first deputy stood back up at full height and swept his beam across the brown tall grass around the wreck.

Kyle lowered his profile until his chin rested on the top of his handlebars. They didn't know he was there. Should he tell them about the second car? How the second car had two men inside and it had forced the other car off the road? He knew what he should do but something held him back.

Then he pushed his bike out from behind the Russian olive bush until he was in plain sight on the trail. The deputy's flashlight hit Kyle in the eyes and blinded him.

"Stay right where you are, son," the first deputy said. "There's something here you don't want to see."

"Who is that kid?" the second deputy asked after finishing up his request.

"Paperboy."

"What's he doing out here?"

"Delivering papers, I'd guess."

"Ha!"

Kyle stopped and held his hand up against the flashlight to shade his eyes.

"What's your name, boy?" the fat deputy asked.

Kyle didn't answer.

"Ask him if he saw anything," the second deputy said as if Kyle weren't there.

"Look, see his face? He won't be any help."

"What do you mean?"

"Now I recognize him," the first deputy said. "It's the Westergaard boy."

Kyle opened his fingers and peeked through them to see the first deputy gesture by rotating his index finger in a circle around his right ear. The other deputy nodded, then looked back at Kyle with sympathy on his face.

He said, "Poor kid. But at least he's got a

work ethic."

"You would too at that age if the newspaper was offering a signing bonus," the first deputy said with a chuckle. "It ain't like when you and me were kids."

Then, more gently, "Son, turn that bike around. Go finish your route. There might be someone out there stupid enough to want to read the *Grimstad Tribune.*"

The second deputy laughed at that.

Kyle didn't respond, and he clumsily turned his bike around in the trail. He felt the light on his back and saw his long shadow out ahead of him. Then the light went out.

"You want to go meet the ambulance up on the road?" the first deputy asked the second. "I'll keep looking around here in case there's another victim."

Kyle was hurt by that index-finger-in-a-circle thing. Of course, he'd seen it before. But he was even more hurt by that look the second deputy gave him, that look of pity. It wasn't fair, but it somehow made him invisible.

And he was confused by the conversation between the fat older deputy and the younger one. There had been *two* cars. How could the fat deputy not have seen the

23

second car take off?

He stopped at the bundle and lowered his kickstand. After transferring all of the papers from the right pannier into the ink-stained left pannier, he lifted the bundle and dropped it in the empty bag. It felt like there were bags of sand inside. The bundle outweighed the newspapers and would make his bike list, but it wasn't as clumsy as he thought it might be if he stood on the pedals and shifted his weight to the left.

Then he started pedaling back up the trail. The incline would make it hard work but it would also warm him up, he hoped.

He still had a lot of newspapers to deliver before six thirty or angry subscribers would start calling the gnome Alf Pedersen and complaining about him. If he got many more complaints, Alf had said, he would lose the job and have to return the signing bonus. Kyle knew it was already spent, so that wouldn't work. His mom had bought a new HD TV at ALCO with the money.

Kyle's hands were freezing.

And that bundle was *heavy*.

CHAPTER TWO

Wilson, North Carolina

As soon as the airplane door was opened to the exit ramp at the Raleigh-Durham Airport, Investigator Cassie Dewell felt her hair begin to frizz. It was subtle at first, and it reminded her of a self-inflating sleeping pad she'd once seen unfurled in a dome tent on a camping trip in the Crazy Mountains.

And there was nothing she could do about it.

She wore the dark blue suit she reserved for funerals and for testifying in court, a white blouse with a string of fake pearls, and low heels. She'd received a few compliments on the outfit that might have been perfunctory but had cheered her nevertheless. Of course, on the occasions she received the compliments she was back in Montana, not the South, and her hair wasn't frizzing out due to the sudden humidity and looking like an oversized helmet made of fur like it was now.

Cassie stood and retrieved her garment bag from the overhead compartment and a bulging black fabric briefcase that weighed more than her clothes.

Inside the terminal, Cassie stepped aside and let the other passengers proceed in front of her toward baggage claim. They all seemed to be in a hurry. She wasn't, although she'd waited two years for what was about to happen. Two years of scanning the ViCAP and RIMN law-enforcement databases every morning for an arrest or verified sighting. Two years of waiting for her cell phone to ring.

Now that it had finally come to pass, she was having trouble putting one foot in front of the other. Her heart raced and she gasped for air. She knew the locals waiting for her in the terminal would start to wonder if she was ever coming out.

The case file in her briefcase consisted solely of reports, affidavits, and testimony concerning one man: Ronald Pergram, aka the Lizard King.

Within a few hours, she would be face-to-face with him — or someone the locals *thought* was him — in the interrogation room of the Wilson County jail.

■ ■ ■ ■

Cassie was thirty-six years old with short brown hair and large brown eyes. She'd lost twenty pounds twice in two years and gained it right back, plus a few. She was self-conscious about being heavy and thought that her suit felt and looked like a sausage casing.

But she didn't care how she felt or looked if she could help put Pergram in a cage for the rest of his life or, better yet, into the ground. Before she boarded her flight in Helena, she'd Googled "North Carolina death penalty" on her iPhone and was reassured to find out the state had put more than forty-three murderers to death since 1977. She wanted the Lizard King to be number forty-four.

The Lizard King had haunted a large part of her life since he'd been unmasked near Park County, Montana, by her former partner Cody Hoyt. Cody paid for the discovery with his life. At the time, Cody had no idea that Pergram, a long-haul trucker, was a serial killer likely responsible for the disappearances of scores of truck-stop prostitutes known as "lot lizards," or that Pergram had local associates who were involved in the torture and murder of the women. Pergram had also likely abducted victims whose cars had broken down on the highways across the nation. Although entire cars had been unearthed where they'd been buried in a high mountain valley, not a single body had ever been found. Cassie uncovered the associates and shot one of them to death in a highly publicized shoot-out. But the Lizard King himself vanished in his truck.

In his truck. It was still incomprehensible to her as well as members of the FBI's Highway Serial Killers Initiative how Pergram and his massive Peterbilt and trailer had simply disappeared. The only evidence they had that he still might be out there was the increase in the estimate of missing lot lizards, from seven hundred to more than a thousand.

Cassie had never seen Pergram in person, but she'd gathered the few photos she could find of him, including his high school yearbook photo from Livingston High and two commercial driver's license (CDL) head shots. Those photos of a doughy and unremarkable man in his midfifties with wavy ginger hair and sullen eyes had in fact been flashed across television screens throughout the nation. His face, as dull and

28

pedestrian as it was, was the cause of parents' nightmares as well as the working girls who crawled from truck to truck at nights.

That face had been in Cassie's nightmares as well, since it was very likely he had seen her even if she hadn't seen him.

Which was why she'd left her six-year-old son Ben in the care of her mother Isabel and had flown to North Carolina. Her idea had been to review the thick file on the airplane. But when she opened it up, she realized she'd practically memorized every page: every documented missing victim's profile and photo, every newspaper or Internet clipping, and every printed report from the FBI on the twenty to twenty-four suspected serial killers who drove long-haul trucks.

Meeting her in the lobby of the airport near baggage claim were Wilson County Sheriff Eric Ernest Puente, County Prosecutor Leslie Behaunek, and FBI task force liaison Special Agent Craig Rhodine.

They stood in an obvious huddle and were easy to spot. Sheriff Puente was round and short in his uniform, and had an easy smile. Behaunek wore a dark suit similar to Cassie's, although it fit her better. She had dark red hair and was tall and lean with a long, almost horselike face. Agent Rhodine looked like every FBI field agent Cassie had ever met: fit, intense, clean-cut, and dressed in a sports coat, tie, and slacks. He looked ex-military even if he wasn't. Any other time, Cassie would have been a sucker for that look. Not now.

"Are you Investigator Dewell?" the sheriff asked, who stepped out, removed his hat, and extended his hand.

"I am," she said, shaking his hand.

"We're glad you could come on such short notice. And bless your heart, I guess I expected some kind of Montana cowgirl in cowboy boots and a hat," he said in a soft Carolina accent. " 'An Angel with a Lariat,' as k.d. lang once sang. Do you know the song?"

Cassie noticed that Behaunek rolled her eyes in embarrassment at the comment.

"Yes," Cassie said, "I've been known to wear boots. I haven't gotten around to the hat and the rope, though. And I don't know what to tell you about my hair. It's the humidity, I guess."

"You think this is humidity?" The sheriff laughed. "My lord, you should come back in August."

"Our car is outside," Behaunek said after

introductions were made. "It takes an hour to get to Wilson and we can go over everything on the way there."

Agent Rhodine tilted his chin up. "We think we just might have our man."

Cassie nodded grimly.

"There's something we want to show you on the way, Miss Cassie," Sheriff Puente said. Cassie knew "Miss Cassie" was a Southern thing and she overlooked how condescending it came across to one not used to it.

"What's that?"

"His truck."

December in North Carolina was brown and gray but not white. Light rain fell from a close granite sky. The hardwood trees were tall and skeletal and a thick brown carpet of leaves covered the forest floor. The walls of pine were so close to the highway she could see nothing through them. It was like driving through a tunnel, and she wondered how anyone who lived there knew where anything was if they couldn't even see forty feet in any direction. She'd grown up in Montana and was used to big skies and vistas.

Back in Montana, snow was on the ground and had been since October and the mountains were snowcapped.

An FBI agent drove the black SUV with U.S. Government plates and merged onto I-40. Rhodine occupied the passenger seat. Cassie sat next to Sheriff Puente in the second row, and Behaunek sat alone in the back. Upon entering the Ford Expedition, Behaunek opened her briefcase and shuffled through documents.

Rhodine turned and draped his arm over the front seat so he could face her. He smiled as if to reassure her, but she read it as "Aren't I a good-looking man?" He said, "I don't know how much you know but I wanted to brief you on everything before you actually meet him. I know you talked to Sheriff Puente and County Prosecutor Leslie Behaunek yesterday, but I don't know if they stressed what an important role you have to play if we want to hold this guy."

"We did," Behaunek said wearily from the backseat.

Rhodine ignored her. Cassie could already discern the tension that had developed between the locals and the FBI. It wasn't unusual when the feds moved into a local jurisdiction to assist, because "assist" was often defined by the FBI as "take over from the stupid locals."

"Basically," Rhodine said, "law enforcement was first tipped off regarding the subject two days ago by a loading supervisor at a grocery warehouse distributor in Raleigh. The supervisor said he'd posted a full load from Raleigh that needed to get to Virginia Beach the next day. I don't know if you know about the system independent truckers use, do you?"

Cassie said, "Yes, I know about it. When someone needs a truckload of something delivered, they post the contents and the weight on a national computer network that is displayed on screens in most big truck stops. If drivers are close, they'll call the customer and make the deal. It's completely different from trucking companies that haul the same freight for the same companies most of the time."

"Exactly," Rhodine said. "Independent drivers compete with each other for work and they make the deals themselves directly with the distributor. There are no dispatchers or trucking companies doing it for them. We've been thinking for some time that Pergram likely went that route once he vanished. It's easier for a man like that to hide in plain sight if he's not working for any one company. And lord knows, we sent his photo to every trucking company in the country. When we never heard anything, we figured he'd likely gone indie.

"So anyway, this warehouse guy gets a call from a trucker who says his name is Dale Spradley and he's just a couple of hours away. The warehouse guy says he asks Spradley if his truck can handle a full load, and Spradley tells him he just made a delivery and he's got a refrigerated trailer and he's rolling empty at the moment."

Cassie knew truckers referred to those trailers as "reefers," but she didn't interrupt.

"So Spradley shows up and backs up to the delivery dock and the warehouse guys start loading the empty trailer with pallets of frozen food while they work out the paperwork. Just about when they're through with the contracts, a guy notices something odd about the trailer of the truck."

"Odd how?" Cassie asked.

"Sheriff, why don't you tell her the rest?" Rhodine said.

Puente cleared his throat. "We got an old boy named Lightning Bates who works at the warehouse. He's a young fellow, and they call him 'Lightning' because he's anything but. It's kind of mean but he don't seem to mind. Anyway, Lightning is pretty dim but when it comes to patterns and

34

numbers he's kind of a genius. When he was in high school here he went to a swim meet at the brand-new pool and afterwards he told the principal the pool wasn't long enough for the races. Keep in mind they'd just constructed that pool and it cost an arm and a leg of taxpayer money. But Lightning *insisted* it wasn't fifty meters. Finally, they measured it just to shut him up and it turned out to be forty-nine point eight meters. You can imagine how that caused a stink."

"Lightning Bates is an autistic savant," Behaunek said crisply from the back as if to urge Sheriff Puente on with his story.

"Yeah," Puente said, "like that. Anyway, Lightning helped fill that trailer at the warehouse but when they were done and closing it up he was real upset. He told his supervisor they'd just filled a fifty-three-foot standard trailer with a forty-eight-foot load. As you know, a trailer is either forty-eight feet or fifty-three feet. Those are the standard sizes in the trucking industry."

"I'm aware," Cassie said. "I've learned a lot about the ins and outs of trucking. My dad was a trucker. He had a forty-eight footer, too."

She was intrigued. She said, "It takes a very trained eye to tell the difference."

"Unless you're Lightning Bates, I guess," Sheriff Puente noted. He obviously wanted to credit one of his own constituents for what happened next.

"Yes," Rhodine said, "so this Bates and the supervisor discussed the discrepancy after the truck pulled away. They started talking about the alerts they'd received urging everyone to be on the lookout for the Lizard King. That guy has become kind of a legend, even though Spradley didn't exactly fit the description of Ronald Pergram. But the supervisor trusted Lightning Bates, and he thought it was suspicious that a forty-eight-foot load fit perfectly into a fifty-three-foot trailer. That made him wonder why five feet of space inside was unaccounted for. So he called the state police. Spradley was pulled over just inside the Wilson county line by a North Carolina trooper and asked to account for the misunderstanding."

"Hold it," Cassie said, raising her hand. "The police responded because a warehouse supervisor had a suspicion?"

Sheriff Puente said, "The supervisor's on the county commission. Some of them guys like to throw their weight around."

Cassie nodded but didn't approve. She'd had it with local politicians influencing county law enforcement. It was no solace that it occurred in other states.

Rhodine said, "But Spradley made a big mistake. He got belligerent with the trooper and refused to open up his trailer. He claimed his load was frozen — which it was — but said if he opened it up and anything thawed he'd take a financial hit. Spradley said he was being railroaded by a bunch of Southern rednecks and worse."

Cassie nodded. She hated to agree with Spradley, but . . .

"The trooper called in backup, which happened to be the Wilson County Sheriff's Department," Rhodine said.

"My guys," Sheriff Puente said. "This Spradley or whoever he is called them every name in the book. They charged him with noncooperation and threw cuffs on him and hauled him in. By the time he got to county lockup, he was going berserk. We had to pepper spray his fat ass just to calm him down."

Cassie asked the sheriff, "When did you suspect Dale Spradley *was* Ronald Pergram?"

Puente said solemnly, "Not until we opened up that truck just up ahead. That's when we called in the FBI."

As he spoke the words, the SUV slowed down and took an exit to a service road that

37

paralleled the interstate. Through the trees, Cassie saw high chain-link fencing and a weathered sign that read:

MISSING YOUR CAR?
ALL VISITORS MUST CHECK IN AT
THE OFFICE.
WILSON COUNTY IMPOUND LOT.

Then she saw the huge eighteen-wheel truck and trailer on the lot.

She said, "That's not it."

Agent Rhodine's formerly confident face went slack.

"Pergram drove a black Peterbilt Model 379," Cassie said as they approached the big rig. Pallets of once-frozen food were stacked unceremoniously on the asphalt. The smell of rotting meat hung low in the air. Cassie wondered who would cover the loss when something like this happened, but she didn't ask.

The driver slowed to a stop with the shiny grille of the big truck filling the windshield.

Rhodine leapt out, followed by Cassie and Sheriff Puente. Behaunek stayed in the SUV with her files.

Cassie said, "I saw his rig once even though I didn't get a clear look at the driver.

38

But I never forgot the truck. He'd stripped all the chrome off it and had even blackened the exhaust stacks with some kind of heat-resistant paint. It was blacker than black."

She gestured toward the truck in the lot. "This is a newer model Peterbilt 389 with an Ultracab Unibilt. And it's bright yellow. This isn't the truck or trailer I saw."

"No one said it was," Rhodine said through clenched teeth. "No one said he didn't trade his old one in on a newer model."

Cassie paused and looked it over. She'd long speculated that Pergram would stay in his profession but figure out a way to change his identity and his vehicle.

"It may be a new rig," Puente said, "but wait until you see what we found inside."

Cassie approached the open back of the trailer with the two men. An aluminum loading ramp was attached to the back floor of the trailer and sloped down to the asphalt.

Before entering, she looked inside. It was empty and cavernous. The inside walls were scarred from hundreds of skids that had been loaded and unloaded. On the far end of the trailer, on the other side of the wall and out of view, was the refrigerator unit to keep the temperature constant inside.

"Go to the front," Puente said.

"Remember the length discrepancy," Rhodine said in a tone that indicated he'd regained his confidence from learning it wasn't the same truck. "Forty-eight versus fifty-three feet. The outside of this trailer is fifty-three feet on the nose. The inside measures forty-eight."

Their shoes echoed inside the empty trailer and Cassie walked to the front of the trailer. She wondered what it was she was supposed to see. The front wall was made of sheet steel and scarred like the sidewalls. Mounted at eye level across the length of the front panel were a series of ringbolts. She knew they were used to secure netting over the top of cargo that might shift or fall. She pulled and twisted each one in turn. Nothing happened. She knocked. The wall seemed solid. With that in mind, she turned to the sheriff and Rhodine and said, "So?"

Sheriff Puente waggled his eyebrows in a gesture that suggested she look again. She got it. It wasn't until she bent stiffly in her too-tight suit on the right side of the wall that she saw the nearly hidden hinges.

"There's a room here," she whispered.

"And we finally figured how to get it open," Puente said, squatting clumsily to his haunches with a grunt. On the bottom of the sidewall, nearly flush with the floor, was an aluminum slide-out panel. When he opened the panel there was a single red button.

"Watch this, Miss Cassie," he said, and pressed it. She was starting to like being called Miss Cassie.

There was a muffled click on the left side of the wall. Rhodine stepped around her and grasped one of the ringbolts and pulled.

She stepped back so the front wall wouldn't hit her as it opened.

Behind the wall was an eight-foot-by-five-foot compartment lined with polished stainless-steel siding. It was lit inside by bright fluorescent tubes on the ceiling triggered on by the open door. A sheet metal conduit from the outside refrigeration unit stretched across the top of the room into the cargo area and there was a small adjustable vent on the bottom of it. This way, she thought with a chill, he could keep both his cargo and his victim cold. A steel-framed cot was bolted to the floor. Ringbolts were secured to the walls. Beneath the cot was a round stainless-steel drain.

Cassie felt a chill shoot through her, and for a moment she almost reached out to steady herself on Puente. He noticed and grasped her hand to steady her. "Bless your heart, Miss Cassie," he said softly, "But it

41

looks like your man took his show on the road."

"Obviously," Rhodine said, "you can't touch anything."

She swallowed hard and gently withdrew her hand from Sheriff Puente's grasp. She appreciated his gesture, though.

"Have your evidence techs been through it?" she asked, wondering how many women had been in the secret room. Dozens? Hundreds? She couldn't take her eyes off the drain.

"Nothing so far," Rhodine said. "No hair, no fiber, no fingerprints, no DNA."

"Nothing?" she echoed. "What about the drain?"

"We've swabbed it inside and out," Rhodine said wearily. "We haven't found *anything*. This monster is thorough and he really thought this out. All he needed to do was wash it down with a high-pressure hose or steam cleaner. No doubt, he blasted the bottom of the drain under the truck as part of his routine. There's nothing inside that room for any evidence or fluids to cling to."

Cassie shook her head. "In Montana, he was known as a knife man. Did you find weapons?"

"Sure, plenty of them," Rhodine said with a sigh. "Butcher knives, filet knives, even a bone saw — the kind big game hunters use in the field. Plus a Taser and a dozen zip ties."

Cassie looked over and arched her eyebrows as if to say, Isn't that enough?

"Clean," Rhodine said. "Everything is meticulously clean. And it isn't illegal to have a Taser. Anyone can buy one over the Internet."

"Frustrating," Cassie said. But her anger was starting to build up. "You guys have the best forensic technology in the world and you can't come up with anything that will stick to him?"

"We're waiting on a team of super techs to arrive from Washington tomorrow," Rhodine said. "They may find something we missed on the first pass."

"For the sake of those girls, I hope so," Cassie said.

"For my sake, too," Rhodine said. "I've got a lot riding on this."

Both Cassie and Sheriff Puente glared at him but neither said anything. The man was ambitious, Cassie thought.

Sheriff Puente folded his arms across his chest and rested them on his belly. He said, "It pains me we can't arrest him for driving around with this . . . *torture chamber* in his truck. But if we can't find any evidence that it's been used for what we know it's been used for, there is no law against it. This is one of those situations where we've got the law on one side and doing what's right — *what we all know is right* — on the other."

Cassie nodded and looked at her shoes.

"Too bad we can't have some kind of accident where he's found hanging by his belt in his cell," Puente said.

"Please," Rhodine said sharply, "I don't want to hear any more of that. We need to nail this guy by the book and we need to do it this afternoon or we'll have to cut him loose."

He turned to Cassie. "That's why it's so important that you're here."

She understood. And she didn't know if she was up to the task.

Back in the SUV on the way into Wilson, Rhodine said to Cassie, "So have you done a lot of interviews with suspects?"

"What kind of question is that?" she snapped back.

"No offense," he said, raising his palms to her in a gesture that read, "Calm down, lady." She hated when men did that to her.

"I read up on her," Behaunek said to Rhodine from the backseat. She had a pair of reading glasses perched halfway on her nose and looked over them at the FBI agent. "Dewell here put down the Lizard King's partner in a shoot-out. Hit him six times and killed him dead. I think she can handle an interview."

Cassie appreciated the defense. But the fact was she hadn't done more than a dozen interviews in her career, and none as important as this.

"Okay, okay, I get it," Rhodine said to Behaunek with mock sincerity. "I just want to make sure she's comfortable with this."

"You two talk like I'm not sitting right here," Cassie said. "I know the situation we're in."

The situation was dire, as Behaunek had explained to her the day before on the phone. They couldn't prove that Dale Spradley was, in fact, Ronald Pergram, aka the Lizard King. Spradley was approximately the same size, shape, and age. He had the same profession and he had a kill room in his truck. But he didn't look the same in the photo Behaunek had e-mailed her of the suspect in custody.

Dale Spradley had jet-black hair, a thick Fu Manchu mustache, and horn-rimmed glasses. He had heavy jowls and was thirty to forty pounds heavier than Ronald Per-

45

gram's most recent commercial driver's license shot. Still, Cassie could see a resemblance that couldn't be disguised: the wide Slavic face, the flat expression, the soulless eyes.

It didn't help that Dale E. Spradley had what appeared to be proper documentation proving who he was, including a valid CDL, a social security card, load insurance, a medical examiner's report, and a federal Compliance, Safety, Accountability (CSA) score sheet that showed he had a clean record.

Cassie had asked Behaunek if Spradley's DNA matched that of Pergram and the answer dismayed her. There was no Pergram DNA to match. None had ever been taken and since he'd burned his childhood home and all of his possessions to the ground when he left Montana, there was no way to get any. The only blood relative Pergram had that could have produced similar DNA was his mother who had died in the fire. No sample was taken of her remains. The same with fingerprints or dental charts: no record of Pergram.

But there was a hole in Spradley's story, Behaunek said. It wasn't enough to invalidate his identity but it was enough to hold him in custody until Cassie could arrive. No one in Oakes, North Dakota, could be found who could corroborate Spradley's claim that he was from there. It was thin, but it was something. Spradley claimed that he'd always kept to himself and had long ago left Oakes for a nomad's existence on the nation's highways, but not a single person could remember him in a small farm town of less than two thousand people?

So, Cassie was told, they had to tie Spradley to Montana and to the events that took place there two years before. If Cassie could get him to admit he lived there, get him to react in a way that would break character, they could arrest him and hold him long enough, they hoped, that the FBI super techs could come through with damning evidence of what Spradley-Pergram had done in the secret room of his semi-trailer. Additional time and publicity might even produce a witness who could place Spradley in Montana, or better yet connect him to the abduction of a truck stop prostitute.

"Does he know I'm coming?" Cassie asked as the SUV pulled in front of the impressive and ancient county courthouse on Nash Street. The building was massive and gleaming with ornate fluted Corinthian columns and a recessed porch. It seemed to Cassie to be more courthouse than Wilson needed.

"No," Rhodine said. "He doesn't know we suspect he's the Lizard King. At this point, he's being held for interfering with a police officer. We're hoping that when he sees you — the one person who knows more about him than anyone else who is still alive — it'll shake him. He'll know what we suspect the second you walk into that room."

"Good."

"And he's waived his right to a lawyer at least for now," Behaunek said from behind her.

"That fits," Cassie said. "He thinks he's smarter than anyone else. He thinks he'll never get caught."

"So far, he's been right," Puente said.

Cassie tried to swallow but her mouth was dry.

Behaunek said, "So it will just be you and him in the room. I imagine he'll be quite surprised to see you in North Carolina."

Cassie nodded. Her hands were cold and her palms sweaty. She flexed her fingers in and out at her sides but kept her hands low so no one could see how nervous she was. "You'll be watching everything?"

"Of course," Sheriff Puente said. "We'll have a deputy right outside on the other side of the one-way mirror. The rest of us will be a few steps down the hall watching the monitors. We'll have one camera tight on his face to record his reaction to seeing you the first time. The other one will be a two-shot of you both."

Behaunek said, "We discussed how far you should go, and you need to be careful. We can't have anything on that video defense counsel can point to later and claim illegal coercion. If you start to go over the line, I'm going to open the door and break it up."

"Got it," Cassie said.

"Do you need anything before you go in there?" Sheriff Puente asked. "Water, or to use the bathroom?"

"I need to check messages and use the bathroom," she said.

"Put on your game face," Rhodine said as he opened the door for her. "We're all counting on you. We know you won't let us down."

"Gee, thanks," she said, fighting an urge to slap him.

Cassie tried to tame her hair in the mirror and failed, then drew her cell phone from her purse. No messages from her mother about Ben, which was good. Isabel didn't text or e-mail — she called. If Cassie didn't answer immediately, she kept calling. Cassie hoped she could get through the interview without hearing from her mother.

And there was nothing yet from the sheriff of Grimstad, North Dakota, where she'd made the short list of applicants for a much better-paying job as chief investigator. The sheriff there had promised to let her know his decision by the end of the day. Cassie checked her watch. It was 2:00 P.M. in North Carolina, noon in Montana, and 1:00 P.M. in Grimstad. She had hours to wait.

Then she raised her head and looked into her own eyes in the mirror and tried to steel herself for what was to come. For two years, the Lizard King had been out there somewhere but still a constant part of her life. She despised him, and wished she could sever the link today, right now, by opening the door to his conviction and his death.

She said aloud, "Let's go get this son of a bitch."

CHAPTER THREE

Wilson

Cassie lowered her head and strode down the hallway toward the interrogation room. She could see Behaunek, Sheriff Puente, and Agent Rhodine gathered around two closed-circuit monitors in the communications center. As she passed them, Puente gave her a thumbs-up.

A deputy swung the door open and whispered, "I'll be just outside," into her ear as she entered the stark white and windowless interrogation room.

The door shut behind her.

He was seated with his manacled wrists on top of a brushed metal table. He was a big man, bigger than she realized. His hands were pink and the size of hams. He had thick stubby fingers with dirty fingernails.

She had the strange feeling that she was watching herself enter the room from above, as if she wasn't really in her own body. She could see her disheveled hair, her too-tight suit. And she could see the man sitting at the table.

When he looked up at her his eyes blinked. There was no other gesture or tic to indicate he knew who she was. He sat absolutely still, breathing slowly with the slight wheeze of a fat man, his dead eyes fixed on her. But she saw it. *He blinked.*

She hoped the camera caught it, too.

"Hello, Ronald," she said. "It's been what — two years?"

Suddenly, she was no longer viewing the scene like an outsider. She was all in.

He cocked his head slightly to the side and he looked at her warily.

"Two years ago on the street in Gardiner, Montana," she said. "I was inside a quilt shop interviewing the owner. But I heard your truck and looked outside just in time to see you leave a package of videos on the seat of my car that would implicate your partner so you could get away. It looks like you've really gained some weight since then. Don't tell me — too much truck-stop food?"

"I don't know what you're talking about," he said. His voice was higher than she would have guessed. His tone had air in it, as if his throat was constricted by the rolls of fat.

"I'm Investigator Cassie Dewell from the

Lewis and Clark County Sheriff's Department in Helena. But you knew that, right?"

"Again," he said, "I don't know what the hell you're talking about. I've never met you and you've never met me. And all I know about Montana is it's a big-assed state that takes too damn long to drive across."

She shook her head as if disappointed and sat down in the chair directly across from him. When she tried to scoot the chair closer she realized the legs of both the chair and the table were bolted to the floor. So she shifted forward until she was on the edge of the chair. She leaned in as close as she could to him and looked directly into his eyes.

He was slumped back and didn't react to her closing in on him.

"I saw in your eyes that you recognized me when I walked in," she said. "Quite a surprise, huh, Ronald?"

He sighed and shook his head. "Them dumb rednecks out there either need to arrest me or they need to cut me loose. They can't just hold me in here without any charges being filed."

He lifted his chin and addressed the camera in the ceiling over Cassie's head, "Yeah, I know you heard me, you dumb rednecks. I know my rights. You can't detain me without charging me with a crime. And you better damn figure out who is going to pay for the load I got screwed out of too, not to mention the time and money I've lost since you dumb rednecks brought me in here."

She was about to speak but he wasn't done talking to the camera. He said, "And come get this goofy bitch out of here. I don't know her and I'm not talking to her. She thinks I'm somebody I'm not. If you don't come drag her out of here I'm gonna get a lawyer to sue your ass for harassment."

"Are you through?" Cassie asked.

He lowered his chin and glared at her.

"You can deal with them later," she said. "Now you need to deal with me."

Was that a slight smirk on his face?

"When I saw you last in Montana you were driving a black truck — a Kenworth or a Volvo or something, right? Now you've got a new one."

She'd hoped he'd correct her and say it was a Peterbilt. Hard-core truckers thought of Peterbilts the way hard-core bikers thought of Harley-Davidson motorcycles. Peterbilts were a trucker's truck. That she suggested otherwise, she hoped, might get a rise out of him.

It didn't.

He said, "My truck is in the impound lot."

"But that's your new truck," she said. "What happened to the old one? The black one?"

"I don't know what the hell you're asking me."

"Sure you do. You used to have a black truck and now you've got a yellow one."

He took a big breath and held it. She knew she'd hit a nerve. But he didn't take the bait and talk about his black truck.

"For years," she said, "you used that black truck to pick up prostitutes at truck stops. You called them 'lot lizards' and yourself the 'Lizard King.' "

Another hit, she thought. He closed his eyes for a moment and breathed deeply, as if counting to ten. But when he reopened them, there was nothing.

She said, "It took a while, but we found where you hid the bodies, or at least some of them. Why don't we talk about that?"

In fact, no bodies had ever been located, despite searches by dogs and sonar finders. Every inch of the small ranch the Lizard King and his associates had used for their crimes was searched. Cars were found buried, but not a single body of a female murder victim. The only identifiable body found had been of Cassie's partner, Cody Hoyt.

Cassie listened for footsteps outside the door in the hallway, half expecting Behaunek to enter the room and shut down the interview.

Instead of talking, he revealed a slight knowing grin as if to say, *I know what you're doing. You didn't find any bodies.*

"I think I've had enough of this," he said. "You're just making things up."

"I'd never do that," she said. "So back to Montana. Emigrant, specifically, where you used to live when you were home off the road. What was it like going to high school in Livingston? Was it tough being kind of chubby and unathletic? Were you bullied by the other boys?"

She expected another hit, but he didn't react at all. It was as if he'd shut himself off from her, as if he'd taken his rage and anger with him someplace else and left his hulking shell in the room. Cassie felt a twinge of panic.

She'd once read that some reptiles had a transparent membrane like a second eyelid that covered their eyes. Spradley seemed as if he had the same adaptation. His eyes were open but shielded from images he didn't want to see. And they seemed incapable of showing emotion.

"Help me make sure I've got everything

that happened in Montana two years ago in the right order, okay? It's something I think about a lot because there were loose ends and nobody left alive to tie them up — except you."

Spradley let out another heavy sigh as she methodically went through the events when the Sullivan sisters from Colorado were abducted on the highway after their car broke down. She recounted finding the concrete bunker on the ranch that served as the staging location for the horrendous abuse and murder of dozens of women by Ronald Pergram and his two associates. She described encountering one of them on the stairs down into the bunker and shooting him dead. He'd been a Montana state trooper named Rick Legerski.

And she recalled standing helplessly by the smoldering ruins of Pergram's childhood home. At the time, she said, they didn't know if Pergram's body was inside. After it was carefully investigated, they did find a body. But it wasn't Pergram. The body belonged to Pergram's mother.

He listened to her with his dead-eye stare, but he didn't interrupt. She reasoned that despite his denials and subterfuge, he was *interested* to hear what Cassie was telling him. All he knew previously about the death of his associate Legerski, she guessed, was what he read in the papers or saw on the Internet.

But he refused to take the bait, to say or do anything that could be used against him. A suspect couldn't be arrested for blinking his eyes.

She paused, her mind racing. There had to be a way to get him to admit he was the Lizard King.

"Excuse me for a moment," she said. She rose and rapped on the door and the deputy let her out.

"It's not working," she said to Behaunek. Sheriff Puente nodded and looked away. He didn't appear to be upset with Cassie but with the hopelessness of the situation. Agent Rhodine, on the other hand, appeared defeated.

"No, it isn't," Behaunek said. "He's too good. Our chance to crack him was right after you walked in. It shook him up, we could tell. But now he's settled in. There's nothing you can say that will make him break character."

"I still like my idea about finding him hanging in his cell," Puente said.

"Please," Rhodine said with frustration. "Maybe he's telling the truth?"

It was a trial balloon that hit the wall with a thud.

The four of them stared at the man in custody in the monitors. He hadn't moved since she left.

"It's him, I know it," Cassie said.

"That doesn't help us right now, you knowing it," Rhodine said, brusquely running his hand through his perfect hair. "Despite what you led him to believe in there, you've never actually seen him in person. It's in your report. Defense counsel will shred us if we try to go with that one."

Cassie stared at Spradley-Pergram on the screen. Rhodine was right and she knew it. She thought about what she knew about the Lizard King, about his past in Montana. About the fact that he'd murdered perhaps hundreds of helpless women and probably his very own mother.

"We're going to have to cut him loose," Rhodine said. "We've held him too long as it is. Sheriff . . ."

"I know, I know," Puente said, his face red.

Cassie said, "I can try something else," and spun on her heel. She didn't reply when Behaunek asked what she was contemplating.

■ ■ ■ ■

Cassie sat back down across from him. He beheld her with a weary expression and said, "Are we done here?"

"Close but not yet."

Then she made her play.

She said, "We know this Montana state trooper who was shot and killed was the mastermind behind the whole operation," she said, continuing in the same tone she'd used to recount the tale. "It was on his property, after all. Of the three of you involved in the crimes, he was the only one intelligent enough to pull it off for so long. He was the only one with a college education. Even his ex-wife conceded how smart he was, even if he was diabolical."

Although he didn't say anything or move in the slightest, she could hear the rate of his breathing increase. The Lizard King didn't like it that she had so casually dismissed his intelligence. She wished he was plugged into a heart rate monitor so they could watch how he was reacting.

"It's such a shame that the trooper was such a deviant," she said. "But he must have been very charismatic and convincing to be able to recruit both of you into his sick world and to make you keep your mouths shut. I know it couldn't have been the other way around.

"I checked up on you, Ronald. I interviewed your old teachers, your neighbors, and the employees at your old trucking company. I think I might know you better than anyone else left alive.

"Let's talk about your new truck. Yellow — that's kind of bright and cheery, isn't it? Kind of, you know, metrosexual or something? Have you come out of the closet, Ronald? Now that you have a bright yellow truck, what are you? The Lizard *Queen*?"

She paused and smiled at him. "You aren't exactly the sharpest knife in the drawer, are you, Ronald?"

His breathing pattern was becoming more rapid. The long wheeze had morphed into a series of quick whistles, but he didn't seem to be able to hear himself. Although his expression was frozen in place, his ears had reddened. And she could see a tiny pearl necklace of perspiration on his scalp beneath his dark hair.

"It couldn't have been easy growing up in that house with no father. And your mother, before she got obese and obsessive, couldn't really see any value in you. Especially not compared to your sister JoBeth, God rest her soul."

Cassie held out her right hand, palm up and gestured to it. "Here we have JoBeth: two-sport all-state athlete, honor roll, Future Farmers of America award winner. She's athletic, attractive, and smart. She was even the homecoming queen. Then she joined the U.S. Marines and went overseas to Kuwait. She was a *hero.* And just like my husband, she was killed in action. Your mother kept the folded flag they sent her on the wall, right next to JoBeth's trophies. She was proud of JoBeth, and who wouldn't be?"

Cassie raised her left hand and expelled a puff of breath as she looked at it. "And here we have Ronald. Dull, overweight, held back in the third grade. The only physical activity he participated in was masturbating in his bedroom. Picked up for DWI the week before he planned to join the army, so even they wouldn't take him. He took one minimum-wage job after the other and had to come home every night and look at that flag on the wall. He is a forty-five-year-old man who still lives at home with his mother."

She paused and nodded to her right hand and said, "Winner." Then to her left, "Loser."

Cassie lowered her hands to the tabletop and shook her head as if she was disappointed in him.

"All those women you tortured and killed, Ronald, just to get back at your mother and sister. It's pathetic when you think about it —"

He exploded across the table and screamed, *"You fat fucking bitch!"* before she had time to react. His huge manacled hands were on her throat, his thumbs crushing her windpipe. She tried to pry them off but he was twice as strong and she couldn't break his grip.

Cassie rose in an attempt to twist away, and she impulsively kicked at him but her toe bounced off the table leg. The pressure on her throat was unbelievable and the sight of his grimacing face darkened and faded out of her sight like a curtain being drawn across a window.

Footfalls, like cascading thunder, echoed from the hallway.

She never heard the door burst open.

CHAPTER FOUR

Grimstad

T-Lock was pacing like a caged panther on the inside of the dirty glass storm door when Kyle got home after school. Kyle climbed off his bike and leaned it against the old washing machine on the side of the house. He used to keep his bike in the front but there had been so many stories of bike thefts recently that he used the new location. The washer had been there for a year. Kyle's mom was always asking T-Lock to take it away to the dump or at least lock it closed with a chain so no little kids could crawl inside and die. Neither had been done.

T-Lock opened the side door and leaned out, his eyes bulging. He glanced left and right down the block, then growled, "You, get in here. *Now.*"

Kyle nodded. He knew he should be scared. T-Lock could be a scary guy and Kyle knew he must be in trouble for something.

Kyle simply stared at the man. He considered turning his bike around and riding away — but where?

T-Lock's real name was Tracy Andersen and he was a roofer. That's what he told people who asked what he did. He said he got the name "T-Lock" because of the shingles he used to work with. So no one would forget, he had the name embroidered above the pocket of his denim jacket and tattooed on his forearm.

"I said move your ass, Kyle. I'm freezing to death standing here with the door open."

It *was* cold. Clouds had blown in from the north and covered the sky in dark gray. Pelletlike snow came in waves, carried by gusts of wind. The brown grass — what little there was of it in the front yard — was catching the snow and holding it there. Kyle wondered how much snow there would be the next morning when he went out to do his paper route. He needed those warm boots and some gloves. Maybe he could convince his mom to take him to Work Wearhouse later that night.

"*Now*, Kyle. Come on, man."

If T-Lock wore clothes other than black concert T-shirts and jeans with big holes in them — and maybe even shoes instead of flip-flops — he wouldn't be so cold all the time, Kyle thought.

Kyle climbed off his bike, readjusted his backpack full of books, and marched toward the front of his house with his head down. Their house was in the older part of town. Big trees, small lots, buckled sidewalks, no fences, lots of cars parked on the street because the homes had been built in the olden days before two- and three-car garages. Some of the houses, usually owned by old people, still looked pretty nice. Others didn't. Kyle's didn't.

T-Lock kept the storm door open for Kyle, who trudged up the cracked concrete steps and ducked under T-Lock's outstretched arm. The storm door was closed behind him, followed by the front door. The inside of the house smelled of cigarette smoke, as usual. T-Lock wasn't supposed to smoke inside except in the attached one-car garage, but he did it anyway. Especially since Kyle's mom worked the afternoon shift at McDonald's and wasn't around.

It was dark inside the house because T-Lock kept the curtains and blinds closed during the day.

Kyle didn't expect T-Lock to grab him by the shoulder and spin him around so they were face-to-face. The move nearly made

66

Kyle lose his balance and fall to the floor because his heavy pack swung around as well.

T-Lock was in his face. "We gotta talk, Kyle, we gotta talk. I went out to the garage to burn one and you know what I found, don't you? You *know* what I found."

T-Lock was his mother's boyfriend and had been, on and off, for a few years. He was tall and wide-shouldered with long stringy hair parted in the middle. He had deep-set eyes and a slow stoner's smile when he smiled. In the winter he grew his beard out and didn't shave it off until summer. T-Lock's whiskers were thin and scraggly and about an inch long. The tips of his whiskers curled white as if covered by frost.

"Do you know what's in that bag you brought home?" T-Lock asked, shoving his face closer to Kyle's. His eyes were bulging and there was a throbbing vein in his forehead that mesmerized Kyle because he'd never noticed it before. Of course, T-Lock rarely got so close. Kyle could smell his smoky breath.

Kyle shook his head. When he'd returned that morning with the heavy packet he didn't know what to do with it. He couldn't leave it outside. His mom was still asleep with T-Lock in their bedroom, so he couldn't ask her. He carried it from the canvas *Tribune* bag into the junky garage and put it on the floor under the workbench. It was tight in there because T-Lock had pushed an old Toyota Land Cruiser into the garage the year before so he could get it running. It was still there and not running. Kyle's mom had to park their old minivan out on the driveway, even in the winter.

"You really don't know?" T-Lock asked.

Kyle shrugged.

T-Lock stood and whooped as if he couldn't believe how dumb Kyle was. Then he bent back down and his face got serious. The intensity of T-Lock's eyes unnerved Kyle because he'd rarely seen him look that way before. Usually, T-Lock was so laid-back it seemed possible he could drift off to sleep any minute.

"First, Kyle, tell me where you found it."

Kyle could talk. He just didn't like to. It was hard, although it seemed to be getting a little easier since he'd started working with the speech therapist and special ed teacher at school. He liked his special ed teacher. She was a kind and roly-poly lady from Mandan. He didn't like the speech therapist, though. She spent most of their session texting with someone on her cell phone. The special ed lady hadn't been there that day, though, and he'd spent the whole time in class with the rest of the sixth grade. They watched movies. Kyle didn't like being in the class with the others because he was a year older than they were and they knew it. All of his old classmates and friends had moved up to seventh grade and middle school and had left Kyle behind.

"In the grass," Kyle said.

T-Lock rolled his eyes. "I mean where, exactly, in the grass? You mean on somebody's lawn or something?"

Kyle gestured to the south. "No. Out in the prairie. It was on the ground."

T-Lock cocked his head while he thought. "Was this around when that car wrecked this morning?"

Kyle nodded.

"Did you see it happen?"

Kyle nodded again.

"And you went down there and found that bag? Did it come out of the car when it rolled, is that it?"

"I think so."

T-Lock cradled his head in his big hands and held it there for a moment.

"Kyle," he said, trying to keep the excitement out of his voice, "Did anyone see you grab the bag?"

No.

"Does anybody know? Don't lie to me, Kyle."

Kyle didn't lie. T-Lock should know that, he thought.

"The cops don't know?" T-Lock asked.

"No one knows," Kyle said.

"You're sure?"

Kyle nodded.

"You didn't tell your mom or nothing, did you? You didn't tell your grandma?"

"No."

T-Lock seemed to be thinking. When he did that he closed his eyes. Then, suddenly, they popped open and T-Lock grasped both of Kyle's hands in his and squeezed hard enough that Kyle took in a breath and held it so he wouldn't cry out.

"Kyle, you can't tell anybody. *Anybody.* You've got to swear to me right here and now you'll keep your mouth shut about finding that bag."

Kyle wasn't sure. He'd planned on telling his mom about it and then maybe taking it to the police. That seemed like the right thing to do.

"Why?" Kyle asked.

"*Why?* I'll fucking show you."

Kyle thought, That word again. Just like the two men in the second car. He wondered if they, or T-Lock, could speak without it.

■ ■ ■ ■

The canvas duffel bag was unzipped on the dining-room table. T-Lock clicked on the overhead light so it shone down on the bag. It looked like the bag was being interrogated — like on television — Kyle thought.

T-Lock skirted the table and stood on the other side of it. He plunged both hands inside and came up with a handfuls of small plastic clear glassine baggies the size of a penny. The tiny baggies were filled with crystalline powder that looked like snow crust at the end of winter. The powder was bluish in color.

"Do you know what this is?" T-Lock asked.

"Drugs," Kyle said. He knew about drugs from drug-prevention movies at school, although he'd never seen drugs in real life. The weed he'd seen T-Lock smoke in the garage didn't count.

"Damn tootin'," T-Lock said, letting the baggies sift through his fingers into the opening of the duffel. "Hundreds of little packets. Maybe a thousand, I don't know. I don't know how many because I haven't had a chance to count 'em yet. But there's fifteen or twenty pounds of them in here, maybe more."

Kyle blinked. Fifteen or twenty pounds sounded like a lot, but not when compared to potatoes or dog food, he thought.

"That ain't all," T-Lock said, digging into the duffel. He came up with a large Ziploc bag bulging with smaller bags of what looked like black pebbles. Kyle frowned. Rocks?

"This is called black tar," T-Lock said. Kyle wondered who would want black tar. To himself, T-Lock mumbled, "Gotta keep this shit away from your mom."

T-Lock shoved the bag of black tar back into the duffel and held up two thick bundles of cash. The money was tied together into bricks by thick rubber bands. It looked like used money, not clean bills. Kyle could only see the denomination of the bills on the top and bottom of the bricks — fifties, twenties.

"I ain't counted this yet, either, but do you know what this could mean?" T-Lock asked.

Before Kyle could answer, T-Lock said, "Yeah, I know, the bills are marked. But there are ways around that."

He showed Kyle where someone had run a light purple highlighter pen up and down the sides of both bricks.

"I heard about this trick," T-Lock said.

"All you have to do is shine a black light on the edge of a bill and that mark will show up. Otherwise, you'd never know. They do that so the courier can't skim."

Kyle had no idea what T-Lock was talking about.

"Back to the subject. I said, 'Do you know what this could mean?' " T-Lock said, his eyes bulging again as he thrust out a brick of cash in each hand, "It means we can take care of your mom."

Kyle hadn't thought of that but he instantly warmed to the idea.

T-Lock said, "You don't know this, but your mom got a notice from the landlord last week evicting our ass. These pricks around here can charge big money for rental houses now that the oil boom is on. They don't need hardworking people like us anymore."

T-Lock only worked when it was warm outside, which wasn't often in North Dakota. The rest of the time, like now, he hung around the house in his T-shirt and jeans and flip-flops. Freezing. Kyle didn't know what else T-Lock did during the day. He guessed he watched TV.

"Well, your mom didn't want to tell you we might have to move, but it's been worrying her sick. She's a good lady, Kyle, you know that. She works her ass off to give you a good home and stuff to eat. You love your mom, don't you?"

Kyle nodded.

"You don't want her to go back downtown to work the pole again, do you?"

"No."

"Damn right you don't. I don't either, even though it was good money and it paid the rent," T-Lock said wistfully.

Kyle had overheard his mom and T-Lock arguing about her job as a dancer. She wanted to quit for a long time and her hours were being reduced now that the club owners were bringing in professionals from around the country. She'd told T-Lock she was used as a backup when one of the "hotties" didn't show up. T-Lock argued that she should keep the job since he didn't have one.

Kyle wanted his mom to be happy. If quitting her job made her happy, Kyle was on her side.

Luckily, she'd quit dancing and had recently gotten a job at McDonald's in Grimstad when they started paying $17 per hour plus benefits. It was weird seeing her come home in that McDonald's uniform, but usually she had a bag or two of cheeseburgers and fries for dinner.

Sometimes it was Big Macs or Filet-O-Fish, Kyle's favorites.

"Your mom," T-Lock said, "she's struggled for you. Just struggled," liking the word enough to say it twice. "She got clean and convinced them people to let you come back. And she's stayed clean. She doesn't deserve to get thrown out of her own house, right?"

Kyle nodded. He visualized the scene: large men in coveralls pitching his mom out the door into the snow so she landed on her rear end.

"Ain't it time you and me took care of her for a change? She deserves better, don't you think? Don't you think your mom is entitled to the life everybody else around here seems to have? Why should she do all the struggling, anyway?" T-Lock asked, raising the bricks of cash as if making an offering to the overhead light.

Kyle was confused. He understood about the money, that was obvious. But what about the other?

T-Lock said, "I know some guys. Other roofers and guys I see around. You think of me as a construction guy, but I got connections."

Kyle never thought of T-Lock as a

construction guy, but he kept his mouth shut.

He continued, "There are what — thirty, forty thousand single men out there in the county now? They're looking for stuff. I'll figure this out. We'll take care of your mom.

"The one thing," T-Lock said, "is if you truly love your mom like you say you do and want to make her happy, the one thing is you gotta keep your mouth shut. You can't tell anybody about this bag. We want to surprise her, you know? Christmas is just around the corner, so you just let me handle it."

Then T-Lock smiled that wide stoner smile and shook his head and chuckled.

"I don't know why I'm asking you of all people not to fuckin' talk."

Kyle said, "Can I take my coat off now?"

T-Lock threw back his head and laughed. Kyle had rarely seen the man so happy, so giddy.

He looked at the duffel bag on the table and the scene that morning came rushing back: that bloody man trying to claw his way out of his wrecked car, the two men who had forced him off the road, the cops.

At least it made T-Lock happy, he thought.

■ ■ ■ ■ ■

Day Two

■ ■ ■ ■ ■

CHAPTER FIVE

Wilson

The previous night at the Wilson Medical Center, the doctor who looked too much like Ed Begley, Jr., had said to Cassie: "It only takes eleven pounds of pressure placed on both carotid arteries for ten seconds to cause loss of consciousness. To completely close off the trachea, you need thirty-three pounds of pressure. If strangulation persists, brain death will occur in four to five minutes. This man has very powerful hands. It's very fortunate they were able to pry him off of you when they did."

She would have nodded if she could.

On the way to the Raleigh-Durham Airport and her flight back, Cassie propped her head uncomfortably against the headrest of the backseat. She wore a stiff plastic brace. In the mirror that morning, she'd seen the bruises under her jawbone that spread down to her breasts like a blue-black lace collar. They looked hideous.

The sheriff's deputy who'd been the first into the interrogation room to save her drove the cruiser. Behaunek sat next to Cassie in the backseat in a much-appreciated show of sisterhood.

The night before both Behaunek and Sheriff Puente had come to see her at the hospital to check on her condition. Agent Rhodine was apparently too busy.

"What you did was brave," Behaunek had said softly, shaking her head in what appeared to be wonder. "You gave it up for the team. You probably don't know that when he attacked you I was in the process of getting up from my chair to come into the room and put a halt to that particular line of questioning."

Cassie had nodded. "I was wondering about that," she said. She could speak either in a reedy whisper or a honking croak and it hurt to do either. Simply swallowing water brought tears to her eyes.

"I've never seen anything quite like it," Behaunek said. "Did you know he would react that way?"

Cassie shook her head. She had to edit her words in advance because each one was painful. "Just guessing."

"Well, you guessed right. You found the one thing that would cause him to flip out. I've never seen a man his size move so fast."

Cassie grunted in agreement.

"There's no way I can spin what happened into an admission of guilt on his part, but the assault charge will keep him locked up for a while. You bought us time, Cassie."

Cassie had tried to smile.

"And it looks like we'll be seeing you again when you come back to testify against him in court."

"How long?" Cassie croaked.

"Three or four weeks, I'd guess," Behaunek said. "We filed the assault charge this morning and the preliminary hearing will be tomorrow. I can't see the judge allowing him to be released prior to the trial. Especially if we show him that videotape."

"Does he have a lawyer?"

"Yes — court appointed," Behaunek said. "I'm curious to see if he hires one on his own. In my experience, monsters like that often think they can represent themselves because they think they're so much smarter than anyone else in the courtroom. I hope he does that because I want to be the one who nails him."

After Behaunek and Puente had left her the

81

night before and before the swelling in her neck had really set in, Cassie had used the landline phone next to her bed to call her mother, Isabel. Although Cassie's sentences were halting and she was still half in shock, she told her mother what had happened and asked her not to tell Ben. She didn't want her son worrying about her condition.

And she didn't tell Isabel who had tried to kill her. She referred to him as "the suspect."

"I'll talk to Ben when I get back," Cassie had said. She didn't recognize her own voice.

"What? I can't hear you."

Cassie enunciated more clearly, grimacing while she did so.

Isabel said, "You don't want me telling him that his mother was strangled in North Carolina?"

Cassie had rolled her eyes. Isabel was a free spirit and a child of the sixties. She'd insisted on being called Isabel instead of Mom or Mother. She made no secret of the fact that she still thought most cops were pigs. She'd never approved of Cassie's line of work and had never hesitated to say so.

"Please, Isabel, not now."

"When will you get back?"

"At least a day later than planned," Cassie

had said. "They need to take photos of my injuries, and the doctor still has to release me. I know I'll be here at least tonight for observation."

"Will the injuries cause permanent damage? Will you always talk like that? No offense, but you sound like a really fat person."

"No offense," Cassie had repeated. Her mother didn't possess any kind of internal governor. Whatever she thought came out through her mouth. It seemed to be getting worse.

Isabel said, "You know I have my zumba class tomorrow night. I'd hate to miss that."

"You might have to." Cassie envisioned Isabel writhing around at the YMCA in her flowing robes, or worse, in tight workout clothes.

"Maybe I can find someone to watch Ben for the night. Maybe I could ask Ripster . . ."

Ripster was a formerly homeless man and recovering meth tweaker Isabel had made her new project. Isabel's life was strewn with failed projects like Ripster who, in Isabel's mind, qualified as victims of bourgeois oppression.

"Mom, *no.* Not Ripster. Absolutely not."

83

"You don't have to be so judgmental, Cassie."

"When it comes to Ben, I do."

Isabel had sighed heavily.

Cassie said, "I may not be able to talk, so I'll text you."

"I *hate* texting and you know it."

Cassie could hear Ben in the background.

"He's right *here*," Isabel said, laying on the guilt.

"I'll talk with him."

"I thought so," Isabel said, handing over the phone.

"Hey, Mom."

"Hi, little man," Cassie said.

"What's wrong with your voice?"

"I'm in North Carolina," Cassie had said. Somehow, it worked. Ben told her a long story about finding a stray cat in the alley on the way home from school. It was the best cat *ever.* But it was lonely and needed a home really bad. He wanted to name it Sergeant, which was a manipulative play aimed straight at his mother's heart. Ben's father Jim, who had died during the Battle of Wanat in Afghanistan in 2008, had been a sergeant in the army. Ben was born after Jim was killed. Jim had never seen his son, but Ben worshipped his father. Or, more

84

precisely, he worshipped the *idea* of his father.

But before she could tell Ben he couldn't have a cat, she heard it yowling through the receiver.

"Grandma Isabel is giving it some milk," Ben said.

"Of course she is."

In the car, Behaunek opened her briefcase and handed Cassie a large Ziploc bag of her possessions that they'd taken away when she was admitted into the Wilson Medical Center.

Cassie nodded her thanks and buckled on her watch and twisted her wedding ring on her finger. She caught Behaunek watching.

"I understand," Behaunek said with a smile. She raised her left hand with a ring on it, and said, "My divorce was three years ago. This helps keep the wolves at bay — or at least most of them."

Cassie powered on her cell phone and saw she had a pending voice message from area code 701. North Dakota.

Before she could retrieve it, Behaunek reached over and touched her arm. "Cassie, there's something we need to talk about."

"What?"

Behaunek took a deep breath. Cassie braced for bad news.

"Unless the FBI finds ironclad evidence in that truck that proves Spradley is the Lizard King he may not serve much time in jail. He has no priors — he looks clean."

Cassie shook her head as if dismissing the prospect in general.

Behaunek said, "If I step back from what we know and look at this entire case the way a criminal defense lawyer will see it, I start to get really nervous. Think about it."

The prosecutor said, "One, the initial arrest is shaky. Spradley was pulled over because of a theory backed by a local politician, not because of true reasonable suspicion of a crime or traffic offense. Then the truck was unloaded and searched. I'll have a tough time making the argument that Lightning Bates's observation comes across as solid probable cause that would allow the police to search that truck. A good lawyer can look at those two things and argue that everything that resulted from the initial stop is 'fruit of a poisonous tree,' meaning it should not be admissible in court."

Cassie didn't want to hear what she was hearing. But she could tell Behaunek was being straight with her. Behaunek was worried, which made Cassie worried.

"So we held Spradley in county lockup for a day and a half without counsel and without charging him," Behaunek said. "It was a chance I was willing to take in the hope you could get him to incriminate himself. But the defense may look at that and say it was illegal coercion — that you were brought down here for the purpose of shocking him and deliberately provoking him. They might say in court that you baited him, hoping he'd lose control."

Cassie tried to nod. Couldn't. She said, "That's what I did."

"And that's between us and will never be spoken of again," Behaunek said. "North Carolina statute number fourteen, thirty-four, seven classifies assault on a law enforcement officer as only a Class F felony, unless we can somehow convince the judge that Spradley's hands are lethal weapons. With no priors, the best we could hope for if he's convicted is five to ten years, and possibly even less. You know how the law works."

Cassie pursed her mouth. She knew how the law worked, all right.

Behaunek said, "Based on what I saw in that interrogation room, he might come after you if he gets out."

"Then don't let him out," Cassie croaked.

"There has to be evidence. *Trophies.*"

She wanted to explain how Pergram had previously kept a collection of DVDs and videotapes of his victims being assaulted. How Pergram had arranged to get two of the DVDs into Cassie's hands two years before in a successful effort to steer her toward his accomplice instead of him.

"We know about these types of killers, how they like to keep trophies," Behaunek said. "But we just can't find where he keeps them. I hope the FBI tears that truck and trailer apart bolt by bolt."

"Maybe the sheriff's idea is a good one."

Behaunek withdrew her hand and said, "You surprise me."

"I learned from the best," Cassie said. "His name was Cody Hoyt and he was my partner. Pergram's accomplice shot him in the face."

At the curbside check-in, Behaunek got out of the car with Cassie and helped get her overnight bag out of the back.

She gave Cassie a hug goodbye, then held both of Cassie's hands for a moment. "You were great."

Cassie said, "Don't let him out."

"I'll do my best to keep him in a cage," she said. Cassie was grateful. She had confidence in Leslie Behaunek. She came across as a bulldog prosecutor.

"And I'll keep in touch with you on everything."

Cassie paused before turning and entering the airport. "Call me on my cell," she said. "Don't call my office or send e-mail to my sheriff's department e-mail address."

When Behaunek raised her eyebrows, Cassie said, "I may not be there very long."

Inside the terminal, Cassie withdrew her phone. The message on her cell phone was from Bakken County Sheriff Jon Kirkbride. He spoke in a slow Western drawl and said, "Greetings from the new energy capital of the world. We'd like to offer you that job we talked about and the sooner you can get here, the better. But there's something you need to remember: this place is the Wild West. I can *guar-and-damn-tee* you ain't ever seen anything like it. And I ain't kidding about that."

She lowered the phone and closed her eyes for a moment.

Cassie couldn't wait to tell Sheriff Tubman in Helena that she was moving on. She didn't know who would be happier.

■ ■ ■ ■

Day Three

■ ■ ■ ■

CHAPTER SIX

Grimstad

The next morning, Kyle Westergaard rode up to the bluff to look over the dark prairie where it had all happened two days before.

Big trucks filled the highway to Watson City like normal. They were moving slowly, though, because of the weather. Kyle could see dust devils of snow kicked up by dual rear wheels caught in the lights of oncoming trucks.

He made a V with his fingers and raised his hand to his mouth. This morning, he thought, he was smoking a big cigar.

He was much warmer than he'd been the morning before although the snow had continued through the night. Steam rose from the collar of his coat when he paused on the bluff because he was sweating. It was hard work pedaling through three inches of untracked snow, and he had to keep stopping and cleaning packed snow from his tires. His new Thinsulate gloves in camo made it a challenge to fish individual copies of the *Tribune* out of his canvas panniers — but he didn't mind.

While pausing to catch his breath, Kyle lowered his new Sorel Pac boots to the ground and balanced his bike. He couldn't stop for too long, he knew, or the chill would set in.

That old gnome Alf Pedersen had told him someone had complained the day before about Kyle tossing the last of his newspapers on their driveway at 6:45 — fifteen minutes late.

"You were here early enough," Alf said. "Why were you so late with the delivery?"

Kyle didn't want to say he'd seen the rollover. He hoped Alf wouldn't ask about it.

But he did.

"Were you rubbernecking around that crash? I heard about that. Some Mexican high on drugs went off the road. Things are crazy around here. That kind of thing never used to happen."

Kyle said he'd seen the car crash from a distance.

"Ah," Alf had said. "I wish I could understand what the hell it is you're saying to me. Anyway, next time deliver the newspapers and *then* go rubbernecking."

Kyle had no idea what rubbernecking meant, but he didn't think he'd told a lie. He just hadn't told Alf *everything.*

The night before when his mom got home clutching a bag of hamburgers, T-Lock had bounded through the small house and had met her at the back door, saying, "Fuck those burgers. We're going out!"

His mom, who had already taken off her thick winter coat to reveal the maroon Mc-Donald's smock, began to protest immediately. She brought dinner home, she said. They couldn't afford to go out. They never went out, she reminded T-Lock, except to fast-food places. She'd spent the entire day on her feet at McDonalds'. And the other fast-food places were packed with men as well and it took forever to get your order . . .

T-Lock wouldn't take no for an answer. He was giddy and his grin was in full beam. He took the bag from her and tossed the burgers on the counter and yelled for Kyle to grab his coat.

Kyle's mom was as thin as T-Lock, with short dirty-blond hair, brown eyes, wide cheekbones, and a slash of a mouth. She was small and wiry and often had a pinched, don't-mess-with-me-or-my-kid expression on her face like she was looking for a fight. Kyle didn't mind.

T-Lock insisted they were going out, and held out her coat for her like she was a queen and he was somebody who dressed the queen.

It had been so long since Kyle had seen her smile like that he didn't mind T-Lock's lie to her about winning $300 in the North Dakota Lottery that day. He said he'd won the Hot Lotto with a Triple Sizzler, to be exact.

Kyle thought that was a pretty specific lie.

T-Lock drove his mother's van. Before going to the Wagon Wheel, he merged dangerously between two huge muddy trucks in a convoy of them on Main Street. The traffic was unbelievable, practically gridlock in both directions. Exhaust rose from beneath the big trucks and swirled with the snow in the streetlights. It was loud inside the van because of the throbbing diesel engines all around them from idly moving or barely moving trucks.

They drove three blocks before T-Lock exited Main into the packed parking lot of Work Wearhouse.

Inside, they waited for twenty minutes in

line behind rough men in muddy and oil-covered coveralls cradling small mountains of thermal underwear, fireproof clothing, Carhartt parkas. It smelled earthy in line, Kyle thought, like what it might smell like after a meteorite blew a hole open in the ground.

At the register, Kyle watched T-Lock peel several bills from a roll and hand them to the salesclerk. Kyle knew where the money had come from. Although he wanted and needed the winter items, he wasn't sure he liked the idea of T-Lock spending money on him when they agreed they'd spend the money on his mother. When he looked at his mom to see if she was suspicious, she simply smiled at him. She seemed genuinely touched T-Lock was buying warm boots and gloves for her son.

"What do you say to Tracy, Kyle?" his mom prompted. She never called him T-Lock.

"Thank you," Kyle said.

T-Lock winked back.

Kyle couldn't remember having eaten as well as he had the night before at the Wagon Wheel, except at his grandmother's house. As he perched on the bluff and looked out over the hundreds of orange flares in the distance — the Indian village — he could still taste the deep-fried cheese, the breaded shrimp, even the bite of cheesecake his mother had offered him from her dessert. The restaurant had been packed with men from the oil fields.

Nearly all the men wore hoodies, jeans, boots, and ball caps. The few women in the place dressed the same way minus the ball caps. There were loud conversations about the prices on the menu, but he didn't see anyone get up and leave.

He was still full when he got up that morning, hoping his mom would remember she promised to drive him on his route because of the weather. But even though he knocked on her bedroom door and stood outside it for five minutes, she didn't get up.

He left the house after T-Lock yelled for him to "Go the fuck away."

As the morning cold started to seep into his clothing, Kyle got ready to finish his route. Then he saw a familiar car slow down on the highway and edge to the side of the road where the crash had occurred. He recognized it by its low-slung, bright-white halogen headlights.

There was no way, he thought, he'd go

back down there to see who it was.

The car stopped and the doors opened and the same two men — at least Kyle assumed they were the same men — got out and descended into the prairie. The crashed car had been towed away, but the men walked to where the car had rolled to a stop. Then two flashlights came on and scoured the snow-covered ground.

Kyle watched as the men circled around the spot where the wreck had occurred, walking in ever-widening circles. It must be tough, Kyle, thought, to see anything under the snow. He guessed they were looking for a lump.

Then, just as had happened the morning before but much slower and without sirens or lights, the cop SUV drove out from the edge of Grimstad and made its way to the parked car. Only this time the two men in the prairie didn't run back to their vehicle and drive away. This time, the men continued to look.

And as Kyle watched and puffed on his big cigar and got ready to go, he saw the deputy join the two men so the three of them could search the ground together.

CHAPTER SEVEN

Cassie saw her first man camp fifteen miles west of Grimstad. It was out there in the snow and mud: a kind of high-tech ant colony made up of portable housing units tightly joined together and sprawling off in different directions across the prairie like word tiles on a Scrabble board. The high chain-link fence surrounding the camp recalled a low-security prison except for the massive lot where hundreds of muddy company trucks were parked in neat rows. There wasn't a single man outside walking around.

Because it was dusk about a third of the outside windows of the camp glowed from interior lights. She caught a glimpse inside of what must have been the dining hall. Dozens of men sat at tables inside, heads bent down, shoveling food.

The very name made her smile grimly.

Man camp.

■ ■ ■ ■

It had been a long, flat, desolate drive of eight hours for more than 506 miles. All of it was in Montana. The route paralleled both the Lewis and Clark Trail and the railroad from Helena, Montana, to Grimstad. Cassie hoped her 2006 Honda Civic would hold together along the route known as the Montana Hi-Line through Great Falls, Havre, Malta, Glasgow, and Wolf Point long enough to get there. Grimstad was located twenty miles across the North Dakota border.

The terrain flattened the farther she drove east, morphing from mountains in the rearview mirror to hundreds of miles of rolling grass prairie and farmland through the front windshield. The sky was huge and gray and endless and the horizon was perfectly horizontal. She knew she was nearing her new job when the grasslands gave way suddenly to pipeline fields, heavy equipment yards, tool companies, and muddy pickups merging onto U.S. Route 2.

Her sense of both excitement and dread had increased by the hour. She was a third-generation Montanan, and had always thought the state was big enough there was no reason to ever move anywhere else. Her father Bill claimed he had driven his semitruck on every single road in Montana and it took him most of his life to do so.

And here she was, soon to uproot her son (and mother) to move east to a state that had always served as the punch line of jokes in Montana. To a place people used to be *from,* but were never headed *to.* To one of the few states that until recently had lost population in every census. To a place where there were Scandihoovian farmers rather than raw-boned ranchers, and where polka music was a staple on the radio and Sven and Ole jokes were relevant.

But that was back before they made the largest discovery of domestic oil in North America and one of the largest found anywhere in the world and figured out how to get at it: by hydraulic fracturing or fracking. That was before, according to the tagline from the single local AM radio station she could get, Grimstad became the "Oil Capital of North Dakota," where nearly a million barrels of oil a day were being shipped out. And that was before the sheriff's department could offer to pay their new lead investigator $80,000 per year in salary plus family health insurance and benefits — including a subsidy for housing.

After returning from North Carolina, Cassie had found Sheriff Tubman in his office looking over artwork for new billboards urging Lewis and Clark County residents to vote for him for reelection. As usual, his Stetson was crown up behind him on the credenza. That used to drive her old partner Cody out of his mind because Cody had grown up on a ranch and knew real cowboys always placed their hats crown down to preserve the bend of the brim. For Tubman, the hat was an affectation.

As soon as Tubman saw her enter, he covered the artwork with his forearms and eyed her warily.

Their relationship had deteriorated since he'd hired her as an investigator, primarily so he could burnish his diversity credentials within the county, and he made no secret of it. In the first year of her employment, she'd been personally dutiful, even going so far as to serve as his spy on other cops, including Cody. But Tubman had betrayed her by citing her findings and firing Hoyt, and he'd followed it up by his active benign neglect of her pursuit of the Lizard King. She knew Tubman saw her as a threat and also knew the only reason she hadn't been fired was because of her gender. But that didn't mean the sheriff wouldn't undermine her at every turn, and plant rumors about her character and morality and sexual orientation as a way to turn up the heat to convince her to leave on her own.

When she told Tubman about the offer from North Dakota and asked if he wanted to match it, he'd laughed out loud. She hadn't been surprised. And when she gave her two weeks' notice, he countered with two *hours.*

They were reprogramming the electronic entry code to the Lewis and Clark Law Enforcement Center even as she left it for the last time carrying a cardboard box of personal items.

When she'd called Sheriff Kirkbride in Grimstad to say she could be available to start the job sooner than they'd discussed, he told her she was already late.

The heavy truck traffic in town surprised her, although she thought she should have expected it. The big tractor-trailers and oil field pickups slowly clotted the few streets and made her think of a highly mechanized army moving through a country village en route to the front. It took her twenty minutes to navigate through the old-fashioned downtown to the county law enforcement center. The downtown obviously hadn't come close to catching up with the impact of the boom — JCPenneys, an ancient movie theater, a couple of packed diners — and near the Amtrak station were three adjacent strip clubs with parking lots jammed with pickups even though it wasn't yet five o'clock.

She found an open space in the lot next to the law enforcement center, which was an obviously new building made of brick and glass, and punched the speed dial for Sheriff Kirkbride's office.

"I'm here," she said. "I'm right outside."

He chuckled. "What do you think so far?"

"I don't know what to think."

"Stay there," he said. "I'll be right down with the keys and show you your apartment. Then we can go on a little tour of Bakken County."

She looked at her wristwatch: 5:30 P.M. Sheriff Tubman would be shutting off his lights in his office to go home.

"Are you sure you have the time?" she asked.

Kirkbride said, "It used to be that way, before the place went twenty-four-seven. Now, though . . . well, I'll show you. Besides, my wife has her book club tonight and I've already been home to feed the horses. Maybe we can grab a bite later. I'll call and get us a reservation or we'll have to wait for two hours to get a table. I'll be right down."

The central lobby of the law enforcement center was lit up like an aquarium at night: lots of glass, a few sofas and tables, and two elevator doors. A stooped man who she assumed was a jail trusty by his orange jumpsuit pushed a mop across the stone floor, and he looked up and greeted the man who appeared as the elevator doors opened.

Sheriff Jon Kirkbride exchanged pleasantries with the trusty. He wore a khaki uniform with a brown sheriff's department ball cap. Kirkbride had a bushy gunfighter's-style mustache. He pulled on his coat as he pushed through the glass doors and walked toward her car. He was a big man with wide shoulders, a slightly stooped posture, and the delicate, bow-legged, and pigeon-toed way of walking she'd observed in many Montana ex-rodeo riders.

He approached her car and held out a huge hand. "Cassie Dewell, it's good to see you again for the first time," he said with a grin.

Their interviews had taken place via

telephone and Skype and, Cassie thought, had a slightly desperate quality to them.

"Glad to be here," she said, climbing out of her Honda and shaking his hand.

"Is it just you or do you have your little one with you?"

"Just me. My mom and son can't get here for another couple of weeks. I didn't want to take him out of school until the Thanksgiving break."

Kirkbride nodded and looked her over in the way cops looked over each other, the way cattle buyers looked at a cow. Like always, she thought, she'd likely disappoint him.

He handed her a set of three plastic keycards held together by a twist tie. "One of 'em is a master and will get you in the building and it'll open every door inside. Like I told you, we share the building with the other law enforcement folks — the local Grimstad Police, the highway patrol, and the Northwest Drug Enforcement Task Force, but we work together as a team. No territorial or jurisdiction bullshit, even though our department is the big dog around here. The other two keys are for your apartment. Do you need some help carrying your stuff up?"

She shook her head. "I've only got a

suitcase at this point and I can handle it."

"Of course you can," he said, rubbing his jaw. "I just never know what to do or say anymore. I was raised to open doors for women and carry their stuff. Now I'm always worried I'm offending them if I offer."

"No offense taken," she said. "If I wasn't traveling so light, I'd take you up on your offer and thank you for making it."

"Whew," he said.

She followed him across the parking lot pulling her rolling carry-on bag to a modern three-story building adjacent to the law enforcement center. He said over his shoulder, "If somebody would have told me twelve years ago when I got this job that I'd be a landlord as well as a sheriff, I woulda looked at them funny."

She laughed politely. She knew how unique the situation was in Grimstad. Cassie had checked rent costs online. Without housing as part of the package, she knew she couldn't have afforded to make the move. Grimstad now had the highest rents in the nation, surpassing even New York City.

"Is it all sheriff's department people inside?" she asked.

"Yeah. A couple of married couples, but mainly single men. It's like a sports-only dormitory — one big happy family."

"Any kids?" she asked.

"One in the oven," he said. "You know about the situation here with men and women in general, right?"

"You told me," Cassie said. "Ten-to-one men to women."

"I've revised that," he said as he opened the door to the apartment building by swiping a card through the reader. "Now I think it's more twenty-to-one."

Her apartment was located on the third and top floor. She thought, Ben will love the elevator.

Sheriff Kirkbride hovered just outside the door, holding his hat in his hands as she went in and turned on the lights. "It's my only three-bedroom unit. You're the first to live in it."

"It's great," she said, parking her rolling luggage near a new couch and looking around. The apartment smelled of fresh paint and new carpet.

When he didn't respond she looked over to see him staring closely at her. Instinctively, she reached up and touched the bruises on her lower jaw with the tips of her fingers. She'd forgotten about them.

"This is what the Lizard King did to me," she said. "You know about him, right?"

"Everybody does," Kirkbride said. "And I know your history with him. But how in the *hell* did he get his hands around your neck and how in the *hell* did you live to tell the tale?"

"It's a long story," she said, forcing a smile so he'd know she wasn't trying to be obscure. "I can tell you all about it later."

"Okay, because I want to hear it. Folks in the eastern part of the state are pretty cheesed off that he passed himself off as a North Dakotan."

She briefly looked around. The apartment was clean, new, modern, and airy, she thought. Two bathrooms. A big-screen HD TV in the living room. It was bigger and cheerier than the place she'd left in Helena. She knew from the Web site there was a fenced-in playground outside. Ben would like that — unless he turned out to be the only child in the complex.

"Let's go on that tour," she said.

"You sure you don't want to make yourself at home?" he asked.

"I'll have plenty of time for that," she said. She'd decided to wait to sort out who would sleep in which bedrooms, how she'd rearrange the furniture, and what she'd put on the stark white walls.

Besides, she thought, if the sheriff was using his personal time to show her around, she felt obligated to participate. Plus, it would be important for her to see the county through his eyes. She'd learned painfully from her time in Helena that the culture of a sheriff's department was set at the top — for good or ill.

After they closed the door and waited for the elevator, Kirkbride said, "I tell all my new guys they'll get ten years of experience in law enforcement in their first six months here. You'll soon see why."

"Are your deputies local hires?" she asked.

"Not hardly," he said. "Locals who might be so inclined go straight to work out in the oil fields pulling in a hundred thousand a year. No, I have my best luck recruiting out-of-staters fresh out of the academy in Illinois, Michigan, and Minnesota — places where the economy sucks and they can't find a job. I've even got one from sunny California — they call him 'Surfer Dude.' It's hard to get experienced cops to move out here. But these guys — you'll meet 'em — are all fresh-faced and gung ho. They like to get right out there and mix it up with the bad guys because they're young and full of beans. I'm glad you're not either."

Then he blushed when he realized how it had sounded.

"Damn, that was a stupid thing for me to say," he said as the elevator opened. Instead of going in, he stood there for a moment looking at the tops of his boots. "My wife would kill me if she heard me say that to you."

"It's okay," she said, holding the door. "I know what you meant."

"I hope so," he said, looking at everything inside the elevator car but her. She liked him instantly.

"We begin our tour," Sheriff Kirkbride said in a put-on television announcer's voice-over tone, "with what Grimstad was five years ago before they figured out how to get all this oil out of the shale underground. When this little desolate hamlet on the North Dakota prairie was home to less than twelve thousand people . . ."

He was at the wheel of his unmarked silver GMC Tahoe. Inside, though, it was a fully equipped law enforcement vehicle. There was a wire screen between the front and back row, both a shotgun and a semiautomatic rifle mounted to the dashboard, and a portable flasher on the seat that could be quickly attached to the roof by its magnetic base. He'd lowered the radio so they could talk.

Cassie smiled and said, "That's how they started the video piece I saw on YouTube. I think it was by *The New York Times.*"

"You saw that, huh?"

Cassie nodded. "When I found the job posted, I Googled Grimstad, North Dakota, Bakken County Sheriff's Department, crime in Bakken County, population of Bakken County, whatever. I found clips from CNN and *The New York Times* and another from a Danish news crew about the boom and how it had impacted the area. I thought you handled the questions pretty well."

"They all ask the same things," Kirkbride said wearily. "They want to know about the growing crime rate, the potential environmental dangers of fracking, and what they call the 'loss of innocence' of Bakken County. These reporters all seem to have their stories written before they even set foot in North Dakota. They want me to give 'em a quote that will confirm their bias. They want me to condemn fracking for oil and the sudden influx of people. If I don't go along with their script they get pissy. And they always find someone who will give them the quote they want."

"I noticed," she said, recalling how hostile he'd come across in the most recent clips.

"I don't even call 'em back anymore. They fly all the way here from the East Coast burning up jet fuel, then rent cars and fill 'em with gasoline to drive all the way to Grimstad just so they can trot me out to say, 'Oil is bad.' I won't play their game anymore. The truth is this town was dying a slow death before they found oil. We were losing all our young people. Farming and ranching is hard damn work, and it doesn't pay much. It gets colder than hell around here in the winter."

She nodded.

He said, "*This* is what Grimstad used to look like, minus all the oil field trucks on the street."

They were on a narrow residential street two blocks from the law enforcement center. The homes were small, single family, close together. Very Midwestern, she thought. There were towering oaks in many of the small front yards. But because of the many four-wheel-drive vehicles parked on both curbs, Kirkbride's big SUV could barely navigate down the street.

There was a flash in the headlights and the sheriff applied the brakes and whispered, "Shit."

Cassie's seat belt restrained her from hitting her head on the dashboard. She looked up in time to see an adolescent boy on a bike dart out from between two of the vehicles and then stop in the headlights and look at them. He obviously hadn't seen them coming.

"Nearly hit him," Kirkbride said.

"Thank God you didn't."

Before the sheriff could roll down his window to speak to the boy, the rider recovered from his surprise and quickly pedaled the rest of the way across the pavement. He vanished between two oil field service SUVs. Cassie noted the empty canvas *Grimstad Tribune* panniers on the handlebars of the bike and the face that looked back bathed in headlights. The boy's face was unsettling.

"Westergaard boy," the sheriff said, shaking his head. "I nearly clipped him good."

"You know him?"

"Kind of," Kirkbride said. "He's not a bad kid, but he's going to get himself killed riding his bike like that. Someone should tell that little shit we have traffic now."

Kirkbride proceeded down the narrow street, but more slowly. Cassie looked out her window and caught another glimpse of the boy riding his bike across a front lawn and then between two houses. There was an old washing machine back there.

She said, "There was something odd about him, I thought."

Kirkbride nodded. "You noticed that. Small kid for his age, kind of a vacant stare."

"Yes."

"Fetal alcohol syndrome," he said. "His mother, Rachel Westergaard, is a piece of work. I hear she's gotten her act together and I hope so because Kyle seems like a good kid. Hard worker, as you could see. I talked to him at the school antidrug deal. He listens and he tries to keep up but he doesn't talk."

"He can't talk at all?"

"Some, I guess. But right now I'm more worried about him getting mashed by some drunk on the street if he doesn't start paying attention."

Cassie grimaced as she reset the shoulder strap of the seat belt. The sudden stop had pressured the most painful part of her injury.

"You okay?" the sheriff asked.

"Fine," she said.

"Anyway," Kirkbride said, "that's what it used to be like around here."

She looked over, not quite getting what he was saying.

"We all knew everybody else. I hauled Kyle's mom in a half-dozen times for public intoxication. I remember seeing her pregnant with Kyle in the cell and I called Social Services to help her out. Who knows who the father was. But it was too late for Kyle, I guess. She was sober when he was born but the damage was already done. He lived with his grandmother for a while after he was born, but I guess she proved to the social workers she'd changed for the better and now he's back home. If I would have had a vote he'd still be with his grandma."

He paused. "That's how it used to be. Now I've got a hundred and twenty-five men in my jail and I don't have room for another. And I don't know a single one of their names."

CHAPTER EIGHT

Kyle passed through the bright headlights of the truck on the road into darkness as he darted between two parked pickups. He thought, That was close.

He jumped the curb and rode across the front lawn of his next-door neighbor toward his house. He hoped the people in the car that almost hit him wouldn't follow. It wouldn't do any good to yell at him or tell him to look both ways before riding his bike across the street. He knew that. But he wasn't himself and hadn't been all day at school. All he could think about was the bag he'd found and what T-Lock had said about being able to take care of his mom. He couldn't wait to see her face when T-Lock told her they were moving. And he couldn't help but think the bundle he'd found could somehow help him put his river plan in place, and he was excited about that.

His friend Raheem would need to know

about the bundle soon. Raheem was in on the plan, and they'd bumped fists on it.

The lights were on inside his house and leaked around the closed blinds. Kyle paused after he leaned his bike against the washing machine. His mom was still at work, but there were two cars parked nose-to-tail in the driveway. That's where his mom usually parked her van.

The car in front was one of the biggest, shiniest, and coolest SUVs he'd ever seen up close: a Cadillac Escalade. There was a sticker in the back window indicating it had just come from the car dealership. Behind the Escalade was a beat-up old pickup with huge patches of gray primer all over it. In the bed of the pickup was assorted junk: piles of discarded asphalt and shake shingles, shredded roofing paper, bent lengths of edging tin.

The pickup belonged to T-Lock's friend Winkie. They called him that because he wore glasses so thick his eyes were magnified through the lenses and when he blinked it was a visual event. Winkie was short and stout, a fellow roofer in T-Lock's crew. Long ago, Kyle's mom had declared that Winkie wasn't welcome in her house after he'd accidentally fired a razor-tipped bolt through the front door while trying to cock his new 250-pound crossbow.

Kyle wondered why Winkie was there, and who owned the Escalade.

"Holy shit!" T-Lock said in alarm as Kyle came in the front door, "What time is it?" Like always, he scrambled for his phone and like always he patted himself down and couldn't find it. T-Lock didn't wear a wristwatch.

Winkie looked up from where he sat on the couch.

Blink.

"Kyle, my man," Winkie said. "How you doin', man? How you fuckin' *doin*?"

He asked as if it was the most important question in the world, liked he *really* cared.

Kyle shrugged and took it in. The coffee table in front of the couch had been cleared of his mom's magazines and picture books. On the edge of the table near Winkie was a small square of dusty-looking glass dusted with white powder. The mustache under Winkie's nose contained the same substance. Next to the square of glass was a twelve-pack carton of beer. Half the bottles were gone.

"You don't talk much, do you, Kyle, my man?" Winkie said, firing the words. "You

120

never did, man. Loose lips sink shits." When he realized his mispronunciation, Winkie roared with laughter and fell back on the couch, repeating it twice. When he recovered he sat back up and stared at Kyle with glassy eyes. *Blink.*

T-Lock fought back laughter himself and tried to play adult to Kyle. He made a serious face and said, "Kyle, I'm wrapping things up here with my friend Winkie. Why don't you go do homework in your room or whatever. Your mom will be home soon."

Kyle squinted and T-Lock misunderstood what he was squinting about.

"Winkie was just leaving, don't worry," T-Lock said.

"I was?" Winkie said. *Blink.*

"Rachel'll be home. You've got to be gone before she shows up."

Blink.

Kyle said, "Who owns that Escalade?"

"What'd he say?" Winkie asked T-Lock. "I can never understand him."

"I can," T-Lock said. "He wants to know who that Escalade belongs to."

T-Lock and Winkie exchanged looks. They looked as if they were both ready to bust out laughing.

T-Lock said to Kyle, "Man, we'll talk about that later. But don't you think your mom deserves a nice ride? She's been nursing that van of hers along for what, ten years?"

"That's my money," Kyle said. "I found it. It's for me and Mom. You said so."

"Uh-oh," Winkie said, looking away with a smirk on his mouth. "I don't have a fuckin' clue what he said but he looks pissed."

Kyle *hated* it when people talked about him like he wasn't in the room, as if he couldn't hear them talking about him.

"Look," T-Lock said, bending toward Kyle with his hands out, looking like he was pleading his case, "It *is* for your mom. Everything is for your mom. But I don't want to talk about it right now. We can talk about it later," he said, drawing out the last word and chinning toward Winkie. "We'll talk about it later man-to-man, okay?"

Kyle frowned. He hated T-Lock sometimes because T-Lock thought he was stupid.

"Go do your homework," T-Lock said again, "I'll clean up before your mom comes home."

Kyle glared at Winkie as he marched to his room and Winkie looked back.

Blink.

Winkie reached inside the beer carton and said, "Here, kid, have a beer. Relax. You're twelve or something, right? I was ten when

I had my first sixer."

Winkie looked up at T-Lock for approval, and T-Lock shrugged. He said, "It might take the edge off, Kyle. Just don't tell your mother. I won't."

Kyle slammed his door closed. His room was small and cluttered, although he knew where everything was. The door was cheap and old and he could overhear T-Lock and Winkie whispering and laughing in the living room.

He sat at his too-small desk and snapped on his lamp. There was math homework in his backpack but he didn't worry about it. Kyle struggled with most subjects but he was good at math and he could usually get it done in just a few minutes. Now, though, he felt an urgent, almost furious need to go over his plan, to look at the list he'd been making for several months. Raheem had been involved with the list when they first talked about it the summer before, but Kyle had taken it over. Raheem wasn't very practical when it came to survival lists. Plus, since it was Raheem's boat in the first place, they both agreed he didn't need to do half the planning as well.

But it was hard for Kyle to really concentrate on the list because he kept overhearing snatches of rat-a-tat-tat conversation in the other room.

Kyle stared at the sweating bottle of beer he'd placed on his desk. He'd always wanted to try to drink beer, but he knew he wasn't old enough. But Winkie had just handed it to him and T-Lock didn't stop him. Maybe he *was* old enough.

He pulled a loose sock from the floor over his hand and used it to twist the cap off the bottle. The *pssst* sound was nice when it opened, and he took a drink.

Buzzy, he thought. Kind of bitter. But cold and nice. Kyle had never liked sweet drinks and beer wasn't sweet. It felt good going down, so he took another sip.

Winkie: "That's some fuckin' awesome shit, you know that don't you?"

T-Lock: "Of course, man. Of course! That first hit just about blew the back of my head off. I don't think this meth has been cut at all, man. Or if it has it hasn't been cut very much. No, they were getting ready to sell this shit. That's why it's packaged the way it is in one-gram hits. This shit was ready to hit the streets, man."

Winkie: "How much did you say you had?"

T-Lock: "Well, I could only use Rachel's bathroom scale, so it may not be perfectly accurate, but I got fourteen and a half pounds. I weighed it twice, man. Fourteen point five fucking pounds of this shit."

Winkie: "Jesus! How much is it worth on the street?"

T-Lock: "I don't know for sure, but —"

Winkie: "Fuck, it's millions. I know hits are going for two hundred a gram and that's shit that's been cut way down. There are a shitload of high-quality meth grams in that bag."

T-Lock: "I got on the Internet today before I got too fucked up. The local yokels did that big bust last year, remember? They got three pounds of meth off one guy, and the article said the street value was two hundred and seventy thousand, remember that?"

Winkie: "Sort of. I know prices went up right after that and a couple of the guys were bitching about it."

T-Lock: "Yeah, they said it went up to two hundred and fifty a gram for a while. Anyway, let's say the price is back to two hundred dollars a gram again now. So I did the math. We're talking ninety thousand a pound minimum. So fourteen and a half pounds is worth one point three million on the street, easy. Maybe one and a half million. Plus that fifty-four thousand in cash.

Yeah, I know the bills are marked, but they worked today when I leased that Escalade, didn't they?"

Winkie: "You're a fucking millionaire! Jesus, I know a millionaire. You ain't gonna forget your friends, are you?"

Kyle thought, That's for me and my mom.

The old wooden boat on the side of Raheem's house had been there when Raheem's family moved here from Detroit. The boat had a deep V hull and had been stored upside-down on the side of the house for years. The finish on the hull had long ago deteriorated and the sun had faded the boat gray. When Kyle and Raheem turned it upright the inside was filled with cobwebs, old leaves, and a nest made by field mice. The oarlocks were rusted and the lines of the gunwales were warped but the floor of the boat was solid and it looked sound. They tested it by filling it with water from a garden hose. It didn't leak. There was a wooden box affixed to the bow with a hasp that could be locked up. There were also two-foot-long storage boxes on the inside gunwales. No oars, though.

Kyle and Raheem spent days cleaning it out, lubricating the oarlocks with WD-40 they found in Raheem's dad's garage, and coating the interior and exterior with a polyurethane topcoat from gallon cans they'd found at a construction site. By the end of the summer they sometimes just sat in it, a white kid from North Dakota and a black kid from Detroit, pretending they were floating down the Missouri River on the world's greatest adventure. Raheem did lots of fake casts and caught dozens of imaginary fish. Kyle sat at the center bench seat and feigned rowing. He waved at passing farmers and ranchers on the shores who waved back. Eagles perched on tree branches that stretched out over the water. Puffy white clouds scudded across a wide blue sky.

That's when the plan was hatched. The idea had come to him after a trip to the Badlands.

Kyle studied his list. He'd crossed out items many times and added new ones. Half the beer was gone, and the words seemed to swim across the page.

Sleeping bags
Food (jerkie, crackers, things like that)
Fishing poles and tackel
Raincoats
Binokulars
Pistol or rifle (animals, hoboes)

Journal for writing
Map
Knife
X-tra clothes
Swimming trunks
Rope
Tent
Plates and utensuls
Matches
Oars (get B4 summer)
Cell phone
Money

At least, he thought, that last item was possible now. It was why he'd taken the paper route in the first place. But money shouldn't be a problem anymore. Unless T-Lock blew all of it.

Winkie: "But you know somebody out there is looking for this shit, right? They'll want it back."

T-Lock: "What if it was just one guy? Have you thought of that? If it was just one guy maybe there isn't anyone even looking for him."

Winkie: "No way it was just one guy. That many pounds and all that cash? No fuckin' way. There are people out there wondering where it went."

T-Lock: "You think I haven't thought of that? Of course they'll want it back. But they don't know who took it, do they? All they know is their guy rolled his car and got dead. They don't know what happened to the stuff inside. Think about it, man. As far as they know it's still out there in the prairie, or hidden inside the car wreck. Or maybe the dead guy sold it all and hid the cash before he took his dirt nap? How are they going to know? They might think even the cops recovered it and are keeping it quiet. Or maybe some corrupt cop grabbed it and took it home. There's nothing that points to me, man."

Winkie (laughing): "Except that Cadillac Escalade out there."

T-Lock: "That's why we drove up there and bought it in Minot, man! Those car dealers up there are used to Bakken workers strolling in with rolls of cash. That's nothing new to them anymore. And I leased it, remember? I didn't buy it outright. That would have raised too many red flags. You've got to give me more credit, man. You're starting to piss me off, Winkie."

For the hundredth time, Kyle studied the map he'd printed off at school. He tried to tune out what was being said in the living room.

The Missouri started in southern Montana and flowed north through Great Falls then across the entire state until it entered North Dakota and Grimstad. On the western side of the river it was Mountain Time and on the eastern side it was Central. From Grimstad, it flowed south and east, through Bismarck, Pierre, Omaha, Kansas City, and Saint Louis. In Saint Louis, the river joined the Mississippi and continued south through Memphis and finally to New Orleans, Louisiana. Even the names sounded exciting and exotic. Raheem said he'd never been to New Orleans but he wanted to go there because it was warm, unlike North Dakota. Plus, Raheem said, that was where the Saints played in the Superdome and women walked around on the streets flashing their bare breasts at everyone.

So when the ice broke up on the river in the spring and after the high water, they'd launch their boat. Kyle still hadn't figured out what he'd tell his mother about it. He knew she'd miss him, and he'd miss her.

But the pull of the plan enflamed his imagination. He thought of long days on the river with Raheem catching fish and

130

camping on the shore. He thought of weeks and months of floating away until they eventually arrived at a city where it was warm and foreign. They'd likely be greeted as pioneers and heroes, he thought: two twelve-year-old boys who took a rowboat from the northern border of the country to the Gulf of Mexico. Maybe they'd call him "Captain Kyle," or "Wandering Westergaard."

Kyle drank to the name "Captain Kyle."

Winkie: "Just because you got it doesn't mean you can just go out and sell it. You know that, right? You can't go out to the bars and man camps with your bag of meth like you was selling hot dogs. And if you just jump into the market, well, you've got competition out there. They aren't going to like that — especially if you show up with this high-quality shit. That is, unless you plan to snort it all up your nose yourself."

T-Lock: "Jesus, I know that. We need distribution. We need to tap into a network that's already there. That's where you got to help me, man. You know guys."

Winkie: "I know users. I don't know many dealers."

T-Lock: "But they know, man. They know who they buy from."

Winkie: "What about Willie Dietrich? I've always heard Willie is hooked up."

T-Lock: "That guy has hated me since we were in junior high."

Winkie: "But he don't hate me. He used to bang my sister, remember? I know him. I can talk to him. But what's in it for me, man?"

T-Lock: "I'll cut you in."

Winkie: "How much? What's my cut?"

T-Lock: "I'm still figuring it out. But it'll be enough to make you rich, I'll tell you that right now. But we've got to do this right. We can't let anybody know I've got all this shit. If assholes find out, they might try to come and get it."

Winkie: "I'm excited but I'm also starting to get a headache. This might not be easy, you know. It might get scary as hell."

T-Lock: "You don't worry about that. I'm the one doing the thinking here. I've got it handled, man. I've waited my whole life for something like this. I've already figured out a way to launder that marked cash. You just go out and sniff around Willie and his guys and see what you can find out. See if you hear about anyone missing a shitload of meth and cash but don't tip anyone off about what we have. Just leave it all to me."

■ ■ ■ ■

Kyle stood unsteadily. The bottle was empty. The sounds from the next room seemed to meld together into a kind of background noise, like when the house was buffeted by wind.

He thought, So this is what being drunk feels like. And he wondered why adults spent so much time and money wanting to feel this way. All he wanted to do was to go to sleep.

Kyle staggered across his room and fell face-first onto his bed. Even though his room was messy he always made his bed. He always had.

He went to sleep with the droning sounds of T-Lock and Winkie scheming and arguing.

Then he dreamed about his boat, and what it would feel like to push it away from the riverbank. What it would feel like when the current took them away.

CHAPTER NINE

After cruising through the pre-boom residential areas and new developments that were going up in every direction on the outskirts of Grimstad, Kirkbride cursed under his breath as he merged into the non-stop convoy of huge muddy trucks on Main Street headed north. Steam and exhaust rose from the pavement and from beneath the vehicles. Kirkbride pointed out the trucks belonging to the major players in the oil boom: Halliburton, Sanjel, Baker Hughes, Whiting, Continental Oil, Marathon Oil, Scorpion, and Nabors.

The problem with the traffic, he said, was that the city and county had not yet had the chance to build new infrastructure that could handle the sudden tenfold increase in vehicles and machinery. The oil field traffic going north or south had to be funneled through the middle of town on roads designed to accommodate residential traffic flow, thus almost impenetrable bottlenecks were created.

"We don't even know what our population is," he said in answer to the question Cassie asked. "It's growing that fast. A few months ago, I would have said thirty-five to forty thousand in the county. There are over ten thousand units in the man camps alone. But I was talking to the director at the water treatment facility and he says they're handling sewage now for sixty thousand plus. Imagine that," he said with a snort, "we guess how many residents we have by the sewage they produce."

She shook her head as he reeled off positive talking points he'd no doubt repeated many times:

- A million barrels of crude from the Bakken Formation were being shipped every day by thirty-five to forty tanker trains that stretched over a mile long each;

- North Dakota was now the second-biggest oil-producing state in the country having surpassed Alaska;

- The state's population was increasing by the thousands each month;

- The unemployment rate in Grimstad was less than half of 1 percent;

- The success rate for drilling of the hydraulic fracturing oil wells was over 99 percent;

- The power companies couldn't keep up with getting electricity to the oil wells and were more than eight hundred behind, which meant generators had to be installed on site;

- Per capita, Bakken County was first in the nation in building permits, Carhartt clothing sales, and the sale of Corvettes;

- The single bustling Walmart paid new employees $18 an hour plus benefits plus employee housing — as did practically every new business going up in town. New fast-food employees, retail clerks, and even newspaper carriers were being given signing bonuses;

- Once with the oldest demographics at sixty-plus, Bakken County now had the youngest population in the state;

- The county which five years before

consisted primarily of Norwegian and German descendants now had residents from all fifty states and dozens of countries, and the previously 95 percent white population was now wildly diverse.

• The average salary in Bakken County was $80,000. Blue-collar oil field workers, drillers, oil service hotshots, and some truckers pulled in well past double that.

Then he outlined many of the negatives.

• Housing was a severe problem. Existing rooms rented for $1,000 each per month and the average two-bedroom house rented for $3,500 per month;

• Locals who didn't own their homes when the boom hit were being evicted for high-paying oil field employees;

• There was no homeless shelter, not a single psychiatrist, and plenty of stress;

• Horses on farms and ranches in the county were dying of dust inhalation kicked up by the sudden army of big trucks on unpaved county roads;

- All local business owners now had to become landlords as well or they couldn't retain employees. Every new business was accompanied by a nearby apartment building;

- Although most of the new workers were men, there were enough women and families to impact the schools, meaning not enough teachers or rooms, schoolkids living in RVs, and transients hanging around the playgrounds;

- Prostitution, drug abuse, and violent crime had all spiked in relation to the increase in population.

Cassie sat back and simply took it in. She was astounded and couldn't decide if she was in the middle of an economic miracle or a disaster.

While he talked, Kirkbride took a muddy side road and parked at the top of the highest hill on the north edge of town. The view, Cassie thought, was astonishing.

As far as she could see out onto the dark prairie were natural gas flares, twinkling lights from man camps, pipe yards, pumping units, truck yards, and heavy equipment operations.

"At night you can see it from space," Sheriff Kirkbride said. "I'm not kidding. There are satellite photos where if you didn't know better you'd say it's bigger and brighter than Chicago or Minneapolis."

She said, "What about the stuff you always hear about with fracking — earthquakes, drinking water that catches on fire, that kind of thing?"

"Hasn't happened," Kirkbride said. "That's not to say that someday one of these companies might get sloppy and screw up. But so far, nada."

When they headed back into town, Kirkbride said, "Like every job you'll ever take in law enforcement, you've always got to remember that most of the people we serve are just good folks. All they want to do is make a good living and take care of their families. They pay our salaries. A big number of the new residents were unemployed for years somewhere else and now they've got a second chance at creating a prosperous life.

"Of course," he said, "we rarely deal with *those* people. We see the pimps, the drug dealers, the whores, and the scum that shows up on the periphery. We've always got to remember they're here to prey on the good people who were here before the boom and the new folks who are living the dream. Our job is to protect the good folks and make sure the bad guys get punished. Simple as that."

He sighed. "It used to be that if I ran across Ole the farmer out driving drunk after a big night of whiskey drinking and polka dancing, I'd follow him home to make sure he was okay and he didn't hurt anyone else. Maybe give him a stern warning or something. We can't do that kind of thing anymore. Ole has sold out and moved to Arizona, and the drunk driver may be some Idahole with a bad attitude and a pistol on his front seat. There's no such thing as North Dakota nice anymore," he said wistfully.

"And when I was talking about the stress of living here, I wasn't kidding. We've always had drugs and we've always had fights. But the types of calls are just more traumatic now. Bar fights are more vicious. Domestic violence calls are more bloody. Bad actors from other parts of the country bring their lack of manners with them. Once in a while the crews from the different oil field outfits get in big fights with each other. It's something out of a Western movie. Think cowboys versus sheepmen or sailors versus marines — that kind of thing. They ride for the brand.

"The drugs of choice have gotten worse also. It used to be weed and blow. Now it's meth and heroin, both the black tar and white powder versions."

Cassie said, "You said there was a lot of stress. Does that come from money, or change, or what?"

"My theory is there's a lot of mourning going on beneath the surface and it builds up until they lash out. The locals are mourning what they had, and the newcomers are mourning what they lost when they moved here."

Cassie sat back and looked at him. She said, "That's profound. What keeps *you* here?"

He grinned ruefully. "You mean because I'm obviously so damned old I could retire?"

"I didn't say that exactly. Remember, you said I was getting old myself a while back."

"I think I'll be hearing about that for a while," he said with a wink. "Just don't tell my wife."

"I won't. So what keeps you here?"

He merged into the heavy traffic for the slow ride back into downtown Grimstad. "My horses, for one," he said. "I used to ride 'em in team penning events. Now they're too old to win me any money and I'm too old to ride 'em. So I keep 'em fed and doctored, and maybe we'll time it right so we'll all ride off into the sunset together."

He paused. "And I guess I just feel like I need to see this thing through. I was here when it started and I want to try to make sure the good guys win in the end."

Then: "You hungry?"

"Starved."

En route to the Wagon Wheel, Kirkbride continued to play tour guide by offering anecdotes on places they passed.

The mega Walmart parking lot was packed with cars as if it were the day after Thanksgiving. "Up until a few months ago, they didn't even bother stocking the shelves because they couldn't keep up. They'd just bring pallets of stuff in and stack 'em in the aisles. There's actual merchandise on the shelves now, so I guess we're gaining a little ground.

"Last year, a garbage truck in the alley started lifting up a Dumpster when a guy jumped out who'd been sleeping inside on old mattresses. The guy started screaming and luckily the driver heard him. Last time I saw him he was working at Walmart."

At the Amtrak station, he said, "Every single day the train stops and a few men get off. Some of 'em don't even have coats. Saddest sight you'll ever see — something straight out of the Depression. You'll see them walking through the parking lot toward the downtown looking for work. If they aren't bleeding or obviously high on drugs, they'll be employed by sundown."

Cassie asked, "The oil companies hire users?"

"Oh hell no," Kirkbride said. "The companies run clean outfits. If you can't pass a drug test you can't get a job out in the field. Same with drillers, pipeline outfits, tool pushers, truck drivers, whatever. But there are plenty of jobs that don't test. And believe it or not, we've got our share of lazy bastards who refuse to work. They'd rather live on government cheese, even though — these days — they could pull down a pretty good income flipping burgers."

As they drove by the strip clubs Kirkbride told her, "The dancers rotate through here from Chicago, Phoenix, Seattle, Denver, Philly. We're talking hot women, and they make top dollar entertaining the troops. Thing is, they wouldn't even have to be all that good-looking around here to get attention. One of the bars has a big sign inside that says, 'Welcome to Grimstad, where even ugly women get lucky.' "

Cassie saw why Kirkbride had called the Wagon Wheel in advance. Despite the cold, Carhartt-clad knots of young men stood outside the front door drinking beer and smoking cigarettes and waiting for a table to open. Inside, every table and booth was filled with rough-looking men and women, the bar area was shoulder to shoulder, and the clamor was ferocious. Above the bar, a live hockey game from Canada and a recorded NFL football game were on.

The owner, a fleshy square-headed man, obviously knew Kirkbride and he waved them over to a booth near the kitchen. Cassie sat down while the sheriff shook hands with a few locals on their way to the booth. The locals seemed to genuinely like him, she thought, in contrast with the reception Sheriff Tubman used to get in public back in Helena.

There was a raucous group of five men at a table. They were still wearing their oil-stained coveralls and they eyed her with interest. Two of them were obviously whispering about her. All five of the men had beards and wore ball caps. Dozens of empty beer bottles littered the table. She looked away and hoped she hadn't flushed red. Cassie couldn't recall a similar situation since the high school cafeteria. It was as if testosterone circulated through the air.

Kirkbride and Cassie ordered beer and cheeseburgers from a teenage waitress wearing a Grimstad Vikings hoodie. She told Cassie her beer was on the house, since it was company policy that women drank for free. When the waitress was gone, Kirkbride said, "You can see why I don't go out much anymore. They're building more restaurants but they aren't open yet because they can't find employees. Do you cook?"

"Not enough," Cassie confessed. "But I can see that I should get better at it. My mother will be in for a shock, that's for sure. She's a vegan and she's into sustainable and organic."

"Whatever that is," Kirkbride said, taking a long pull of his beer. "She's in for a culture shock."

A line of foam stuck to his mustache. "So tell me about the Lizard King."

Cassie relayed what had happened in North Carolina. Kirkbride leaned forward so he could hear her over the din. A frown formed on his face.

"So they haven't charged him with any abductions or murders yet?" he asked.

"Not that I've heard," she said. "I'm in close contact with the county prosecutor, and she's good. But right now the only thing they've got to hold him is his attack on me."

"From what you tell me it sounds a little shaky," Kirkbride said. "Not that I don't admire the hell out of what you did to provoke him — I do. That took guts. But I wish they had more than that. If there ever was a beast that deserved the needle or the chair or whatever they do down there, it's that guy."

She agreed. "The FBI has their top people going over his truck and trailer, so I'm confident they'll find something that will tie him to a murder. The guy is smart and cagey, but no one is *that* smart and cagey. They'll swab every inch of that truck for DNA."

Kirkbride nodded, but his frown remained. "Let's say they find some," he said. "Then they have to try and tie it to one of a thousand or two thousand missing truck stop lot lizards who may or may not have left any usable DNA to match up with. Man, talk about a needle in a haystack . . ."

He paused and looked hard at Cassie. "Are you sure it was him?"

"Ninety-five percent. He's changed his appearance."

Kirkbride shook his head.

Cassie felt herself go cold. She hadn't considered how near to impossible it might be for the forensics experts to identify a specific victim — even with tangible evidence. Not without a body. Again she was reminded how difficult it was to catch serial killers who were long-haul truckers. Not only was the driver likely ten states away when a woman was reported missing, but he had thousands of highway miles to dispose of a body.

"At this point, I can only hope," Cassie said. "I bought them some time and I can only hope they come up with something."

Kirkbride nodded in agreement. "Me too," he said.

After their cheeseburgers arrived, Cassie inadvertently glanced over toward the table of five men. They were still staring at her. One of them waggled his eyebrows at her as he took a long pull from his beer mug. She quickly looked back to Kirkbride.

"What about prostitution?" she asked.

"Oh, it's here," Kirkbride said with a laugh.

"Is it organized?"

"Not really. The days of whorehouses are over. There's a few lowlife pimps who show up with a carload of girls, but most of it's done over the Internet. Check out a Web site called 'North Dakota Backpage.' You'll see how it's done. It's quite a marketplace.

"But to be honest, we really don't want to make it a high priority. Look around you. Unless these guys are crossing the line seeking underage girls or getting involved with human traffickers, we'll kind of look the other way. We've got tens of thousands of single men out there and I'd rather they blow off steam that way than busting a beer bottle across someone's face. We've got bigger fish to fry, is what I'm saying."

She understood that.

"What about homicides?" she asked.

"Up until the boom, we averaged one every three years. Usually domestics. Lena had it up to here with Ole and brained him with a cast-iron skillet in the farmhouse. But there are seven so far this year and two are unsolved. Maybe even three. That's one of the reasons I'm happy you're here," he said with a slow grin. "You'll find the files on your desk in the morning. I *hate* unsolveds. It jacks my stats. The worst thing is two of 'em look like professional contract hits."

Cassie stopped chewing. She'd never worked a contract murder investigation.

"That's right," Kirkbride said. "As crazy

as that is to believe out here."

"Tell me more," she said.

"Those guys over there at that table are ogling you."

She blushed and wished there was a way to take it back. She sighed, and said, "I know. Tell me more about the two and maybe three contract hits."

Kirkbride said, "Two months ago, we found two bodies dumped in a field ten miles from town. Males, tatted up, tortured, killed, and dumped. I've never seen anything quite like it but I won't get into the details until you finish your dinner. Each of 'em were still in their colors."

"Colors?"

"Have you ever heard of an outlaw motorcycle gang called the Sons of Freedom? They're originally out of Colorado but they've got chapters all over the country. They do it all — strong-arm robbery, murder, meth, heroin. They're one of the original One Percenter gangs."

Cassie knew a little about One Percenters — Hell's Angels, Warlocks, Sons of Freedom. They wore patches on their vests proclaiming it.

"We've heard the Sons started a chapter here a while back."

"Wouldn't they be obvious?" she asked.

"I know what you're thinking. You're thinking they all ride around on Harley choppers wearing their colors, so why haven't we picked them up and questioned them? The thing is, some of those guys still do that, but a lot of them don't anymore. They have to operate under the radar to get a foothold in a community. The colors come out once they're established and they've intimidated everyone to the point that no one will try to take them on."

She asked, "Any idea who was responsible?"

"Only a guess. But I hate to even think it."

"Think what?"

Kirkbride sat back and said, "Finish your burger and I'll show you something. I want to see if you come to the same conclusion I did."

Bakken County didn't have a morgue, Kirkbride said as they drove downtown. There were two funeral homes — Gundersen's and Schneider's — and they used to alternate years as to which one would serve as the official county morgue. That had been changed with the increase in homicides. Now both funeral homes stored bodies until they could be autopsied locally if necessary, or sent to Bismarck for examination by state crime lab technicians.

They stopped in front of Gundersen's Memorial Chapel. There were no lights on inside.

"I have a key," Kirkbride said. "You're not real squeamish, are you?"

"No," she lied.

As she waited for the sheriff to open the side door, she noticed how much colder it had become. She hugged herself and vowed to get a warmer coat. She'd heard about winter in North Dakota, how bitter it was. Now she knew it to be true.

Unfortunately, it wasn't much warmer in the steel and tile backroom used by Gundersen's for embalming the deceased. Harsh white fluorescent lights reflecting off the steel and tile in the room made it seem even colder.

A body, covered by a plasticized sheet, was on a gurney outside of two steel half-doors. She assumed there were other bodies inside the drawers.

"The paying customers get to use the pull-out shelves," Kirkbride said. "Our county bodies have to wait out in the open like riffraff. Which they usually are."

She nodded. His attempt to lighten the moment hadn't worked.

"Ready?" he asked, grasping the top corner of the sheet. She nodded quickly. Her hands were in her coat pockets, fingernails digging into her palms.

"I'll only peel it back halfway," the sheriff said. "The bottom half, well, it's nearly detached. No reason to see that. Right now we're classifying him as a victim of a one-car rollover."

She tried not to shiver from the cold.

The body unveiled on the gurney was male, olive-colored, well-muscled, and heavily tattooed, even on its face and neck. Both arms had full-sleeve tattoos. The face tattoos were so elaborate and dark they made it look like he was wearing a mask. He had a shaved head, gold earrings, and a heavy brow. Light-colored knife blade scars showed on his face, forearms, and torso.

A discernible tattoo on the breast was of a clenched hand with clawlike fingernails. The pointer and little finger were outstretched, the two middle fingers were held down by the thumb. She was puzzled by it.

Kirkbride noticed. He said, "Think what it looks like upside down."

She said, "An 'M.' "

He nodded and then said, "And if anyone still doubts what we've got here" — he grasped the body by the arm and tugged it over — "we've got *this.*"

The victim's back was also a mass of swirling tattoos. Most were amateuristic: angels with fangs, naked big-breasted women, daggers, a stylized AK-47. But the bad tattoos framed the words "MS-13" inked in a Germanic-looking font. The letters covered most of his back from shoulder to shoulder.

"*Mara Salvatrucha* 13 or MS-13," Kirkbride said. "Also known as the most violent gang in America. I looked them up. Salvadoran origin out of Los Angeles but they've spread out across the country. They're known for drug distribution, murder, rape, child prostitution, robbery, home invasions, kidnapping, human trafficking, carjackings . . . they do it all, as long as it's violent."

Cassie took a deep breath. "So you find two outlaw motorcycle gang members tortured and killed and two months later you've got an MS-13 member laid out in your morgue."

Kirkbride nodded.

She said, "If we assume that this was more than a one-car rollover, it sounds like you've got some kind of vigilante out there keeping bad people out."

Kirkbride shook his head. "I gave that some thought, but I don't believe it. Not after I saw what happened to those two bodies we found out in the field. Someone used blowtorches on them, Cassie. They used drills on their kneecaps and bolt cutters on their fingers and toes. It was drawn out and terrible and it was the work of more than one man."

She said, "Then it could be the beginnings of a gang war."

"Right here in Bakken County," Kirkbride said.

Then he said, "I want you to dig into this. We've got to make sure this isn't what it looks like. And if it is, we've got to get in front of it."

Cassie nodded.

"There's something else, and this needs to be kept strictly between you and me," Kirkbride said. "You need to do this investigation completely on your own. You can't recruit any deputies to help, or even talk to them about it. You only report to me, understand?"

She was confused and she knew she showed it. "Why? Why wouldn't we want to put all of our resources into finding out?"

Kirkbride nodded. He said, "Just trust me on this for now. I know it's asking a lot since you barely know me and you haven't even worked your first day on the job. But I ask you to trust me."

"I was in a situation before I came here where the sheriff asked me to be his spy within the department," she said. "He used the information I gave him to railroad my partner. I swore I would never get into a situation like that again, and I won't. You have to assure me that isn't what you're asking me to do or I'll get in my car tonight and drive back to Montana."

Kirkbride was silent. Their eyes were locked and she was angrier than she wanted to be. She knew there would be nothing in Helena for her, but she couldn't back down.

"I'm not going to use what you tell me to railroad anyone," Kirkbride said firmly. "That's as much as I can say right now. So I guess it's your choice to trust me or not. There's a reason why I reached outside the department to hire my new chief investigator. I did my research before I offered you the job. I read about how you gunned down a corrupt state trooper who had a dozen years on you and how the guy had been operating under the nose of local law enforcement for years. I read about how you stayed on the Lizard King case even though it was out of your jurisdiction and beyond your authority. What I see in you is a bulldog. I need a bulldog."

Cassie blinked hard and understood. "You think someone in your department —"

"Stop," Kirkbride barked, raising his hand palm up to cut her off. "Leave it where it is. I'm not going to say any more. It's your choice to stay under my conditions or leave under yours."

She took a deep breath and expelled it. So much, so quickly. She had yet to internalize the situation in Grimstad, much less the possibilities of a nascent gang war or internal corruption within the sheriff's department. But she was flattered by what he said and God knew she needed the promotion and the challenge. She wasn't sure she was up to it, though. Kirkbride didn't know the whole story when it came to the gun battle with the trooper — how she'd ambushed the man in a stairwell and made it look like he fired first.

She said, "I'll stay."

On the way back to the law enforcement center and her apartment, Kirkbride said, "Get a good night's sleep and I'll see you at seven forty-five tomorrow for the morning briefing. You'll get to meet my team."

She nodded. But she wasn't sure she'd be able to sleep at all.

■ ■ ■ ■

PART TWO:
DAY FOUR

■ ■ ■ ■

Chapter Ten

It was late at night when Kyle woke up. His stomach churned and his head felt foggy. He was afraid he might throw up, and he hovered for a moment over the trash can in his room trying to keep it in. He couldn't remember eating dinner, but he thought he could recall his door opening earlier followed by an argument between his mom and T-Lock. But Kyle wasn't sure he hadn't dreamed it.

He didn't like the way his mouth tasted, either. It was dry and he needed a drink of water.

Kyle opened his bedroom door cautiously. The lights were still on in the living room, and there were more empty beer bottles on the end table. But Winkie was gone, and so was the square of glass.

He could hear talking — a soft, high-pitched conversation — coming from inside his mother's bedroom. Luckily, the door was closed. He didn't want anyone seeing him. Kyle tiptoed past it toward the kitchen.

On the table was a full McDonald's bag with the top folded over. Kyle opened it and looked inside. She'd brought burgers and fries home but they were all cold so apparently they hadn't eaten anything either. He tried a French fry but it was cold and stiff and it nearly made him gag.

Kyle drank two full glasses of water from the tap. He thought he could make it back to his bedroom before anyone saw him, but his mom's door opened just as he passed it.

She didn't see him at first because she was looking back over her shoulder. She was wearing a thin black nightie Kyle had never seen before. Her legs were white and bare. He didn't like it that he could see her curves through her clothing because she was backlit. She was looking back at T-Lock, who was sitting up in bed in his boxer shorts lit by the dim light of the table lamp. He was smoking a cigarette *right in the open.* The square of glass was next to him on top of the covers, and several little squares — baggies from the bundle — were on the glass. So was a candle, a syringe, and a little black ball.

Just then, his mom turned and nearly bowled him over. She could barely walk and her eyes were glassy.

She bent down and hugged him and buried her face into his neck, and said, "Oh, my little man. My little sweet man."

She said it in a slurred little girl voice Kyle had never heard before.

Kyle kept his eyes closed tight. He didn't want to see anymore.

From the bedroom, T-Lock said, "Shut the damned door, Rachel."

CHAPTER ELEVEN

At two forty-five in the morning, Fidel "La Matanza" Escobar and Diego "Silencio" Argueta drove their silver Toyota Tundra pickup into the parking lot of the Missouri Breaks Lodge east of Grimstad. The truck was beaded with water from the industrial wash at the truck plaza outside of town and it streamed in rivulets from the back tailgate. As they passed by the large lighted window of the man camp office, Escobar saw a pudgy Caucasian inside sitting at a desk. The Caucasian wore a denim shirt with a name badge on the breast and a patch on his shoulder.

The Caucasian, who had a thatch of straw-colored hair and a ruddy complexion, looked up and squinted as the Tundra passed by.

"Labriego," Escobar said, meaning "farmworker."

Argueta laughed.

Escobar swung the pickup over and parked between two muddy four-by-four company vehicles. He kept the pickup running as he got out and pulled on his heavy distressed brown leather jacket. Twin jets of condensation came out of his nostrils as he exhaled into the cold night air, and he wrapped a newly purchased fleece scarf over the top of his shaved head and around his face below his nose. He tucked the ends of the scarf into his collar. Oh, how he hated the cold.

Escobar wasn't quite five foot six but he had broad shoulders and a thick chest. He had an egg-shaped shaved head, a flat wide nose, a soul patch under his bottom lip, and huge protruding ears. His ears got cold easily, he thought, because they weren't close enough to his scalp so they froze on the inside and the outside at the same time. He had flat black eyes.

He did a walk around the Tundra under the harsh light of the LED floods that lit up the parking lot like a used-car lot. Water pattered on the pavement from the undercarriage and truck bed. Within the hour, he knew, it would be turned into ice. That was fine, he thought. As long as the ice was clean.

He glanced over at the window of the office to see the *labriego* leaning back in his desk chair to check him out. No doubt, the *labriego* didn't recognize the pickup as belonging to any of his current residents. Either that, or the man was easily distracted. Maybe seeing a pickup that was actually clean was an unusual sight, Escobar thought.

Escobar looked around the fenced perimeter of the lot. There were security cameras mounted on each distant corner post. The cameras could see the activity in the lot in abstract, but weren't close enough or high enough to see into individual vehicles. From the angle he was parked, he knew the *labriego* couldn't see well either, so he opened the tailgate.

His tools were splayed across the metal ribbed floor of the pickup. Bolt cutters, drill bits, tin snips, ball-peen hammer, pliers, bar clamp, stainless-steel commercial bone saw. And the two eighteen-inch-high carbon stainless-steel Condor El Salvador machetes, which were unique because of the slot in the blade and the knuckle guard grip. The tools were beaded with rinse water from being blasted with the same high-pressure hand-wands they'd used to clean out the bed of the pickup as well as the inside bed walls. The tools glistened in the bright overhead lights, although the beads of water were already starting to freeze into translucent buttons.

He walked around the pickup to the passenger side as Argueta powered down his window.

Argueta said, "*Ayee* — it's a cold motherfucker, La Matanza." *La Matanza* meant "the Massacre." The Massacre was an infamous event in Salvadoran history, when tens of thousands of peasants were slaughtered by the ruling elite in 1932. Escobar's great-grandmother had been hacked to death by machete. He'd never known her.

Escobar said, "You've been in there with the heater blasting. I've been the one out here, Silencio."

"You said to stay inside, man."

Argueta was even shorter than Escobar and much leaner. Everything about him was sharp angles — nose, cheekbones, chin. He reminded Escobar of a bird — bird frame, bird bones, bird eyes, bird swiftness. Argueta did everything fast and jerky. He wouldn't have been La Matanza's first choice but for the fact that Argueta didn't have face and neck tattoos. Now that he'd seen him swing a machete, though, Escobar knew he'd made the right choice.

Escobar said, "I'll go inside and talk to the *labriego.* You gather up all my tools and put them in my toolbox. Make sure they're dry. If there is any ice on the metal — chip it off. Put the Condors under the seat so nobody can see them from outside."

Argueta nodded, then chinned over Escobar's shoulder. "It's too fucking cold in this place, man. Human beings aren't made to live in this kind of cold."

"Get a better coat."

"You know what I mean, man. This is *brutal.*"

"Stay here and don't bring the toolbox in until I signal you," Escobar said, looking over his shoulder at the man camp office window. The *labriego* was still there behind the desk, but he'd switched his attention to a computer monitor and he was no longer looking out the window. "Let me go check this place out and make sure it will work for us."

Escobar tugged on the front door handle but it was locked.

"Forget your keycard?" said the electronic voice of the *labriego* through a speaker grill.

"I don't have one. I wanted to see about renting a couple of rooms. Me and my buddy out there heard you can rent rooms for the night at these man camps."

"Hold on — I'll buzz you in."

The lock clicked and Escobar tugged the door open. It felt good to be inside out of the cold. The door eased shut behind him.

The *labriego* looked up from behind his desk in the office. There was a counter and a Plexiglas slider separating them. The *labriego* bounded up and opened the slider and extended a meaty hand. He was young, Escobar thought. Maybe midtwenties. He wore a gold wedding band on his finger.

"Welcome to the Missouri Breaks Lodge," the *labriego* said. "First of all, we don't use the term 'man camp'. That's for some of the other places out there, I guess you'd say. I'm Phil."

Escobar nodded at the name badge on the *labriego's* shirt, as if to acknowledge his name.

"Nice pickup you've got there, mister. I've been looking to trade up myself and those Tundras have caught my eye. You like it?"

"Sure."

"And that's the full-sized CrewMax, right? Five point seven liter V-eight engine? Fully loaded?"

Escobar nodded.

"Cold out there, isn't it?" Phil said with a chuckle. "We aren't even in the worst of it yet. We consider this downright balmy. Wait until January when it never gets above freezing all day long, and it's twenty below at night."

"Nice place," Escobar said. He still had not unwrapped his scarf or unzipped his heavy jacket.

"You bet it is," Phil the *labriego* said. "We've got the cleanest, brightest, and best-run lodge in Bakken County here. When people think of man camps they think all kinds of things. But I can give you a short tour and you'll see what I mean."

"What's it cost a night?"

"One-sixty per unit," Phil said. "But that includes everything. Breakfast from three to nine, lunch from eleven to one, dinner from three thirty to nine. Since we've got guys coming and going on shifts twenty-four seven, we're always open and available. Entry by keycard only, as you saw."

He went on to describe the massive lounge area with televisions and computers, the industrial self-serve laundry, the full-service kitchen, and the on-site convenience store.

As the *labriego* swiped his keycard through a reader on the second set of doors, he said over his shoulder, "We've got eight hundred men in this facility right now and there's no better lodging anywhere in the county. No one can get in without an authorized card, and we have absolutely zero tolerance when it comes to alcohol, drugs, or weapons."

"That's good," Escobar said, a few steps behind the *labriego,* who gestured to big open rooms on their left and right.

"These are the the gear rooms," he said. Escobar saw hundreds of sets of dirty and muddy outdoor clothing hanging from pegs with big dirty boots lining the floor. "Every man entering the facility has to change into clean clothing here and put on a pair of plastic booties to go down the hallways."

The *labriego* paused and looked at Escobar expectantly. At first, Escobar didn't understand.

"Even you," the *labriego* said with a smug grin.

While Escobar slid orange-tinted plastic coverings over his lizard-skin cowboy boots, the *labriego* said, "You can take that big coat off, you know. It's very comfortable inside. We keep the interior at a set seventy degrees in the winter and sixty-eight in the summer. Each unit has its own temperature controls inside."

Escobar grunted, but he didn't remove the scarf or his coat.

The *labriego* toured Escobar through the huge dining hall, and explained that the food was so good sometimes locals drove out just to eat it. He said the lodging company brought in chefs from all over the country to make special meals on special nights. Men with food allergies just had to fill out a form and get a doctor's slip and they'd be fed special meals.

The *labriego* showed Escobar a standard unit, which he called a Jack and Jill room: a small, spare room with a television, small desk, double bed, and closet. The Jack room had a side door that opened into a shared bathroom with a shower. The Jill room, which was identical in layout, was on the other side of the bathroom door.

"Some of the guys hot bunk it," the *labriego* said, "They occupy the same room but switch on different shifts. That means we can go up to four guys in a Jack and Jill.

"Here's our only open VIP room," the *labriego* said, opening the door to a larger unit that included a personal bathroom, a larger bed, a microwave oven, and a refrigerator. "When the company execs come up from Texas or Oklahoma, they like to stay in these."

"Nice." Escobar thought, This is like a fucking spaceship — entirely self-contained.

"So," the *labriego* said, "Do you want to fill out the paperwork? We take cash and company credit cards if they're on our approved list, but sorry, no checks."

"I've got cash."

"Then follow me and we'll get you checked in."

The *labriego* strode back down the hallway toward the office. He said, "I noticed your California plates. I guess the economy is pretty bad out there, huh? I heard something like twenty percent unemployment."

Escobar had no idea. He knew no one with a traditional job.

"I've never been out to the Golden State," the *labriego* said. "I can't even imagine living someplace where they never have winter. I'm from Minnesota originally — a farm outside of Bemidji."

Escobar smiled at that. *Labriego,* all right.

He continued, "My wife and kid are still there, but I'll move them out by next spring. So this cold weather doesn't bother me at all. Are you married?"

"No."

"So no kids?"

"I didn't say that."

The *labriego* laughed uncomfortably. He said, "Being from sunny California — all those bikinis and surfboards — you guys are in for a culture shock."

Escobar nodded.

"So, what brings you two out here? Who are you working for, or are you looking?"

"Looking," Escobar said.

"Well, this is a good place to make contacts. It's pretty rare that an able-bodied guy who can pass a drug test doesn't hook up with one of the big boys within a day or two. I assume you can pass a drug test?" he asked while cocking an eyebrow.

"Of course."

The *labriego* was a chatterer, Escobar thought. He looked around the entryway and the office. It was as clean and stark as a hospital. A closed-circuit camera was mounted over a set of glass doors that led to a long hallway. Inside the office was a bank of closed-circuit television monitors with divided black-and-white images of the parking lot from four angles, empty hallways within the complex, a closed dining area where the only movement was a man with a mop, what looked like a game room, and several exterior views. A mass of cables snaked behind the monitors to an Apple server.

Escobar said, "You got cameras everywhere?"

"Yes, sir. We keep this place as secure as possible."

"So everything we did — everything you just showed me — was recorded?"

"Absolutely. That way if a room gets

broken into or one of our guest's property comes up missing we can go back and pinpoint the bad guy for the police. We've got top-of-the-line video technology," Phil said. He swiveled in his chair and toggled a switch and a camera zoomed in on Escobar's eyes. The image filled one of the monitors.

"Amazing, huh?"

Escobar looked at his own eyes looking back in the monitor. He narrowed them.

"Isn't that scarf getting hot?" Phil laughed.

It was, but Escobar said, "No."

The *labriego* shrugged and said, "We see more and more of you California guys around here these days. There's even a few on this floor. Hell, you might even know 'em."

Escobar thought, *Idiota labriego.* But he said, "Maybe."

"So there's only one way in and one way out?" Escobar asked.

"Yes, sir. That's for security."

"Can I bring my tools inside?"

"You can leave them in the storage area we saw. It's completely secure and we've never had a theft."

"More cameras?"

"Absolutely. Like I said, this lodge is the cream of the crop. Believe me, there are places where they let guys just come and go at all hours and bring in alcohol and prostitutes. The local cops are called there all the time. In fact, you probably saw that place out on the highway called the Home Away from Home. That's as low-rent as it gets."

Escobar nodded as he followed the *labriego* through the doors into the lobby area.

"I'll get the forms if you want to call your buddy in. Is he from California, too?"

"Yes."

"What's your name, anyway? We like to be on a first-name basis with our residents."

"Fidel."

The *labriego* snorted a laugh. "Like Castro? Man, I bet you got a lot of ribbing in school. The guys used to call me Phillips-head Screwdriver."

"That's a good one."

"You know how kids are."

"Do you want to see my Tundra?" Escobar asked.

The *labriego* paused. He said, "I'm not supposed to leave the facility . . ." but he said it in a way that indicated he was willing to break the rules. "Okay. I want to see that outfit."

Escobar led him out across the parking lot.

He made it a point not to look at any of the cameras directly. The *labriego* followed, still chattering, something about playing ice hockey on a pond when he was younger, while he pulled on a thick company parka.

As they neared the Tundra, Argueta saw them coming and looked at Escobar with a puzzled face through the back window.

Subtly, Escobar lifted his right hand and adjusted the scarf around his neck. Argueta nodded in understanding.

"It's easy to find, isn't it?" The *labriego* laughed. "It's the only clean pickup in the whole damned place. Man, if I had an outfit like this I'd keep it looking good myself. I read where the base price is forty-two thousand, before loading it up. Is that right?"

"It's right," Escobar said as Argueta opened the passenger door.

"Premium audio, navigation — the whole nine yards?"

"The whole nine yards," Escobar said as he stepped back. Argueta came out of the truck and flipped a machete through the air.

Escobar caught it by the handle in mid-flight and took two steps forward and swung it like a baseball bat and buried the blade so far into the *labriego's* throat under his chin that it hit his neck bone at the back.

After they'd thrown the body of the *labriego* into the back of the pickup along with the Apple server from the office and cruised out of the lot, Escobar said, "We'll dump him and go back to the truck wash."

After a long silence, Argueta said, "Why did we do that?"

"Too many cameras. And the *labriego* — he talked too much."

"Did anyone see you?"

"No."

"Where are we going to stay until we find the other guy?"

Escobar gestured toward the flickering HOME AWAY FROM HOME CAMP sign across the highway from the truck plaza. He said, "There."

"Why there?"

"The farmhand in back recommended it."

■ ■ ■ ■

DAY FIVE

■ ■ ■ ■

CHAPTER TWELVE

It was uncomfortably warm inside the briefing room of the law enforcement center at 7:30 A.M. the next morning, Cassie thought. The room was packed with jostling sheriff's department deputies as well as representatives from the Grimstad Police Department, the highway patrol, and the Northwest Drug Enforcement Task Force. The warmth of the room contrasted visibly with the cold outside the windows which dripped with condensation and puddled on the sills. Through the fogged glass, poker chip–sized snowflakes floated through the predawn to the icy street three floors below.

Cassie stood uncomfortably in the back of the room behind the last row of chairs. It was obvious to her when she entered that the men inside had certain chairs they sat in every day within certain groups, and she didn't want to encroach on anyone's territory and be thought pushy on her first morning on the job. Several other men, two in sport coats and ties — no doubt the federal drug guys — stood in back as well, as if signaling they were participating in the briefing at arm's length.

The room smelled of freshly shaved and showered men and brought-in hot coffee going on day shift, and lingering cigarette smoke from the fabric of some of the uniforms ending their midnight shift. It was the one time in the day when everyone could be there. Deputies stole glances at her in the back and when they did she nodded in acknowledgment. She'd been in these situations before.

At the front of the room was a podium occupied by Undersheriff Max Maxfield, whom Cassie identified from his name badge. Maxfield reviewed a three-ring binder before him. Sheriff Kirkbride was on his left leaning back in an office chair. He looked affable and slightly bemused. Kirkbride sipped on a mug of coffee and joked with his employees, chiding them for one thing or other. When she'd entered the room he smiled at her.

To Maxfield's right was a middle-aged woman at a small desk. She was tiny, pert, and had a severe black haircut. She wore a dark suit. She was the only other woman in the room, and she and Cassie nodded to each other with a kind of silent kinship. She was Judy Banister, Cassie guessed, Kirkbride's office administrator. Cassie had communicated with Banister previously on employment details. Banister had at one point said, "It'll be nice to have another female in the building." Cassie, though, reserved judgment on that. She'd found that in too many situations, a lone woman could be the most territorial of all.

Most of the forty-plus deputies in the room fit a certain type, Cassie noted. Generally, they were fresh-faced, eager-looking, and young. She recalled Kirkbride saying that when he first became sheriff the department had six deputies.

What was unusual — for Cassie — was the impression of camaraderie she got from interactions of people in the room. Unlike full-staff briefings she'd experienced countless times back in Helena that were charged with resentment and ill feelings, this group seemed to be bubbling with a shared sense of purpose and high morale. She'd never been in the middle of a unit of well-trained soldiers or a close-knit football team, but she thought it must be something like what she was observing. And she knew that the atmosphere of an organization was set at the top, whether for good or ill. Sheriff Tubman in Montana ruled by fear, dirty politics, and innuendo and his people resented it. Kirkbride, in contrast, created an atmosphere of energy and professionalism.

It was a good first impression.

The exception were two older men sitting together in the back row who, she guessed, had been around for a while. They had that old cop I've-seen-everything weariness in their eyes. She wondered if they resented all the young, gung ho deputies in their midst.

She'd been up most of the night too wired to sleep, and she'd read and reread the files and case reports Kirkbride had given her. There were three men she wanted to identify right away: Cam Tollefsen, who was the first on the scene of the rollover, Lance Foster who was second, and Ian Davis, the department's only undercover operative. She guessed that one of the old guys in the back row was Tollefsen because the incident report was written in a terse, cover-your-ass style that was perfected only through years of law-enforcement experience and countless court appearances in front of aggressive defense attorneys. Davis was easy to pick out because he was the only young deputy with a scruffy beard, long hair, and street clothes. Lance Foster, though, could be anyone in the room.

"Before we get started," Kirkbride said, rising from his chair and pausing until he had everyone's attention, "I want to introduce everybody to our new Chief Investigator Cassandra Dewell."

With that, every head in the room swiveled toward her. She tried to smile but she was afraid it came across as a grimace.

"Investigator Dewell comes to us from the Lewis and Clark Sheriff's Department in Helena, Montana," Kirkbride said. "A few of you might have come across her name before if you read anything about the Lizard King case a while back. She's the one who broke up the kidnapping and sexual abuse ring and she had a shoot-out with a corrupt Montana state trooper. We're just happy as hell to have her on our team."

The Lizard King reference got the attention of several of the deputies, who immediately whispered to their colleagues around them. She knew she was blushing now, and she could feel her neck get hot. Especially when most of the men in the room applauded.

She said, "I'm happy to be on your team, Sheriff, and I look forward to working with all of you."

She didn't think she was expected to go

on, and she didn't.

Kirkbride asked all the personnel in the room to briefly introduce themselves to her, even though, he said, "You probably all look alike to her right now — like the bunch of square-headed Midwestern boys you are," which was true and also brought a laugh.

One by one the deputies stood up, stated their names, and sat back down.

"Jim Klug."

"Tom Melvin."

"Shaun McKnight."

"Bryan Gregson."

"Fred Walker."

Cassie made eye contact and nodded toward each deputy as they said their names.

"Lance Foster, or as the guys call me, Surfer Dude."

She smiled and recalled when Kirkbride mentioned him earlier. Foster was blond and beefy, with a buzz-cut haircut and cherubic red cheeks. She noted who he was but didn't let her eyes linger on him.

A dozen other deputies barked out their names and sat down.

"Cam Tollefsen."

Tollefsen was, in fact, one of the older men in the back row. He was nearly as tall as Kirkbride and he had a thick cowboy-style mustache that was flecked with silver.

His large gut strained at his uniform shirt. Unlike the younger deputies, he seemed put out having to introduce himself.

The round-robin of confusing introductions wound their way to the front of the room.

"I'm Leslie Maxfield, the undersheriff. Everyone calls me Max."

Then, "And I'm Judy Banister," she said.

"She's the one you want to talk to if you really want to know anything that goes on around here," Kirkbride said, turning to Banister. "Judy has been with the department since before I came on the scene. She knows where all the bodies are buried, don't you, Judy?"

Banister demurred and shook her head, but Cassie could tell she appreciated the recognition. In Cassie's experience, every sheriff's department had a Judy Banister, and every department needed one. She was the individual who kept the place running and who provided institutional knowledge as employees came and went. Along with Sheriff Kirkbride himself, Cassie thought, she vowed to never cross Judy Banister.

Kirkbride gestured to Maxfield, and said, "Take it away, Max."

"Before we get to the new stuff," Maxfield

said, "there are a couple of updates."

Cassie listened as Maxfield went over cases and crimes that were familiar to everyone in the room except her. "Honchos from Halliburton" were putting more and more pressure on the department to both find the thieves who were stealing their equipment from their facilities and to recover the stolen vehicles. A long-running property and mineral rights dispute between a local farmer and a drilling company could result in trouble between the farmer's sons and company employees. A restraining order had been granted by the judge for an ex-wife against her ex-husband who she swore she'd seen sneaking around the neighborhood.

Although her eyes were on Maxfield, she had trouble concentrating on the initial part of the briefing. She was running primarily on a combination of adrenaline and caffeine and there was a dull headache growing in the back of her head. Some of the details she'd read in the files on the two unsolved homicides had horrified her and set her on edge.

The two Sons of Freedom victims had obviously been tortured, and by professionals. The coroner speculated that both men had been kept alive for hours while the murderer snipped off their fingers joint by joint, severed the tendons of their legs, drilled into their kneecaps, mutilated their sexual organs, gouged out their eyes, seared their skin with blowtorches, and finally beheaded them. The abuse was systematic and well-planned, it seemed, and specific tools were used to carry it out. It was awful, she thought. There was no way to know if the murderer was trying to get information, send a message, or he was simply enjoying himself. Maybe all three. She wasn't easily shocked or sickened, but reading through the files and seeing the photos had gutted her.

She contrasted the Sons of Freedom victims with the body found at the rollover. That vic appeared to simply be on the losing end of a fatal car wreck. There were no outside injuries beyond those occurring from the crash itself, although his body had practically been severed in two.

If there was a gang war taking place, she thought, she knew which side she'd bet on.

Maxfield finished up with status reports and updates before turning the pages in his binder.

"New items," he said. "First, somebody found a foot." He paused and his silence attracted the attention of the entire room, including Cassie.

"Just a foot?" someone asked.

"Mine's right here," someone else said, and half the room laughed.

"Just a foot," Maxfield repeated. He didn't smile. "Four miles east, in the middle of the prairie between two pumping units. Couple of Schlumberger guys found it this morning when they reported to a well to replace a part. They nearly ran it over in their truck."

"Just a *foot*?" one of the deputies echoed.

Maxfield held up an eight-by-ten color photo, displayed it, then handed it to a deputy in the first row to pass along. Cassie noted that it was a man's bare foot cleanly severed at the ankle. The photo was taken against a background of blood-flecked snow.

Maxfield said, "Because it's bare and not still in a boot, it indicates something other than a run-of-the-mill oil field accident. We've checked at the hospital, and nobody walked in on a bloody stump. We're checking hospitals and clinics in a two-hundred-mile radius, but so far no hits."

"What happened, then?" a deputy asked Maxfield.

"Too early to say," the undersheriff responded. "All we know is the coroner packed it in snow and brought it back to the building. He says it was barely frozen, which says it might have been cut off last night or early this morning. No one has called in and reported missing a foot as yet."

Cassie saw several deputies repressing smiles at that.

"Seriously, though, the lack of significant blood on the ground where the foot was found suggests it was cut off postmortem. So keep your eyes open for other body parts, gentlemen."

Kirkbride gestured to Ian Davis, the undercover cop, and Davis nodded that he understood. Cassie watched the wordless exchange: Davis should ask around on the street about who was missing a foot . . . or missing in general.

"Item two," Maxfield said, "is another weird one. The morning man at the Missouri Breaks Lodge called in to say the night shift manager was missing when he showed up to relieve him at the registration desk this morning. Just wasn't there. The missing man is Phillip Klein, thirty-four. There are no signs of foul play, but the computer server that stores all the video from the interior and exterior closed-circuit cameras is missing as well."

Cassie could tell from the murmuring in the room that item two aroused more puzzlement than interest, but she didn't know why.

"Here's his photo from his company ID," Maxfield said, handing around a second print.

"I don't get it," one of the deputies said. Cassie recalled his name as Jim Klug. "Guys go missing all the time from administrative positions. They decide they can make more money out in the oil field, and they just take off for the hills like old-time gold prospectors."

Several deputies agreed.

Maxfield shook his head. "Klein is a thirteen-year manager with a wife and kids back home in Minnesota. The wife says she hears from him every morning when he gets off his shift — he calls her or texts her — except for this morning. His company vehicle is still in the lot. According to the morning manager, Klein isn't the type to get oil fever."

"So he left with somebody else," a deputy said.

"Probably a whore," Cam Tollefsen said from the back in a weary voice. "She showed up, did her thing with him in the front office, and he panicked when he realized the whole act was caught on video. So he jerked the server out, climbed in her car, and he's shacking up with her in a double-wide outside of Minot."

Several deputies nodded their agreement to Tollefsen's speculation. Cassie looked from Tollefsen to Maxfield.

"That could be," Maxfield said. "Stranger things have happened. But we'll get copies of Klein's head shot out to all of you and we want you to ask around to see if anyone's seen him."

"Maybe this is his foot," a deputy said, holding up the first photo. "Maybe it's connected."

The photo finally was passed to the rear of the room and Cassie studied it. There was a crude skull-and-crossbones tattoo on the top of the foot a few inches from where the ankle would have been. But what alarmed her was how similar the amputation looked to the photos she'd seen during the night of the mutilated Sons of Freedom victims. The cut looked to be scored through the flesh with a sharp knife, then the bones cut cleanly with a saw.

She looked up to find Kirkbride watching her. His eyes said he thought the same thing she did: a third torture-murder victim.

"According to Klein's wife, the foot doesn't belong to Klein," Maxfield said to the deputy who'd inquired, "unless Klein got the tattoo very recently. When he was home two weeks ago in Bemidji he didn't have it. So a direct connection between the two cases is pretty unlikely."

Cassie stepped back as the deputies milled out of the room. She wanted to talk to both Ian Davis and Lance Foster, but not together. She hoped to have a few words with Davis first.

As the men gathered their coats and left the room, she heard most of a bad joke Jim Klug was telling to another deputy.

Klug said, "So Ole is walking down the railroad tracks with his wife Lena and he sees a foot and he says, 'Lena, that looks like Joe's foot!' Then he walks a few hundred feet further and sees a hand and says, 'Lena, that looks like Joe's hand!' Then a trunk, and he says, 'Lena, that looks like Joe's trunk!' Finally, Ole sees a head on the tracks and picks it up by the ears and shakes it and says, 'Joe, Joe, are you all right?' "

The other deputy laughed but stopped abruptly when he noticed Cassie was watching them.

"Cop humor," Klug explained, "mixed with Norwegian humor."

"It's okay," Cassie said with a smile. "I kind of like that one."

■ ■ ■ ■

Lance Foster went by in a scrum of other deputies and Cassie let him go. She didn't want to single him out.

Cam Tollefsen gave her an inscrutable dead-eye cop stare as he passed her and she gave it right back although she felt a shiver go up her spine. She didn't even know the man but she knew, right then, that he'd be a challenge to her. And maybe worse.

Ian Davis shouldered on a ratty backpack and was one of the last to leave.

"Officer Davis, could I talk to you for a minute?"

He gave her the once-over, then chinned toward the far corner of the room, and ambled over there. She followed.

He stopped and turned. He was Cassie's height — short — and had soulful brown eyes that were slightly suspicious. But he looked the part he played, she thought. Scruffy, a bit down on his luck, like he'd recently walked off the Amtrak train at the station.

After introducing herself again, she said, "How long have you been working the street here?"

"A year and a half. Six more months and

I go back to patrol. Believe me, I never thought I'd look forward to shaving in the morning and putting on the uniform again, but I am. It's pretty raggedy-ass out there."

"So would you say you've got a pretty good handle on the local players?"

Davis shrugged, but said, "Yeah. It's harder than hell to keep track of the transients through here these days — there's a lot of them. But there were knuckleheads here before the boom and a few of them are still around. They're like the farmers — if they stuck they're getting rich."

"Interesting. Are you talking about dealers in particular?"

"Yes. Everything pretty much starts and ends with drugs around here."

"Is there a go-to local guy? Someone you'd point to who has his ear to the ground?"

"Oh, yeah," Davis said. "Willie Dietrich. The sheriff's run him out of the county more than once but he keeps coming back. He's learned how to operate in the shadows, you know? He's got guys to take the fall for him so he can still look clean. I've sort of met him and I know he's got his fingers in everything around here. My goal before I go back on patrol is to nail that douche bag."

"Willie Dietrich," she said, committing the name to memory.

"What else do you know?" she asked, careful not to reveal why she was asking. "What are they talking about on the street?"

He looked away for a moment, as if gathering his thoughts. Then, "It's kinda weird out there right now. I told the sheriff about it last week, and it's nothing I can put my finger on. But it's like all the players are bunkered in and keeping their mouths shut. They've gone all low profile. Do you watch movies?"

"Less since my son was born," Cassie said.

"You know how in *The Godfather* the bad guys all 'go to the mattresses' before a war? It's like that.

"But the biggest topic of conversation," he said, "is that meth and heroin are at a premium right now and that's unusual. I have to say that as hard as we work it, there's usually like a flood of drugs coming in from every direction. But the flow's been cut off and nobody is saying why because I think they don't know. I wish it was because we've done a huge bust or put the screws to the douche bags, but that isn't the case. When the supply goes down the price goes up, and tweakers get desperate."

Cassie asked, "Has the supply line been cut?"

Davis shrugged. "It seems like it, at least temporarily. Blue meth has gone from two hundred a gram to four hundred in the last week. Funny thing is it isn't really blue at all. The cookers make it blue with food coloring because of that TV show. But whether it's white or blue, that's a big jump in price. Same thing with heroin. I'm sure they'll figure a way around it, though. They always do."

She thanked him and asked for his cell phone number.

He nodded and told it to her which meant, she thought, he felt he could trust her at least to some degree.

"Don't worry if I don't answer it right away," he said, "I'll call back when I can. Sometimes I'm in the middle of a situation and I can't have the caller ID come up, 'Bakken County Sheriff.' "

"I understand," she said with a chuckle, and gave him her cell number. "It's my private phone and it has a four-oh-six Montana prefix, not the department. If something of interest comes up, call me direct."

He said he would.

■ ■ ■ ■

Cassie caught up with Sheriff Kirkbride in the hallway as he was headed for his office.

"How's the apartment?" he asked. "Did you get settled in?"

"It's wonderful," she said. "I'm fine. I was wondering if you had a minute to talk about a couple of things. Plus, I want to know about a guy named Willie Dietrich."

Kirkbride shot out his arm and looked at his watch. "Willie, huh? He's a piece of work. But I can't meet now. I've got a county commission meeting starting in ten minutes. They have an item on the agenda to ban any further man camps in the county, and I've got to weigh in what a dumb idea that is."

"It is?" Cassie asked, surprised.

"Think about it," Kirkbride said as he paused at his door. "We've got hundreds of men showing up every week who need a place to crash. They're building houses like crazy right now but not fast enough to keep up with demand. Those man camps are clean, safe, and well-run — most of 'em, anyway. Where are those men supposed to live while the new housing units are being built over the winter? It's a dumb idea.

"Plus," Kirkbride said, his face flushing red, "they've invited twelve damned Red Chinese politicians to the county who say they want to invest. Commie reds, Chicoms — here in North Dakota! The commissioners want me to provide security for them while they walk around in their suits and loafers. Can you believe that?"

"Anyway," she said, prompting him. "I read the files and I agree we have a gang problem. And maybe more than that."

"I'll be back this afternoon," he said. "Come by after lunch."

"Okay."

"Cassie" — he grinned at her — "I'm glad you said *we.*"

CHAPTER THIRTEEN

Kyle arrived home from delivering newspapers and noticed that T-Lock had finally wrapped a thick chain around the washing machine and secured it with a stout padlock. That meant, Kyle thought, T-Lock was trying to get on his mom's good side by finally doing what she'd been asking him to do for more than a year.

T-Lock and Kyle's mother were sitting at the kitchen table. It was obvious to him they'd been having an argument they didn't want him to overhear by the way they both shut up the instant he came in through the back door.

Their silence hung in the air while Kyle untied his pack boots and hung his heavy coat on a peg. His cheeks were numb from the cold and his skin hurt as the warmth from the kitchen enveloped him.

"Cold out there?" T-Lock asked, fake jaunty.

Instead of answering, Kyle looked at his mom. She was wearing her McDonald's tunic and black pants, her hair in a ponytail. Her uniform and the way she put up her hair made her look young. She shot a glance at him and he was taken aback by how she looked. Her eyes were red and half-closed and her face was puffy. She must have realized what she looked like to him because she quickly turned away and stared at the table. She held a coffee mug between her hands as if trying to crush it into powder.

Kyle said, yes, it was cold.

"Kyle, why don't you go get dressed for school now? Your mom and I are in the middle of a discussion," T-Lock said. Even from where he stood, four feet away, Kyle could smell T-Lock's morning breath. It hung in the air and it was a rancid combination of coffee and cigarette smoke.

"I'm hungry," Kyle said, eying a half-eaten box of powdered donuts on the table. While delivering newspapers that morning all he could think of were two things: eating a hot breakfast when he got home and asking T-Lock for enough money to buy a hand-held GPS. The GPS would come in handy on the river in Raheem's boat.

"Here," T-Lock said as he closed the box and flung the whole thing at Kyle. He

caught it against his stomach. "Go eat that
— we're done with it. Just give your mom
and me a minute, okay, *Kyle*?"

He said Kyle's name with a nasty inflection.

Kyle said to his mom, "You okay?"

"I'm fine, honey," she said, looking up
again briefly then back to her reflection in
the mug of coffee. "I'm sorry about last
night. I didn't mean to upset you."

"He's *fine*," T-Lock said, raising his voice.
"He's fine. You're fine. We're all fucking
fine."

"Tracy, please," Kyle's mother said.

T-Lock glared at Kyle with strange
intensity, Kyle thought. He looked
unhinged. Kyle decided he would stay
where he was to prevent T-Lock from hurt-
ing his mom.

She said to Kyle, "It's okay, Kyle. Let us
talk for a minute."

Kyle didn't like it that she was on T-Lock's
side. But she didn't seem frightened. Kyle
shrugged and took his half full box of
donuts to his bedroom. He'd ask about the
money for the GPS later, when T-Lock was
in one of his mellow moods.

After all, Kyle thought, it was really *his*
money — not T-Lock's.

And T-Lock had been stupid about saying

he should get "dressed for school," Kyle thought. He was dressed for school already: jeans, Grimstad Vikings hoodie. They were the clothes that he had. It's what he wore every day.

He sat down at his desk with the box of donuts and took one out. They'd been in the kitchen for a few days and were dried out, but the powdered sugar coating was good. After he'd devoured the first one he licked his fingers and plucked out another.

Kyle could overhear the conversation going on in the kitchen but he couldn't understand it all. He knew, though, that if T-Lock tried to hurt his mom he'd protect her. So he got prepared.

He dropped to his hands and knees and reached under his bed to retrieve the cardboard box he called his "River Box." It was filled with things he'd been collecting from Dumpsters, construction sites, and lost-and-found boxes for the last few months that he thought he might need when they pushed off on the Missouri: rope, wire, electrician's tape, hand tools, fishing line and fishing lures, extra clothes, a cool captain's hat. It was amazing what people threw away or left behind. Kyle dug into the box and found the crossbow arrow Winkie had shot into their door when his mom got so mad at T-Lock's friend.

The twenty-inch arrow was bent from the impact and from pulling it out of the wood and it was of no use to Winkie and his crossbow again. The paint was scraped off the shaft and the fletching was fouled. But the four-blade broadhead was razor sharp, even though it had been fired through the wood door.

If T-Lock ever hurt his mom, Kyle vowed, he'd stick that arrow into T-Lock's neck.

Kyle ate donuts and fingered the tip of the arrow as their voices carried.

T-Lock said, "I already told you, I've thought this all out. You've got to trust me on this. Quit worrying about it so much. *You're* not doing anything wrong."

"But it feels wrong. You're asking me to wash all the cash."

"It's called laundering, not washing, for Christ sake. And you're not stealing from anybody or cheating anyone. You're just replacing cash in the register with cash from that bag. You replace a twenty from the register with one from the bag. A ten for a ten. A five for a fucking five. It's simple as hell. And when they count up the money everything balances and nobody will even know."

"Still, you said the money is marked. What

if somebody checks it out and finds it?"

"For Christ sake, woman, how would they even know where it came from? You don't replace it all at once like a dumbass. You slip it in one bill at a time through the day. If you give some rube two fives in change, you give him one marked five and one clean one from the drawer. But you've got to keep the count in your head and make sure you put a marked five back in the drawer to take the place of the one you handed out. That's the only tough part of this — remembering not to get the money mixed up. You don't want the count to come up too short or too long. You want it to balance at the end of the day."

"What about the cameras, though? What if someone sees me?"

"We've been over that. The cameras are set up in back of you over your shoulder so they can see anyone at the counter trying to rob the place. They can see the top of your shoulders, the back of your head, the counter, and the rube ordering hamburgers. They can't see anything you're doing below waist level. So when you take the cash from your pocket and put it in the drawer they can't see it."

"What if one of my team members sees me swap out my cash for the money in the drawer?"

"They won't! They're all too fucking busy running around doing their own shit. Besides, if on the off chance somebody sees something and accuses you of stealing, you just get your back up like you do to me sometimes and *demand* they count the money in the drawer if they don't believe you. Just fucking demand they do it right there. They'll find it all balances out like it's supposed to and you're not only off the hook, you could sue their ass for harassment."

"I'd never do that, that's stupid."

"*They* don't know that."

Silence. Kyle waited.

T-Lock said, "If you do this right, if you do this like we talked about, you should be able to get through the whole pile in about a week. Then we're completely clean and you'll never have to do it again. We'll be home free, little lady."

"But what if somebody discovers the marked bills are floating around town?"

"What if they do? How in the hell are they going to figure out where they came from? There's a shitload of places to spend cash and get change. Money circulates — that's why they call it money."

"Really?" She sounded skeptical.

"Damn right. So just try it today. Take a thousand and work on your technique. You'll do fine. And I'll tell you what — I'll come in around noon and order up some burgers. If you're still feeling nervous about doing this, just put the rest of the marked cash in my sack and hand it over to me and I'll take it from there."

"Why don't you just do it in the first place?" she asked. "Why me?"

"How many times do we have to go over this? I'd raise red flags if I showed up around town with a huge wad of cash. People know me here. They *know* I'm not flush in the winter. But you work in an all-cash business. Thousands, hell, tens of thousands, in cash go in and out of the doors every day. If I worked there, I'd do it. But I don't. You work there."

There was another long pause. Kyle could sense that she was ready to do whatever it was T-Lock was asking her to do.

"But you'll take that car back today and get something smaller and older, right?" she said. "You say you can't go around town flashing cash but somehow you can drive around in that *thing* out there?"

"Yeah," T-Lock said with regret in his voice.

"You promise, right?"

"That's our deal. I'll stick to my part of the deal if you'll do yours."

"Get something practical that won't stand out," his mom said. "Get a nice used minivan."

"I hate those fucking mom cars."

"Tracy, you promised."

T-Lock emitted a long and loud groan. It was a groan of agreement, though.

"And there's one more thing," his mom said. "I don't want those drugs in my house. No one can know they're here or even guess they're here. You've got to take them out of my house. What if someone comes for them and Kyle is here? I would never forgive myself."

"It's done," T-Lock said with triumph.

"What's done?"

"You said you wanted that bag out of your house and it's out of your house. I heard you last night and I handled it this morning. The bag is not in your house."

"Where is it?"

"I ain't saying. That's for your protection, darlin'. If you don't know, nobody can get you to say. Same with Kyle."

"T-Lock, I need a bump."

"Maybe one."

Kyle put the arrow back in the box and slid it back under his bed.

207

A *bump*? What did that mean?

But Kyle recalled the square of glass on their bed and he had the feeling things were going to go bad again with his mom.

CHAPTER FOURTEEN

Cassie's new office was two doors down from Sheriff Kirkbride's. It was simple — new construction like the rest of the law enforcement center — with a cheap desk, an empty bookshelf and credenza, blank walls marred by nail holes left by the last occupant, a window overlooking the patrol parking lot behind the building, and a desktop PC and monitor. The only chair was an ancient hardback that would have looked more at home at a college apartment poker table.

She slid the chair behind the desk and placed her briefcase on the credenza in back. The phone set was high-tech and complicated, with half a dozen blinking lights and buttons without instructions.

Inside her briefcase were three framed photos: Ben's recent school picture, a fading photo of Jim in uniform standing outside a helicopter in Afghanistan, and one of Cassie and Ben on horseback the summer before at her uncle's ranch outside of Choteau, Montana. She debated placing the frames on the credenza where visitors to her office could see them or on her desk so she could see them. She opted for the desk.

Uniformed officers streamed past her door in both directions. Some glanced in and waved in mid-conversation.

The desk drawers were empty except for discarded paper clips, tiny scraps of paper, and a single business card wedged into the back corner of the top desk drawer that had probably been overlooked when the office was cleared out.

She extracted it. It read:

CAM TOLLEFSEN
CHIEF INVESTIGATOR
BAKKEN COUNTY SHERIFF'S DEPARTMENT

Which explained why he already resented her. She wondered why Kirkbride hadn't told her she was replacing a man who still worked in the department but had been demoted for some reason to patrol.

"Are you making yourself at home?" Judy Banister asked as she peered around the door frame to Cassie's office.

"I found my desk. I seem to be missing

210

some chairs, though. And I don't know how to turn on my computer or work the phone."

Banister clucked, and said, "The guys around here seem to think an empty office is okay to raid for furniture and supplies. I'll do what I can to at least get you a comfortable chair."

"Thank you."

"And I'll print out a sheet with all the access code passwords you'll need for the computer and our other databases. It also has instructions for the phone. It's not as complicated as it looks. Just make sure never to lose that password sheet."

Cassie nodded.

Banister said, "It will be nice to have some female company around here. As you can see, the makeup of the department is similar to the makeup of Bakken County — practically all men." She still looked around the door frame, as if waiting for an invitation inside.

"I see that. You're welcome to come in, you know."

Banister shook her head. "I'll go see about finding you a chair."

"Judy?" Cassie called out after Banister had ducked away.

In a moment Banister reappeared again, still loath to enter. "Yes, Miss Dewell?"

"Call me Cassie."

"Yes, Cassie."

"Did this office used to belong to Cam Tollefsen?"

"Yes. How did you know?"

"I found his old card. Why did he get busted down to patrol?"

Banister shook her head quickly, as if shedding the question. "You'll have to talk to the sheriff," she said, her voice trailing off as she retreated down the hallway.

While Cassie waited for Banister to return so she could access her computer, she looked out the window and saw Lance Foster and another deputy strolling across the ice-covered parking lot toward a departmental SUV.

Cassie pushed back, grabbed her coat, and went down the three sets of stairs.

Although she'd been out earlier when she left her building and walked across the outside lot to the law enforcement center for the briefing, the still bitter cold of the morning braced her. Snow crystals hung as if they had been created in the air and hadn't come from the sky.

Foster looked up and saw her as he threw a gear bag into the back of the SUV.

"Deputy Foster?"

"Yes, ma'am?" Foster said.

The deputy Foster was with looked from Cassie to Foster, trying to figure out why his partner had been singled out.

"You can get in and start up the car," Cassie said to him. "I'm sure you want to get that heater going."

The deputy got her meaning and jumped in and shut the door. Foster shut the hatchback on the SUV and waited for her expectantly, if a little anxiously.

She was used to this kind of slightly false deference, which was a nod to her superior rank. Officers answered her questions with plenty of "yes, ma'ams" and "no, ma'ams," and then snickered about her when she was out of earshot. That had been the way it was in Helena, and she'd hoped to avoid it in North Dakota but she didn't know how. She didn't want to be one of the boys, because she wasn't. The best way she knew how to proceed was to be straightforward and hardworking and hope they'd eventually respect her for it.

"Deputy Foster, I won't keep you long in this cold but I had a couple of questions for you regarding that one-car rollover you worked a few days ago."

"Shoot," he said. She was grateful he didn't say "yes, ma'am" again.

"You were the second officer on the scene, correct? That's what I read in the report."

"That's right. I was patrolling the south side of town and I saw a vehicle peel out to respond to the crash out on the prairie."

Cassie withdrew her notebook from her pocket and reviewed it, then said, "That would have been around six eighteen A.M., right?"

"Right."

"And the accident occurred at six fifteen or sixteen?"

"That was our best guess. It had just happened and it was still dark out."

"Deputy Tollefsen was the first on the scene?"

"Yes."

"And he was the one who wrote up the accident report?"

"Yes."

"Did you read the report?"

"I did," Foster said, a suspicious note entering his voice. "Was there something wrong with it?"

"No, no," Cassie said quickly. "I just wanted to make sure you agreed with what was in it. I've read a lot of accident reports over the years and I've been a responder on way too many crashes. It just seemed to me the sequence of events was . . . compressed."

He hesitated for a moment, then said, "Yes, I thought the report was accurate."

"Thank you. So the accident likely occurred at six fifteen or six sixteen and Officer Tollefsen responded within two or three minutes?"

"Yes. He said he saw the headlights rolling across the prairie so he hit the gas and booked it down the highway to the scene."

"I don't remember reading that he hit his lights or siren."

"He didn't."

Cassie paused and waited for a further explanation.

"Cam said he was so surprised by the rollover right out there in front of him that he just responded instantly," Foster said. "I hit my lights, though."

Interesting. "And you didn't hear anything over the radio? Officer Tollefsen didn't call it in?"

"No, not right away. He called it in at the scene, though."

"A two-minute response is really fast."

Foster shrugged. "It's still a small town. If there's no traffic it doesn't take long to get from one place to another."

"And there was no traffic that morning?"

"Nope. Which is pretty unusual for that highway. It's usually bumper-to-bumper with trucks, like now." He gestured south, and Cassie followed his arm.

From where they stood in the parking lot, she could see the highway out on the prairie between two older buildings on the other side of the block. Like Foster said, the road was clogged with morning oil field traffic.

Cassie made a note in her notebook.

"So that's where it happened," she said.

"Yeah. You can almost see it from here. In fact, if you drive out there you can still see where the dirt's all churned up from the accident. It wasn't far from town at all."

"But there was no one to witness the accident except for Officer Tollefsen that you know of."

Foster shook his head. "Not that I know of."

Cassie thanked him and asked him to let her know if he thought of anything that might not already be in the report.

As she turned to leave, Foster said, "Investigator? Do you mind if I ask why you're following up on a one-car traffic accident?"

Cassie said, "The sheriff asked me to try and follow up on the fatality and try to see if we can come up with a name on the victim before we get the DNA results back from the state lab. Someone somewhere

216

must be missing him."

"Ah," Foster said, obviously not completely convinced Cassie's answer was all there was.

"Thanks again," she said, before he could ask more questions.

Instead of going back to her new office, Cassie scraped the ice from the windows of her Honda and climbed inside. Something about Tollefsen's report and Foster's answers didn't jibe, but she couldn't put her finger on it. The motor ground shrill but finally turned over and she sat in it freezing. It would take a while before the heater began to work. She looked forward to being assigned a new departmental SUV.

She drove to the end of the street and waited for a gap in the southbound energy trucks before merging onto the highway. It took less than five minutes to reach the scene of the accident, and she eased off the road onto the shoulder. The ice crystals no longer hung in the air, but they'd been replaced by lightly falling snow.

Foster was right — the place where the accident occurred was easy to locate. A delineator post had been knocked down flat by the rolling car, and frozen chunks of upturned black soil littered the surface of the short grass prairie. She could see tire tracks beneath the fresh snow from the tow truck that had retrieved the vehicle. At the rate the snow was coming down, she guessed, it might all be covered up by the end of the day.

Cassie kept her car running and the heater on high as she walked down the embankment into the prairie. The car that crashed had rolled a surprisingly long way, which meant it had been going at a high rate of speed when it went off the road.

She walked in the depressed tire track of the tow truck as she approached the place where the car had stopped rolling. Although the crash had been cleaned up, there were still telltale signs: a small sliver of red plastic from the broken taillight, a foot-long length of tread that had been sheared off one of the tires.

Cassie stood in the field with the cold worming its way down her collar and up her sleeves. Her feet were freezing.

She turned and looked back at Grimstad and thought, Yes, if Tollefsen was on the edge of town he could be out there in minutes. It wasn't far at all, just as Foster had said.

Then before turning and going back to her car, she looked to the west. A half mile beyond the brush-covered field was a bluff partially obscured by falling snow. On top of the bluff was a slew of newly constructed homes and houses in the process of being finished. She wondered if anyone had been up that morning looking out their window at the highway. Then she thought, No, too far to see much in the dark.

She ventured into the high brush, careful not to snag her coat on the sharp thorns of the Russian olives. That's where she noticed a white line in the snow. The thin line extended from a V in the bluff and continued across the field toward her, bending around high clumps of brush. If it weren't covered by a thin layer of new snow, she thought, it wouldn't have been obvious to her at all in the short grass.

Despite how cold her feet were — she needed her heavy pack boots from Helena! — she walked west. The snow was littered with heavy boot tracks for the first twenty yards. She guessed it had been trampled by the first responders Tollefsen and Foster, as well as the EMT crew and the tow truck driver. Cassie walked farther to where the snow was untrammeled to the end of the thin white line. It was a trail. Either a wildlife trail or a bike trail or both.

And she could see beneath the growing

layer of cottony snow the depression of a single narrow knobby tire. The track didn't proceed any farther toward the road from where she stood. Whoever had been on the bike had stopped there. In fact, when she looked a few feet to the right of the trail she could make out where they had turned and gone back toward the bluff.

Cassie had learned on the job in Montana how snow could preserve a story if the investigator learned how to read it. Cody Hoyt, her mentor, had taught her that.

The track had been laid down on top of the last significant snowfall three days before, which was the day of the one-car rollover. It would remain there until it was covered by new snow or melted away. But it had been too cold to melt.

She squatted to her haunches, then to her hands and knees. The track was between her two gloved hands in the snow. She took a deep breath of icy air and blew hard, removing most but not all of the fresh snow from the narrow trail.

Someone, probably a kid, had ridden his or her bike down the trail from the bluff two days before when the rollover occurred. Maybe they'd seen the accident happen, or maybe they arrived well after. But school was in session, she recalled. Because of the short days, students went to school in the dark and came home in the dark. Kids wouldn't be out riding their bikes around during daylight hours. Something, she thought, had drawn the biker across the field from the housing development. Since the wreck had been cleared away during the day, it didn't make sense that there would be anything to look at later that night.

She withdrew her cell phone to take several shots of the bike tire track before the snowfall obscured it for the rest of the winter.

Unfortunately, the screen of her phone was fogged over from the cold and she couldn't view it well enough to get a good shot.

She stood and cursed. By the time she hiked back across the field to her car and returned to the law enforcement center to borrow a camera, whatever that procedure entailed, the track would be covered up.

Cassie thought about covering the exposed tire track with something so she could return later with a camera. She looked around, saw nothing she could use, then sighed and removed her parka and unfurled it over the trail.

The cold was vicious. Her arms and neck were stinging as she trudged across the field toward her Honda. It snowed harder. It was melting in her hair and on her exposed face and neck. She was glad she'd kept her car running and the heater on full blast.

When she looked up she saw that another vehicle had pulled over to the shoulder behind her Honda. It was a sheriff's department SUV.

Cam Tollefsen was at the wheel. He grinned and shook his head at her.

As she climbed the embankment toward her car, his passenger window slid down. "Kind of chilly for a nature walk, isn't it, Miss Montana?"

Before Cassie could respond, the radio inside his unit squawked loudly and the Bakken County dispatcher said, "All units, there is a report of another severed body part located on the southwest corner of Taco John's . . ."

"Gotta go," Tollefsen said to Cassie as his window rolled up. "Somebody's gotta do some real work around here . . ."

He hit his lights to stop the truck traffic on the highway, then shot through an opening in the trucks and turned on his siren as he roared back toward town.

Cassie lost her footing climbing the embankment and rolled back to the bottom. She angrily slapped snow from her clothing once she was on her feet again, and a trucker tooted his air horn and gave her a laughing thumbs-up through the window.

She raised her hand and extended her middle finger at him and she could see him still laughing in his side mirror as he passed.

CHAPTER FIFTEEN

Later that night, Cassie sat exhausted in the parking lot of the law enforcement center in her new sheriff's department Yukon. She'd kept the motor running and the heater on and she leaned back in her seat and briefly closed her eyes. She was too tired to jump out and face the cold and walk across the snow and ice to her apartment building. She had to rest and regroup.

It had stopped snowing during the day but the temperature outside was twenty-two degrees below zero, according to the digital temperature display in the corner of her rearview mirror. An untouched bag of McDonald's hamburgers and fries sat on the seat next to her, as did a six-pack of beer and a bottle of red wine she'd bought at a discount liquor store. It was a typical cop's dinner, she thought: bad food and bad wine. The beer was simply so she'd have something in her refrigerator.

She knew what it was that had affected her so: lack of sleep the night before, mental exhaustion from the first day at her new job, and a fourteen-hour day filled with horror after horror. She'd rarely experienced a day like it.

Eight or nine sheriff's department vehicles responded to the call that morning about the finding of a human hand behind the Taco John's fast-food restaurant. Cassie had joined them after returning to the county building. Judy Banister had met her in her office with a set of keys to a department GMC Yukon as well as a heavy-duty Bakken County Sheriff's Department parka. The parka was too large, but Cassie didn't complain since she'd left her coat in the field. Before leaving, Cassie filled out a request for the evidence tech to make a cast of the bicycle tire track, then located the big new Yukon in the lot behind the building.

When she arrived at the Taco John's on Main Street, she found nearly a dozen deputies standing around in the snowfall in the alley talking about the hand.

Without examining it closely before the medical examiner arrived, the consensus among the law enforcement personnel was that the hand had belonged to the same body as the foot found earlier. It looked cleanly severed, it was Caucasian, and it was frozen into a meaty claw. Although the skin was discolored, she could see there was a tattoo of a rat holding a saber on the top of the hand and letters on the top of the first joint of each finger that spelled R-I-D-E. On the top joint of the thumb was either an O or a zero.

Before the examiner arrived, another call came in. Schoolchildren at the elementary school had discovered what looked like a severed human leg frozen to the gravel of the playground. The principal had placed the school on lockdown until the police could arrive, and the word was getting out to parents what had happened. It was pandemonium.

It hadn't stopped there.

Throughout the day, the sheriff's department responded to call after call of discovered body parts. The victim's other hand was found on the roof of the Work Wearhouse as if someone had driven by during the night and tossed it up there. A severed ankle was identified in the parking lot of Walmart, even though it was barely identifiable because it had been run over so many times by shoppers. A stay-at-home mom called from a house in a new southside development saying that when she let her Labrador in from the backyard he showed up with "a human arm in his mouth." She was on the brink of hysteria.

Sheriff Kirkbride had canceled his meetings with the county commissioners and he now managed his department on-site, dispatching teams of deputies to each discovery to secure the scene until the techs could catch up.

"We need to postpone our meeting," Kirkbride said to Cassie.

"Of course," Cassie said.

He sent Cassie to the stay-at-home mom's house, where she sat with the woman in her living room until she calmed down. While she did, they both tried not to stare at the discolored upper arm — again, covered with tattoos — while it thawed on the fabric of the new carpet.

The headless trunk was discovered impaled on a metal fencepost on the edge of the town park. Somehow, it had been missed all day as officers drove right by it responding to calls of other body parts.

Kirkbride complained that no matter what he did or said, the word was out that someone had dismembered a body and thrown the parts around Grimstad "like the Rotary Club throwing out candy during the

Fourth of July parade."

Kirkbride issued an order to all of his deputies that became a mantra throughout the day: "Find that head before a member of the public does."

Find that head.

It was grim, cold, and horrible. Cassie wasn't surprised when a couple of deputies dealt with the discoveries with macabre humor.

"It looks like Joe's head," Deputy Jim Klug said over the radio from the location of another body part discovery near the Dumpster behind a Chinese restaurant.

"Joe, Joe, are you okay?" someone else responded.

Even Cassie laughed.

But the body parts — sans head — didn't belong to Joe. According to Deputy Ian Davis who was working undercover, they matched up with a man named Rufus Whiteley, a local biker and suspected meth dealer.

Whiteley was not at his home — a double-wide trailer on the west side of town — and no one had reported him missing. But Davis said the local drug subculture had all but vanished into hiding, and the word was someone had gotten to Whiteley the night before. Davis described tattoos on Whiteley that corresponded with tattoos on the body parts. Specifically, Davis said Whiteley had B-O-R-N T-O R-I-D-E inked on the top of his fingers and the phrase stretched across both of his hands.

Deputies on site at the Work Wearhouse confirmed that the letters B-O-R-N-T were tattooed on the fingers and thumb of the hand found on the roof.

At the sheriff's request, the driver's license photo of Rufus Whiteley was e-mailed to every law enforcement cell phone. Whiteley had a round squat head, stringy black hair, a flat nose, and a full dark beard. He looked like trouble.

Of special interest to Cassie was Davis's statement that Whiteley was rumored to be starting a chapter of the Sons of Freedom in Bakken County. And the fact that although he no doubt preferred riding one of his fleet of the three Harleys parked next to each other in his garage, he also drove a black Dodge Challenger that had been found burned to the ground and was still smoldering on the road next to the wastewater treatment facility.

Cassie responded to the call in the early evening — when the temperature really began to drop — that something had been found at the iconic old drive-in on the north side of town.

"Did we find the head?" Kirkbride asked over the radio.

"Not quite," the deputy on the scene answered.

"I'm on my way," Kirkbride said wearily.

She'd seen the old drive-in earlier in the day. As she drove under an ancient marquee that read CLOSED FOR THE WINTER, it brought back memories of going to the double feature with her father during the rare summer nights when he was off the road. He'd pop enough popcorn to fill a grocery bag, load in blankets and pillows for the backseat, and watch both movies although Cassie rarely made it through the second.

She'd arrived to find Sheriff Kirkbride and two other departmental vehicles already there at the far end of the lot near the base of the old screen. The men were outside but they'd kept their vehicles running, the tailpipes puffing out blooms of exhaust. She slowed her Yukon as she approached them, the wheels bucking up and over row after row of small berms where moviegoers parked for the best viewing angle. She passed by dozens of frost-covered metal poles where the speakers were mounted.

As she pulled behind Kirkbride's vehicle, she saw the sheriff look back at her and shake his head.

Puzzled, she got out.

"You probably don't want to see this," Kirkbride said. He spoke loudly because one of the many mile-long oil tanker trains was passing by a half mile away on the tracks.

"What is it?"

Two of the deputies suddenly found the tops of their boots fascinating.

"What do you think?" Kirkbride said. "More parts."

"Did you find the head?"

"Worse."

She hesitated. It was so cold that when she breathed in she could feel the hairs freeze inside her nostrils. Kirkbride's expression warned her off, but she was curious. The man had shown her the severed body of the MS-13 victim the night before. What could be worse?

At that moment a deputy who'd been out of earshot walked out from around the back of the screen with his long Maglite flashlight and shot the beam toward something stuck to the white screen about eight feet from the ground.

She thought at first it was viscera. Then she realized with a shudder that the bloody mess was a man's penis and testicles. She could see where it had hit the white screen and slid down its face until it froze solid on the surface.

Kirkbride said, "I know the guy who owns this drive-in. It's been a money-loser for years and he was trying to dump it until the boom hit. Now I hear Halliburton bought the land from him for three million so they could put in another equipment yard. It's kind of sad to think that the last thing on the movie screen was Rufus Whiteley's family jewels."

One of the deputies fake coughed to disguise a laugh.

Cassie closed her eyes and took another deep breath of frigid air.

At an impromptu debriefing held under the marquee of the drive-in, Sheriff Kirkbride stood in the middle of a loose circle of twenty-five of his men — and Cassie. It was so cold she could no longer feel her face. The men huddled close together without embarrassment to keep warm. Clouds of condensation from their breath rose over the group and hung there like their own private snow cloud. She realized she was standing next to Cam Tollefsen. The events of the day had been so all-consuming and wild she'd almost forgotten about him.

She *knew* her request to the evidence techs to go out to the rollover site and make a foam cast of the bike tire track had been rightfully shunted aside.

Cassie recognized a few of the deputies — Lance Foster, Max Maxfield, Ian Davis, Jim Klug — and already felt a little more part of the team.

"It's been a long day," Kirkbride said, "and I'm proud of you all. I always told you you'd get ten years of experience in law enforcement in your first six months here, but I may have to change it to *one day.*"

A few men laughed and Cassie tried to smile but her mouth was too frozen to move.

"Obviously, we've got a lot to sort out. It looks to all of us that somebody cut up Rufus Whiteley and drove around town and threw out the parts. They didn't try to cover up what they did — just the opposite — which says to me it's some kind of warning or message. Whether that message is to us or to someone else, who knows?"

Kirkbride paused and said, "*Damn,* it's cold."

"Yeah," Maxfield said through chattering teeth, "Too bad we don't have someplace warm like the briefing room of the law enforcement center or something."

Which brought some rough laughter and a couple of calls of "Hear, hear."

"The reason we're out here," Kirkbride said, "is because the horse has already left the barn. What happened today in Bakken County is all over the wires and Facebook and Twitter and everything else. I've got a dozen calls from reporters stacked up on my desk and television vans from Bismarck, Fargo, and Minot downtown waiting for me to show up for a press briefing. We've got hysterical parents and pissed-off county commissioners and I don't blame them one bit.

"What I want to tell all you guys is let me handle the press and handle the heat. That's my job. Your job is to do damned good police work so we can put this all together and throw the bad guys in a cage. Whatever you were doing before today goes on the back burner. The first order of priority is to find the guy — or guys — who did this. Are you all on board?"

Cassie saw no signs of disagreement, although Tollefsen remained mute. She thought she detected somewhat of a smirk on his face, but it could be the cold, she thought.

As they broke up and returned to their vehicles, Cassie realized Kirkbride was walking alongside her.

She said, "Drop everything and concentrate on this?"

"Except for you," he said under his breath.

On the way home she'd waited in the drive-in lane at McDonald's for fifteen minutes. She'd never been in a fast-food line that took longer, but when she thought about bailing out she realized she was pinned in by other vehicles both front and back. The line extended out into the frozen street and around the block.

She'd ordered, received her change from a flinty blond woman who was at least a decade older than most fast-food workers she was used to, and had driven back to the county apartment building. It wasn't until she shifted her Yukon into park that the pure exhaustion hit her and swept her away.

After twenty minutes with her eyes closed, Cassie sat up with a grunt. Something had awakened her, and she realized she'd fallen asleep in the Yukon outside her own building. She cursed herself for being so stupid. The warmth of her apartment was thirty yards away. She'd promised to call Ben before he went to bed. And although the Yukon was a late model, the potential for carbon monoxide poisoning in a stationary car was always a possibility.

She realized what had jarred her awake was the vibration of her cell phone ringing in the inside pocket of her new sheriff's department coat. By the time she retrieved her phone it had stopped.

There were two messages. One was from Isabel, her mother. The other was from County Prosecutor Leslie Behaunek in North Carolina. Cassie looked at the clock display on the dashboard — eight thirty. Which meant ten thirty in Wilson. Pretty late to call with something mundane, she thought.

Cassie grabbed the McDonald's bag, the bottle of wine, the six-pack, and her briefcase and went out into the stunningly cold night.

"You won't have to do anything," Cassie said to Isabel on her cell phone while she put all the items on the kitchen table and shed the parka. "They'll come in and pack everything up and label each box. Then they'll load the boxes into the truck and head east to North Dakota. All you'll need to do is put Ben in the car with some of his books or toys and drive here next week."

"I've never heard of such a thing before," Isabel said, offended. "They just walk into our place and pack our things?"

"Yes. That's what moving companies do."

"Well, needless to say, I've never used one before. I've probably moved a dozen times in my life and you know what that was like."

Cassie did, and they weren't pleasant memories. Isabel filled her VW bus with most of their possessions leaving just enough space for Cassie and drove across town to whatever cheap hovel was replacing the last cheap hovel. Whatever couldn't fit into the bus was piled on the sidewalk with a sign that said, FREE STUFF — TAKE IT. PEACE.

Isabel didn't believe in crass materialism, she had explained.

"We can afford it now," Cassie said, rolling her eyes. "The sheriff's department here will pay for the move."

"But it's such a waste of taxpayer money."

"It's their money to waste," Cassie said. "Now can you put Ben on?"

"Yes, he's right here waiting. But first you have to tell me about what I heard on the news today. Something that happened in the town you want us to move to."

Cassie sighed. The sheriff was right: it was all over the news. "Not with Ben right there," she said.

"Why — so he won't be scared to come there?" Isabel asked. "Doesn't that tell you everything one needs to know about us moving to North Dakota? That you can't even talk about it?"

"We're handling it," Cassie said. But she had to concede that her mother had a point. "Now please put Ben on."

While she talked to her son about his last days of school — his friends wanted to throw him a good-bye party, which brought unexpected tears to her eyes — Cassie put the bag of hamburgers and fries into the microwave and set it at thirty seconds to heat up the food.

The wine had a screw top for which she was grateful because she didn't have a corkscrew. She filled a drinking glass three-quarters full and took a long pull while listening to Ben. The bad wine was good.

Ben asked Cassie if he could buy a fishing license and a fishing pole when he got to North Dakota.

"Yes, but it's cold here right now. Everything's frozen over. But yes, we can do that."

Ben told her he might want to go ice fishing, maybe, as she secured the phone to her ear with her shoulder so her hands were free. She opened the refrigerator door for the beer, put it inside, and closed it.

Then she stood still, frozen inside, suddenly unable to make out a single word Ben was saying.

She thought, No. It had to be a hallucination brought on by what she'd been through that day.

"Honey, can you hold on for a minute?" she said.

"Okay," Ben said impatiently.

Cassie put the phone on the counter and braced herself and opened the refrigerator door once again as the microwave chimed that it was done. She paid no attention to it.

Rufus Whiteley's head was on the top shelf next to the six-pack of beer. She recognized it from his driver's license photo that had been circulated through the department. The eyes were closed but there was a black pool of blood that had drained down through the shelving onto the glass top of the vegetable bin.

"Ben, please put your grandma Isabel back on."

"Why? What's wrong?"

"Do it, please." Somehow, she didn't shout it.

When Isabel took the phone Cassie said, "I'm postponing the moving truck until further notice."

CHAPTER SIXTEEN

At the same time, on the darkened porch of a dilapidated farmhouse just outside the city limits of Grimstad, Willie Dietrich burst out the door and shoved the muzzle of a pistol deep into the mouth of the man who'd knocked to come in.

As the man struggled and gagged, Dietrich said, "Well look who's here. It's the Winkster."

"You said to come by," Winkie tried to say. But it came out as a series of squeaks and grunts. Dietrich stepped back and withdrew the gun and dried the barrel on his jeans. Winkie spat the taste out. His spittle froze instantly between his boots on the concrete stoop.

"Yeah," Dietrich said, as if forgetting was no fault of his own. "You know there's no product now, right? You know that."

"Of course, man. Jesus, that gun hurt. You mighta broke my tooth, man."

Blink.

"You're *fine,* asshat." Dietrich laughed huskily.

He was big, blond, and manic. Winkie could never be sure if Dietrich acted crazy because he was high or because he was naturally crazy or because he wanted everyone to think he was crazy. Dietrich had been so violent as a middle linebacker on the high school football team that opposing coaches boycotted playing the Grimstad Vikings. It had been quite the controversy when Winkie was a junior. Not that Winkie ever played football, but Friday nights were party time during and after games and the boycott ruined the month of October that year.

Despite hard living and a couple of stints in jail, Dietrich still had the intimidating physique of the middle linebacker he'd once been, Winkie thought. Broad shoulders, slablike pecs, and six-pack abs all on display because Dietrich wore only a tight wife-beater, jeans, and no shoes or socks.

"Fuckin' cold, man," Dietrich said, as if accusing Winkie of the weather. He hopped from one bare foot to the other like the concrete was hot instead of cold.

"Twenty-three below, man. I seen it on the bank sign in town."

He paused, then asked, "Can we go inside?"

"No, dude, let's stand out here on the porch all night."

Blink.

"Come in, Winkie. But like I told you, there's no product and I ain't selling you any of my private stash so don't even fuckin' ask."

"I won't."

"Don't, douche."

"I *won't.*"

The shabby front room was overheated from a glowing woodstove in the corner of it. There was a large pile of split hardwood stacked up next to it, and the floor was littered with bits of bark. It was a cheap stove, Winkie thought, because the top was glowing red and he could glimpse yellow flames through cracks on the side. Winkie shed his coat while he stood in the entryway but Dietrich didn't indicate where he should hang it. The room was dim and lit with a dozen or so candles for effect, Winkie guessed, because there were a few unlit lamps in the dark corners.

ESPN was on the big-screen TV but the sound was muted. "SportsCenter."

Two women — a blonde and a tall black

beauty — were in the kitchen down the hallway. Winkie could smell baking. The women looked more like prostitutes on their night off than bakers, Winkie thought: big hair, high heels, tight tops. The tall black woman squinted to see who he was in the gloom of the living room, but she apparently wasn't very impressed when she saw him because she turned away and went back to baking.

"Hash brownies," Dietrich said. "They're making hash brownies. Don't even think of asking."

"I won't."

"Drop the coat," Dietrich said, "arms out and spread 'em."

Winkie did as told and Dietrich patted him down like a professional, even pulling his pant legs up to grope inside the shafts of his boots.

"You wearing a wire?"

"No."

"Gotta check," Dietrich said, roughly unbuttoning the front of Winkie's flannel shirt and opening it with a rough flourish.

"Fish-belly white," Dietrich said. "You ought to get some sun, Winkie."

Winkie smiled uncomfortably while he buttoned back up and tucked his shirt in his jeans.

Dietrich sprawled on an overstuffed chair, one leg cocked up over an arm of it. The pistol was in his lap.

Winkie took a step toward an old couch strewn with clothes and Dietrich said, "I didn't say you could sit down. Did I tell you you could sit down? Did you hear me say that?"

"No." Winkie stood there, his coat pooled in a clump near his boots.

"You told one of my friends you might have a lead on some missing black and blue, is that right?"

Blink.

"The county has dried up, as you know. I've got good customers who are getting pissed off. Some of 'em are driving as far as Rapid City to score. My guys are getting antsy because their customers are leaning on 'em. So if you know where I can get my hands on real product, you better speak up."

Winkie tried to remember everything T-Lock had told him to say. It sounded so smooth and good when T-Lock said it.

"I don't know the guy personally, but I heard through a buddy of mine that this," Winkie hesitated, "this *guy* might have found a whole shitload of blue. He's sitting on it right now because he doesn't know what to do and he doesn't know who he can trust."

"*This guy,*" Dietrich repeated. "This guy who your buddy knows. So who is your buddy?"

"I don't want to say. He doesn't have anything to do with this."

"Who is this guy?"

"I don't even know his name. All I know is he's local. I mean, he ain't one of the newbies."

"So why hasn't this guy taken the shit to the sheriff's department? Turned it in for a reward and a write-up in the paper or something?"

"Man, I don't know."

"The fuck you don't," Dietrich said, his neck tensing. Winkie was impressed. He could actually see Dietrich's muscles and tendons dance beneath his taut skin. "*This guy* wants me to pay him big bucks for the shit sight unseen. *This guy* thinks he's smart enough and I'm stupid enough and desperate enough to set up a meeting and show up with what, a few million in cash?"

"I don't know nothing about prices," Winkie said.

Blink.

"Give me a name," Dietrich said. "Your buddy's name or *this guy's* name."

"I told you I don't know."

"Then get the fuck out of my house before I shoot a bullet into each one of your stupid blinking eyes," Dietrich said, sitting up straight, getting ready to spring like some kind of lion, Winkie thought.

Winkie realized he was sweating. He could smell himself sweat. Then he remembered and said, "I brought you a sample."

Dietrich's eyes narrowed. He didn't spring.

Finally, he said, "Hand it over."

Winkie reached very slowly into the front pocket of his jeans. He knew better than to try a sudden movement. Dietrich's eyes locked on Winkie's hand as he moved. The gun was back in his hand.

Winkie eased the clear plastic baggie out and held it up by his fingertips.

"Give," Dietrich said, holding out his hand palm up.

Winkie placed the packet into Dietrich's hand.

"Blue," Dietrich said, sitting back and studying it. "I know this stuff."

Dietrich pulled apart the Ziploc top and licked his little finger. Almost daintily, he probed into the bag with his finger until it was covered with tiny crystals. Then he stuck the finger up his nostril and inhaled.

He sat and waited. The look on his face

was vacant but expectant. Winkie knew it was the real stuff but he was scared anyway and he felt like his legs might collapse on him.

Dietrich briefly closed his eyes as if in awe, then opened them and smiled.

"This is good shit," he said. "I know where it came from."

Winkie shrugged as if he had no idea.

"I know who really, really, *really* fucking wants it back. Was there a lot of cash in the bag as well?"

"I don't know." It sounded hollow, even to him.

"Sure you do, Winkie." Dietrich said with confidence. He seemed to be studying Winkie's face for cracks.

Then Dietrich slapped the tops of his thighs and stood up. "I want to show you something, Winkster."

Winkie blinked.

Dietrich reached into his front pocket and withdrew a wad of cash that was folded in two. He smoothed the bills on the table in front of him and then fanned them out as if they were a hand of cards.

"Watch this," Dietrich said, holding an odd-looking penlight over the bills. He thumbed a switch and suddenly the faces of the bills revealed glowing swoops and curlicues marked on them.

"This is what they do to prevent skimming from their dealers," Dietrich said. "A dude's less likely to peel off a few bills if he thinks somebody might go through his wallet and flash an ultraviolet light on his stash. And guess where these marked bills came from?"

Winkie shook his head.

Dietrich sang, " 'Ba-da-ba-ba-bah, I'm lovin' it.' That's right, our very own Mickey D's. Two of my guys went there today and they both wound up with some of these bills in change. We've been checking all the cash that comes through here and we got two hits from the same place. Crazy, huh?"

"I have no idea what that means," Winkie said. But he was thinking T-Lock might have put Rachel up to it. He didn't know why. But Rachel worked there.

"See," Dietrich said, "here's what I was thinking before you showed up. I was thinking we could make a deal where everybody wins. You — or your mystery guy — could keep the cash. Just keep it. Consider it payment for the product and everybody's happy. Well, maybe your guy isn't completely happy, but at least he's not cut into a million tiny pieces along with every member of his family. But if *this guy* is already circulating the cash through town like this, it's a matter of time before the cops figure it out and shut him down. Which means he don't get anything, and I don't get any product. And the people who the product belongs to, believe me, they don't fuck around with losers like you and *this guy.*"

"Look," Winkie said, "I'm just the messenger, you know? I don't have the stuff and I don't know where it is. I really don't want to be in the middle of this."

Blink.

"But you are in the middle of it," Dietrich said with a laugh. "You came to me, remember? Now what we've got to do is figure out what comes next."

Winkie didn't know what to suggest, other than he just wanted the last hour of his life back so he could do something else with it.

Dietrich leaned back in his chair and angled his head toward a closed door over his shoulder. His eyes never left Winkie.

"Did you get all that?" he asked, raising his voice.

The door opened.

"I heard it," said a dark, short Hispanic man with big ears. He came into the front room and stepped to the side so a birdlike man could exit.

250

The second man moved swiftly and positioned himself a few feet behind Winkie.

"Meet my friends La Matanza and Silencio," Dietrich said. "Silencio is the one behind you, but La Matanza may have a few questions. They came all the way from California. Push one for English and two for Spanish."

"I don't speak no Spanish," Winkie said.

Dietrich laughed, and said, "Don't worry."

Dietrich then said to La Matanza, "So it wasn't the bikers after all. They might have run your guy off the road, but they didn't get his product. But my friend the Winkster seems to know who did."

La Matanza looked dangerous to Winkie just standing there. Part of it was his stillness. Unlike Dietrich, there was nothing manic about him. He looked at Winkie with what almost looked like sympathy or understanding.

"I don't want no trouble," Winkie said.

"There doesn't have to be any trouble."

He spoke clear English with just a hint of an accent.

"I can go talk to him," Winkie said. "I'll explain the situation to him. I'll ask him to drive out here and work out the details with you guys. I don't want no part of this anymore."

La Matanza nodded thoughtfully. He said to Dietrich, "We thought that guy last night was one tough hombre. It turns out he really didn't know anything. But I think we can see here our message got through."

"Loud and fucking clear." Dietrich laughed. It was a forced laugh, Winkie thought. Then he realized even Dietrich was a little scared himself of the two men in his house. Dietrich wasn't in charge. They were.

The only topic of conversation all day on the job were the body parts being found all over town. Winkie was pretty sure he was staring into the eyes of the man who'd been responsible.

Maybe T-Lock deserved it, Winkie thought. T-Lock had put him in this position. But Rachel didn't, and Kyle didn't.

And *he* didn't.

Winkie said, "I'll go right now and bring him here. I'll tell him to bring the duffel bag. Then I'm out of it, okay?"

"Who is this man?" La Matanza asked.

Winkie hesitated. If he gave up the only thing he had to bargain with so quickly . . .

La Matanza turned and shut the door that led to the kitchen. Winkie could no longer see the two women.

Then he felt two hands on his head from behind, one on top and the other in back, gripping his hair. Silencio.

Winkie was wrenched back and to the side and even as quickly as it happened he knew better than to reach out to try and shield his fall with his bare hands.

But he wished he would have when his face was pressed hard into the top of the glowing woodstove.

The pain was incredible but short-lived because it just reached a crescendo and blinked out after a second or two. What frightened him even more was the sizzling sound it made, like a raw steak dropped in a hot frying pan. And the horrible acrid smell.

"Don't burn his mouth," La Matanza said calmly to Silencio. "We need him to be able to talk."

"Holy *shit*, man," Dietrich whispered.

■ ■ ■ ■

PART THREE:
DAY SIX

■ ■ ■ ■

CHAPTER SEVENTEEN

As he rode home from his paper route, Kyle was thinking he'd never been out in such cold in his life. The vinyl covering of his bicycle seat had actually shattered into shards that morning when he sat on it. He knew it was more than twenty degrees below zero because Alf Pedersen had been complaining about it when he picked up his newspapers two hours before.

Kyle had covered his entire face except for his eyes with a scarf Alf lent him that smelled of Alf's cigarettes, but even his eyeballs were cold. He could barely feel his feet and hands. His tires made a high-pitched squeaking sound in the fresh snow that was irritating, and the chain to his rear wheels was stiff. It had been an awesome sight, though, to look out over the prairie from the bluff that morning: steam rose from the frozen river and made the flares in the distance glow and pulsate. The sight made Kyle imagine the aftermath of a great battle.

It had been the first time since he'd started his route that people were waiting for him when he delivered their newspaper. The headline on the front of the paper that morning was: *SAVAGE: BODY PARTS DISCOVERED THROUGHOUT TOWN.* One lady offered to let him come inside to warm up, but he said he'd be late if he did that.

If there had ever been a morning he could have used some help with his route — like driving him from house to house — this had been it. But he hadn't even asked his mom because he'd overheard her and T-Lock fighting most of the night. He knew she needed some sleep before she went to work.

He didn't know what the argument was about. Something about T-Lock's friend Winkie not showing up. T-Lock cursed his friend and his mom said he'd never been any good anyway, and T-Lock got mad at her for saying that. Kyle had buried his head in his pillows to drown out the argument but not before doing a couple of practice grabs for the arrow under his bed in case he needed to act. Eventually, the house got quiet.

In his dream, Raheem caught a fish in the river and reeled it up to the boat. It was huge and so heavy Raheem couldn't pull it in. It took the two of them to wrestle it over the gunwales where it flopped around. Kyle didn't know what kind of fish it was but it was impressive. Some people having a picnic on the bank saw the size of the fish as they hauled it in and they started cheering. Kyle tipped his hat to them as they floated by.

When Kyle had gotten up that morning he found out why the house was still. T-Lock had taken the new van he'd traded for and left. Kyle hoped he never came back, although he'd sure like his money back so he could take care of his mom.

He bucked a frozen berm of ice that had been pushed to the side of the street by a snowplow and took the sidewalk the last block and a half toward his house. As he turned the corner on his street he saw a vehicle idling in the road directly across from his house. It was so cold that the exhaust from the big SUV ballooned out the back and was tinted cotton-candy pink from the brake lights.

Then he saw the light bar on top of the car in the glow from a streetlight and recognized it as one of the sheriff's department SUVs like he'd seen three days before at the site of the car crash.

It was just sitting there, idling. Like the driver inside was looking at Kyle's house.

Kyle slowed to a stop, hidden from the SUV by a camper trailer parked on the street. He wasn't sure what to do. Probably, he thought, T-Lock had gotten himself into some kind of trouble. The cop was there to tell Kyle's mom about it.

But no one got out of the vehicle.

Kyle knew he couldn't stay hidden very long and keep still or he'd freeze to death. At least riding the bike home had kept him warm. Now, though, he could feel his legs stinging with cold even through his long underwear and jeans.

He heard a second motor but stayed out of sight on the side of the trailer. The tires of the second car squeaked in the snow-packed street. The car was going the same direction as the SUV, and it would have to go around or wait for the SUV to move out of the way, Kyle thought. He leaned forward so he could see around the corner of the trailer, hoping the cop car would drive off.

Instead, the second car — a flashy silver pickup truck — slowed down until it was right behind the SUV. It stopped. Kyle could see three forms in the pickup, two in front and one in the back.

Then he saw the glimpse of an arm, the cop's arm in the headlights of the pickup, through the back window of the SUV. The cop was gesturing toward Kyle's house, as if pointing it out for the people in the pickup.

Then the cop slowly drove off.

As he did, a pair of headlights came around the corner at the far end of the street. The SUV and the oncoming car went by each other. Kyle noticed that two of the heads in the pickup, the front passenger and the person in back, both ducked as the oncoming car approached them.

The oncoming car seemed to slow as it got near the pickup and Kyle's house, then picked up speed and drove by. Kyle got a good look at T-Lock's profile in the new van as he passed by the trailer. T-Lock looked scared.

Kyle frowned beneath his scarf as the pickup moved up the street a few houses before finding a space on the curb to park. No one got out. Like the SUV a few minutes before, it just sat there idling. But no doubt, Kyle thought, watching his house. Maybe waiting for T-Lock to show up.

T-Lock had fooled them by showing up in a car no one had seen before. But rather than stop and go inside and protect his mom, T-Lock had driven away.

261

Kyle thought he had to warn her. He could retreat back down the street and get to his house through the alley in back. That way, the people in the pickup wouldn't see he was home.

Before he turned his bike around, though, another car — smaller, beat-up — came down the street and turned into the driveway of his house. Kyle's mom, pulling on a heavy coat over her McDonald's uniform, came out through the front door and climbed into the little car. Kyle figured his mom had called a coworker for a ride since T-Lock had taken the new van.

He was happy she was safe and he started to sit back on his bike when the bare metal post poked him hard in the butt. He'd forgotten about the missing seat.

As the little car took his mom to work, Kyle decided as long as that pickup was there he didn't want to go into his house.

He knew where he'd go, and it wasn't school.

The eastern sky was turning a cold purple but it was still dark when Kyle reached Grandma Lottie's house at the end of the road. The horizon bled through gaps in the trunks of trees that bordered the frozen dirt road. Her house was at the end of the road and it was small but lit up. Of course she was awake.

He leaned his bike against the trunk of a tree in her front lawn and stiffly walked to the front door. He could smell wood smoke from the chimney, which was something he always liked. The smoke seemed to hang suspended in the icy still air.

Kyle's boots scrunched in the snow as he walked to the side of her house to the woodpile and gathered six or seven lengths, enough to make him sag under the weight. He returned to the front door and because he couldn't used his hands, he rapped on it with his forehead like a woodpecker.

The inside door opened and he could see her silhouette through the frost-covered storm door window.

"Kyle!" she said, surprised. She was in her old red housecoat and slippers. Her gray hair was in curlers. Grandma Lottie was the only person Kyle had ever met who wore curlers. "Come in, come in. You little angel — you brought me some wood for the stove."

He nodded. He remembered she'd always said a good person always brings something when he visits someone's house. The wood was the best he could do.

"Just dump it over there by the stove," she

said. "Why aren't you at school?"

Kyle stepped inside her house and she closed the door behind him. He knew it was warm in there — probably hot, even — but he couldn't yet feel it. He'd never been so cold. The lengths of wood tumbled out of his arms into a cast-iron bin.

"Let me make you some hot chocolate," she said, helping him unzip his coat because his fingers were too stiff to grip the zipper. "We've got to get you thawed out. Do you think it's July? What are you doing out there riding around on your bike?"

"My job," Kyle said. His voice was thicker than normal. But Grandma Lottie had always been able to understand him when he talked. "I deliver the *Tribune.*"

"I didn't *know* that," she said, drawing out the word "know." That's because Kyle's mom and his grandma Lottie rarely spoke anymore. They'd ask him about the other, but they didn't talk directly.

She said, "You'd think on a day like this the paper could wait. Or maybe someone could drive you."

He knew who "someone" was.

"So why aren't you in school?" she asked again. The warmth from the stove was starting to penetrate his clothing. His entire body ached as it did and he felt like hopping around.

He said, "My speech teacher is still sick. She's the only one I like. And Mr. Pedersen said he heard they'd cancel school today because it's so cold."

She nodded and said, "Mr. Pedersen?"

"He's the newspaper guy."

"Alf Pedersen?"

"Yes."

"I've known Alf all his life. I didn't realize he was still around. I thought maybe Alf was, you know, somebody with your mom in your home."

No, that would be T-Lock, he thought.

She said, "They never canceled school when it got cold when I was a girl. This is North Dakota. It gets cold. But I guess they do that these days. Now go over there and stand by the stove. I'll make you breakfast while you get warm. How does bacon, eggs, and lefse sound?"

How did she know he hadn't had breakfast?

"It sounds really good," he said. Lefse was a kind of flat potato pancake made by Norwegians. Grandma Lottie made the best lefse Kyle had ever had. She riced potatoes and added ingredients and rolled the dough into sheets before frying them on an ancient Norwegian lefse griddle. It was an all-day process.

For breakfast, Grandma Lottie cooked the eggs in bacon grease to make the edges crispy, then swabbed the lefse in the grease and folded it over the eggs. No one else Kyle knew ate lefse that way, but he loved it.

"So how is your mom?" Grandma Lottie asked from the kitchen while Kyle warmed up.

"She's good," he lied.

"I'm happy to hear that. One egg or two?"

"Two, please."

The summer before, Grandma Lottie had taken Kyle and Raheem to the Badlands south of Grimstad. Raheem had just moved in and Kyle had just met him but he asked his new friend to go along. Kyle had never been there before and "going to the Badlands" sounded exciting. The two boys piled into her old Buick. Grandma Lottie turned to them with a smile and said it was the first time there had ever been a Negro in her car, but Raheem was more than welcome.

Although Raheem was kind of bored with the scenery, Kyle was not. Kyle was so used to flat farmland that he couldn't believe there was land so foreign-looking and alien just a couple of hours away.

The Badlands were crazy with rock formations, deep crevices, and spires that looked like they should have been inside a cave. There were places where egglike rocks were piled on top of each other and there were long narrow bands of grass that coursed through the rock formations. They saw buffalo, deer, and golden eagles along the river. Kyle especially liked the prairie dogs.

They ate a picnic lunch in the national park on the grassy lawn at an old castlelike home called Medora. Grandma Lottie said it was called a château, which was French. When they finished lunch, Grandma Lottie urged the two boys to join in a talk given inside the château by a park ranger to a bunch of tourists. It was mostly boring, Kyle thought, but one story the ranger told captured him in a way that was completely unexpected.

It was about Theodore Roosevelt, who had once lived there as a cowboy. He later became the president.

In the late winter, when the Missouri was just breaking up and still filled with huge plates of ice, three outlaws had stolen Roosevelt's boat from his ranch and had taken it downriver. Roosevelt and his ranch hands built a new boat of their own and gave chase. After three days of harrowing travel on the cold river with huge chunks of ice all around them, they found the camp of the thieves and captured them at gunpoint and got their boat back. The ranger went on to tell a long story about how many days it took for Roosevelt to deliver the thieves to law officers a long distance away and how all the locals thought he should have just shot them or hung them on the spot, but Kyle couldn't take his eyes off an old photo of Roosevelt holding a shotgun and guarding his three prisoners on the bank of the big river.

Raheem had asked Kyle why he was staring at the photo, and Kyle said, "Don't you have a boat?"

Raheem got it and immediately grinned.

Grandma Lottie had no idea what the boys were thinking, but she said on the way back to town how pleased she was they'd enjoyed the trip.

"I suppose I should call Rachel and let her know you're here," Grandma Lottie said while Kyle shoveled in the eggs, bacon, and lefse. "I don't suppose she knows, does she?"

Kyle shook his head. Grandma Lottie sat at the table with him and sipped a cup of coffee. She was always drinking coffee, just like all the old people Kyle had ever met.

"If Grandpa Sven was here I'd ask *him* to call her."

Kyle had vague memories of his grandfather. All he could remember was he had jet-black hair and he wore bib overalls and he died. He'd been a wheat farmer.

"She's at work," Kyle said.

"Ah. Still at the McDonald's?"

Kyle nodded.

"That's better than where she used to work, for sure. I heard they pay their people seventeen dollars an hour plus health insurance. Is that true?"

Kyle shrugged. He had no idea.

"I don't even know this town anymore. The stories I hear are just . . . unbelievable. And most of the people I know have either died or moved away. Sven always said we'd *never* move. But I think maybe he'd forgive me now.

"So she's doing okay?" she asked.

Kyle nodded but didn't look up and meet his grandmother's eyes.

"It was so rough for such a long time," she said. "She was out of control. She . . ." Then nothing.

Kyle looked up. Grandma Lottie just shook her head. She'd never told Kyle what had happened between her and his mom, but he knew it had a lot to do with him.

"Should I call her at work?" she asked after a long pause.

"No," he said. "I'll ride my bike there later because I need to talk to her." He needed to *warn* her.

"You will not," she said. "I'll get the car warmed up and I'll take you there. It's not supposed to get warmer than twenty below today. I've got a hair appointment at eleven."

"Okay."

After breakfast, Kyle curled up on the couch under an afghan Grandma Lottie had made a long time ago that had always been there and he watched cartoons on her old television set. Her cat Duchess formed a ball near his stocking feet.

It felt good to feel safe and warm. He'd almost forgotten what it was like to feel secure, which is how he'd always felt with Grandma Lottie when his mom was sick. He tried to imagine his mom living in this same house as a little girl, but he couldn't.

He thought about the pickup and the three men in front of his house, and the cop in the car who had pointed it out to them.

He now knew for sure that T-Lock had actually been right about something: he could never go to the cops and tell them what he knew.

And he thought about Theodore Roosevelt and that boat.

Chapter Eighteen

Cassie waited impatiently inside her office at the law enforcement center for Sheriff Kirkbride to arrive for the morning briefing. She looked expectantly every time the elevator announced its arrival with a chime, but thus far he hadn't showed. She checked her wristwatch: ten minutes until the briefing began. Most of the deputies had already filed in, and she could hear the general hum from the briefing room down the hall.

She'd been pleased to find that Judy had either scrounged or repatriated office furniture: a decent fabric-covered chair on rollers, two hardback chairs for guests, and a plastic fern that looked very out of place in North Dakota.

Finally, Kirkbride strode down the hallway and paused at her door. He held up his phone so she could see her own text to him, which read:

I NEED TO TALK TO YOU BEFORE
THE BRIEFING.
IT'S VERY IMPORTANT. CD

"This is from you, right?" he asked.

She nodded, and stepped aside so he could come in. She shut the door behind him.

"I don't have any names programmed into my phone," he said, shedding his departmental parka. "So I never know who leaves me a message or sends me a text except by the numbers. I've got to hire one of my grandkids to do that for me, I guess. But in this case the four-oh-six Montana area code gave it away."

He glanced at his watch to emphasize how little time they had, then looked up expectantly.

She said, "I found this in my refrigerator last night," and handed him her phone with the photo on the screen.

He took it and looked at it and then at her.

"That's Rufus Whiteley's head," Kirkbride said.

"I know."

"And you found this in your refrigerator?"

"Yes."

He lowered the phone and glared at her.

273

"And you're just telling me *now*?"

"Yes."

"Shit, Cassie," he said, leaning back on her desk and rubbing his forehead with his free hand, "You found a human head — the head of a man we've all been looking for — and you sat on it all night long?"

"Listen to my reasoning before you go off on me," she said. "I almost called. I had the phone in my hand and I started to dial dispatch, then I thought about it. I almost called you but it was late and I had to work this out."

"Work what out? These animals threw body parts all over my county and put the head into the refrigerator of my *new chief investigator.* It's like they're telling us they're in control. We could have done a sweep last night and maybe nailed 'em."

"I doubt that," she said, "because I doubt whoever put that head in my apartment was the same person who mutilated Whitely."

Kirkbride closed one eye, trying to anticipate where she was going.

"Look," she said, "All of the body parts were scattered the night before or in the early morning hours. They didn't hold the head back and deliver it to my place later. They probably don't even know who I am or what I do here. They sure wouldn't have

274

access to the building. But whoever put the head in my apartment does."

The sheriff arched his eyebrows as if to say, "Go on."

"One of our own did it," she said. "He found the head during the day when we were all searching for it, and he got into my apartment and put it there to scare me off. He probably thought I'd see it, go hysterical, and drive back to Montana. He doesn't want me here and this was his way of running me off."

Kirkbride nodded but still looked skeptical.

"I didn't call it in because I wanted to see what happened this morning at the briefing," she said. "I want to see who looks at me wondering why I haven't reacted. They'll wonder, 'Did she even open the refrigerator door? And if she did, why hasn't she said something?' He won't know what to think and he might give himself away.

"Besides," she said, "what's the hurry calling it in? We know the head belongs to Rufus Whiteley."

"I'm not sure I completely agree with this tactic," he said. "But I see where you're coming from."

"Tell me about Cam Tollefsen," she said. "He's who I wanted to talk to you about

275

yesterday. I get this vibe from him and it isn't a good one. Believe me, I used to work with a guy who gave off that vibe at times."

Sheriff Kirkbride sighed and said, "Cam used to have your job, but you probably know that. I busted him down to patrol because I thought he was insubordinate and running his own show."

"What's that mean?"

"Cam is an old-timer around here, like me. We joined the department just a couple of years apart. We used to be pretty close, but when I ran for sheriff he thought I'd gotten too big for my britches, you know? I think he resents me and I think he's bitter that most of the people he knew around here either got rich or moved away. He feels entitled to a bigger part of the action. I thought he'd find that when I named him chief investigator, but he built his own little empire and froze me out of it. I'm not saying he's corrupt, but I always get the feeling he's like a train running down a parallel track to his own destination, you know?"

Cassie said, "He showed up yesterday when I was checking out the field where the rollover occurred. I got the feeling he might have been guarding it from me."

"That's nothing we can take action on," Kirkbride said. "But it's something, that's for sure."

"I want to see how he acts this morning when he sees me," Cassie said. "You watch him, too. You know him better so you'll know if he seems bothered or upset."

Kirkbride said he would.

"Several things in the rollover report seem hinky to me," she said. "The times don't make sense. Tollefsen was on the scene so quickly it's almost like he was waiting for that car to show up. He didn't hit his lights or siren and he didn't call it in right away — Lance Foster did. I don't think Tollefsen expected Foster to show up as backup so fast."

"You know what you're implying, don't you?" Kirkbride cautioned.

"That's all I'm doing at this point — implying."

"That's right."

"But isn't this exactly what you expected me to find?" she asked. "Isn't that why you asked me to run an independent investigation?"

Kirkbride didn't answer but his eyes told her she was right. Instead he said, "We better get into that briefing. Max won't start until I show up."

As she gathered her notebook and pen to follow him, he said, "Give it a few beats before you show up. I don't want anybody to think we were conspiring in here, if you know what I mean."

She did. She asked, "What do we do about the head?"

"I'll figure something out." He puzzled over it a moment and a smile formed.

"What?"

"You'll see."

He handed back her phone and left her office. Before she dropped it in her pocket, she realized she had forgotten to call Prosecutor Leslie Behaunek back in North Carolina the night before.

After the briefing, she thought.

Cassie took several deep breaths and tried to take control of her composure. Her plan wouldn't work if she entered the room looking concerned or rattled. She tried to think of something that made her happy, and thought of her son Ben and his crazy plan to become a fisherman in North Dakota. It made her smile, how determined he was. And it put her in the right frame of mind.

Max Maxfield had already begun the briefing when Cassie walked in and took her position in the back of the room against the wall. Her arrival resulted in a hitch in Maxfield's presentation and he lost his place for

278

a moment before resuming, which took Cassie by surprise.

She exchanged looks with Kirkbride in the front and Kirkbride cocked an eyebrow. He was puzzled also.

Cassie felt more than saw a sustained sidewise stare from Tollefsen, who sat where he had the day before in the last row of chairs. She had no doubt he was looking her over closely for some kind of tell. Because she was prepared for it, she turned in his direction and nodded and followed it with a curt smile. It wasn't what he expected, she guessed, and his eyes snapped back to the front of the room.

Again, she locked eyes with Kirkbride and again he raised an eyebrow. He'd seen it too.

There were no leads on the disappearance of Phillip Klein. Twenty-four hours had passed and there was now reason to begin a legitimate inquiry. The photo of Klein and his description had been transmitted to law enforcement agencies throughout North Dakota, South Dakota, Minnesota, and Montana. Maxfield assigned two deputies to work the case and interview Klein's colleagues at the man camp.

There were also no solid leads on who had

mutilated Rufus Whiteley or why. Maxfield said the department had received six or seven calls from people offering information or naming suspects. Whiteley had more than his share of enemies, including other bikers, coworkers, and people he owed money to. Cassie hoped at least one of the leads panned out. She knew from experience that more than 95 percent of felony crimes were solved as a result of citizens volunteering information to law enforcement. Maxfield assigned teams of two deputies to follow up on each lead, even though a couple — a reporting party had claimed he saw an Arab-looking "Al Qaeda–type" man get off the Amtrak train two days before and a second RP said he had a theory on how Whiteley could have mutilated himself — seemed less than promising.

"As to potential motive," Maxfield said, "I'd like to ask Ian to come up to the podium and share some things he heard on the street yesterday while the rest of us were running around town picking up the pieces."

Ian Davis stood and started to make his way up to the front of the room when Sheriff Kirkbride rose and said, "Before we do that, I'd like to commend the newest member of our department for doing something far beyond the call of duty —

Investigator Cassandra Dewell."

Cassie was flummoxed. All of the deputies in the room rotated in their chairs to look at her.

"Cassie here found Rufus Whiteley's head. When most of us were home in bed last night she went out in the thirty-below weather and found it. It seems we all looked everywhere for it except for the alley behind the building. And because the forensics folks were not on duty, she marked and photographed the scene before taking it to her place. She put it in her *refrigerator* until this morning so we could examine it."

"Her refrigerator?" someone asked incredulously.

"Right next to a six-pack of beer," Kirkbride said with a smile. "So we can all stop looking for that head and worrying that some schoolkid might use it to kick around instead of a soccer ball. We can concentrate on our efforts to find the killer."

There were a few laughs and several deputies gave her a thumbs-up. Then they turned back to Kirkbride.

Except for Tollefsen, who narrowed his eyes and seemed conflicted.

Although she didn't like to be surprised like that, she saw the cleverness of what Kirkbride had just done. He'd provided enough misdirection to confuse the man or men who'd set her up. They wouldn't know if the sheriff had been told an outright lie by Cassie, what her motive was, or if he was conspiring with her. And he'd provided a plausible foundation for the retrieval of the head.

Ian Davis had paused near Judy's desk while the sheriff was talking. Kirkbride said to him, "Ian, let's table that presentation of yours for now. Some new information has come to my attention and I want to go over it with you to see if it jibes with what you heard out there."

Cassie was confused, and so was Davis. The undercover officer said, "Sure, I guess."

Kirkbride approached Davis and whispered something to him and Davis nodded reluctantly. Then Kirkbride said to Maxfield, "Continue, Max."

As the briefing concluded, Kirkbride signaled to Cassie to walk with him in the hallway.

"Did I surprise you?"

"Wasn't it obvious?"

"It was." He chuckled. "But the look on your face was perfect. I think everyone bought it."

"Except for Cam Tollefsen," she said.

"I noticed he was the first to leave the room."

Cassie paused. "What about Max? Did you catch that?"

"I did, but I'm not sure we're on the right track thinking Max had anything to do with it. I think he's still not used to a female investigator in the department, and you showing up a minute after he started threw him off track. But it did get me to thinking there's a possibility we might have more than one guy in that room we need to be wary of."

She nodded. "Ian Davis?"

"No, he's a good egg," Kirkbride said. "That's why I asked him to come to my office in half an hour. I want to hear what he has to say and I'd like you there, too."

She got it. Kirkbride didn't want anyone hostile to her investigation to know what Davis had learned. The sheriff wanted to keep any unfriendlies within the department off balance and guessing.

"At some point I'm going to need some help on this case," she said. "I can't continue to work it alone without any resources."

"We aren't there yet," he said, and went into his office and shut the door.

There was a message on Cassie's desk to

call Brandi Atnip in evidence.

Since she had a half an hour before meeting with Kirkbride and Davis, Cassie found Atnip's extension on the list Judy had given her and punched the button.

"Atnip."

"This is Cassie Dewell."

"Ah, right. Well, I've got that tire track cast you asked for."

"You do? With all you had to do yesterday you found the time?"

"I worked late last night."

"Bless you."

Brandi Atnip looked up from the counter wearing a white lab coat, jeans, and high-topped hunting boots. She had close-cropped magenta hair, hipster glasses, and a sly smile. It was amazing, Cassie thought, how evidence techs looked the same everywhere.

"I've got your coat in back, too," Atnip said. "At least I assume it's your coat."

"It is. I really can't thank you enough."

Atnip said, "Not a problem. You asked nice. A lot of these yahoos don't ask nice and I keep 'em waiting for a while. Besides, it felt kind of right to go outside of town in the nice quiet snow last night after the day we had yesterday. Peaceful, even. And from what I just heard, I need to go to your place and bag up a head."

Cassie laughed at the way she said it.

"It's okay, it won't be my first. I get to go to a lot of traffic accidents."

She hopped down from her stool. "Wait here, I'll bring it out."

Atnip walked through a frosted glass door and it hissed shut behind her.

After five minutes, Atnip pushed through the door again with Cassie's coat and a puzzled look on her face.

"It's gone."

"What?"

"It's not where I left it. And damn, it was a good piece of work if I do say so myself. That track was frozen solid and the foam cast picked it up perfectly. It was kind of technical because it was so damned cold out there — but I was able to get it back home in one piece so it could set up. You could see every lug on the tire and you would have been able to match it up with the original."

Cassie shook her head. "Who could have taken it? Who came in here from the time you left me the message to when I called you?"

"Nobody. That's just it. You're the only person who came in here."

Cassie started to ask about other evidence techs or deputies when Atnip said, "Except for when I went to get some coffee."

"What?"

"I've been here all morning except for when I left to get some coffee across the street. I can't stand that crap they make in the lunchroom."

"When was that?" Cassie asked.

"About ten minutes ago," she said. "I got back just when you called me."

At the same time the briefing broke up, Cassie thought.

"Who else has access to your lab?"

"Shit, everybody," Atnip said. "Our key-cards work on every door. Sheriff Kirkbride has a thing about it. He doesn't like the idea of his people getting all territorial. Except for the evidence room, of course."

Cassie said, "This might make him rethink that policy."

Atnip shrugged. "Don't count on it. He's a stubborn old guy. He likes to think everybody in his department is on the up-and-up. Like it was before the boom, I guess."

"I'll talk to him. But in the meanwhile, please let me know if that cast turns up or somebody gives it back. Maybe someone took it by mistake."

"Maybe," Atnip said without conviction. "I hope that happens because there's no way I can get another cast. The snow last night buried the track out in the field and now it's just part of the snowpack. We wouldn't be able to find it until spring — if then."

Cassie checked her wristwatch. Time for the meeting with the sheriff and Ian Davis.

Then, maybe, returning the call to the North Carolina prosecutor . . .

Cassie handed the keycard to her apartment to Atnip.

"Make yourself at home," she said.

"Trust me. You won't even know it was there. I'll leave an open box of baking soda in there for the odor."

Chapter Nineteen

Ian Davis seemed apprehensive about meeting with Kirkbride, Cassie observed. The undercover cop couldn't stop fidgeting and his fingertips pounded out a silent drumbeat on the top of his left thigh. The sheriff couldn't see that, though, because he was behind his desk. Cassie sat next to Davis and sympathized with him. Any cop would be nervous about being asked to come see the boss, even if he had nothing to be ashamed about.

"Sorry to throw you a curve in there," the sheriff told Davis.

"No problem," Davis said cautiously.

"I've asked Cassie to sit in because she's new here and I wanted an outside opinion," Kirkbride said. "Sometimes we all get too close to the locals and the day-to-day, and I find it helpful to get that extra input."

Davis nodded and looked at Cassie, assessing her. Cassie couldn't read what

Davis's conclusion was.

"So please forgive me if I ask dumb questions," Cassie said. "I don't know all the players like you and the sheriff do."

"Okay."

"So what were you going to brief our guys about this morning?" Kirkbride asked. "I know you and Max went over it but I didn't hear what it was."

Davis didn't open his notebook. He said, "I wasn't going to do any speculation, if that's what you were worried about. I was just going to share what I'd heard out and about in town while all that body parts stuff was going down."

"Which is?"

Davis looked to Cassie and then to the sheriff. "The word is new meth will hit the street by tomorrow. You can't believe how antsy some of the tweakers are getting. But the rumor is, one more day."

Kirkbride looked pained. "Is there any way we can stop it?"

Davis shrugged. "I'm not sure, but maybe."

"So how do we do it?"

Davis took a deep breath and sighed. He looked at his hands as if he hadn't noticed them before. Then he said, "What I told you about new blue hitting the street is solid information. I heard it from too many guys not to think it's true — or at least *they* think it's true. But anything else — it's speculation. I just want to go on the record with that, boss."

Kirkbride nodded gently. He had a way, Cassie thought, of putting his guys at ease. "Okay, it's speculation. I won't hold you to anything if it doesn't pan out."

"Good," Davis said, "and one more thing."

"Shoot."

"I think I need to get off the street. I know it's a couple of months early and all, but I think my days are numbered."

Kirkbride sat back, genuinely concerned. "Why — what happened?"

"It's cumulative, not just one thing. But I can feel it coming. You know what I do out there: I hang out at the strip clubs and bars and talk to people and hear things. It's one thing to ask a guy when the crank will be available — that's self-serving and all those guys can get down with that. But I've been pressing lately, and asking about details. 'Where is the meth coming from? What's going on that it's dried up?' That kind of stuff.

"Anyway, a guy I know who is well-connected pulled me aside last night and said, 'Willie Dietrich thinks you're asking too many questions.' "

Davis shot a glance at Cassie. He looked embarrassed.

"He didn't threaten me," Davis said, "but the message was clear. They're starting to wonder about me. And if they think they can't trust me, well, based on what's been going on around here lately . . ."

"No need to explain," Kirkbride said quickly. "You're back on patrol. I don't want you out there anymore. You're making the right call at the right time."

Davis was obviously relieved. "Thank you, sir. I'll report to patrol tomorrow morning."

"No, you won't," Kirkbride said. "You'll ride with Cassie today and show her the ropes. Then you'll take two weeks of vacation and a week of unpaid leave. Go someplace warm, or go home to Wisconsin — whatever. Clear your head, get a haircut, and shave. Then come back and go to work."

Davis closed his eyes and smiled. It was as if he'd won the jackpot, Cassie thought. Davis was a good cop and he needed the firm push from Kirkbride.

"Now that we've got that cleared up, I want to hear your off-the-record speculation."

"That's all it is," Davis said. "But it's based on snippets of conversation, and who is hanging out with who, that sort of thing."

"Shoot."

"Okay," Davis said, opening his spiral notebook and glancing at his cryptic handwriting, "this is what I think is happening. For the last year and a half, Rufus Whitely got control of his bunch of rogue bikers and negotiated a charter with the Sons of Freedom in Denver. Once he had that bunch behind him, Rufus consolidated territory from here all the way to Tioga, Dickenson, Watford City, and even some of Minot. They took over distribution from little independent guys and muscled their way to controlling all of the Badlands. But with all of the new people flooding into the Bakken and all the money around here, the market keeps getting bigger and that fact got around. So we've got organized competition moving into the market."

"Go on," the sheriff said.

"I'd not done much research on MS-13 until about a month ago," Davis said. "I told you about it then, but I didn't have anything to go on besides a rumor. According to the FBI info I read on them, they really didn't exist until about 1980. Salvadorans were involved in a violent civil war and a bunch of 'em moved north to L.A. In order to protect themselves against the more well-established Mexican gangs, they formed Mara Salvatrucha. Because they were outnumbered and outgunned, they figured out pretty quick that the way to hold their territory and gain more was to be over-the-top vicious.

"Now they're in a growth mode. When MS-13 moves into a new territory they don't take prisoners. They're not like other kinds of organized crime gangs who want to stay below the radar and not risk calling attention to themselves. These guys don't negotiate for market share or cut deals. They just show up and say, 'Get the hell out of the business or we'll cut your head off.'

"I think they moved in here fast like they do and told the bikers to get the hell out. These guys are ruthless. The bikers are thugs but they're nothing compared to MS-13.

"MS-13 supposedly has better product from Mexico and they charge more for it, but if you've got a monopoly you can do whatever you want."

"So far," Kirkbride said, "I'm buying it. It goes along with something Cassie and I talked about."

Davis said, "So like I said, the word on a street a few days ago was that really high-quality meth would be hitting. There was a shipment on the way. The slimeball losers I talk with didn't know where it was coming from or who was behind it — they just seemed to know that good shit was coming. That's when I started asking too many questions, probably. I could feel a shift in the market but I didn't know who, or why, or when.

"Then something happened," Davis said. "The shipment somehow didn't show up or got intercepted along the way."

Kirkbride and Cassie exchanged glances. The timing conformed with the date of the rollover.

"I think the bikers learned about the blue meth coming and derailed it. I don't know how they found out or who did it. But they took it out of the pipeline."

Cassie wanted Davis to jump ahead to what she thought she knew was coming, but she refrained. Davis wanted to weave it out.

"So MS-13 retaliated the way they do — violently and over the top. They went straight to the head of the Sons of Freedom, Rufus, and cut him to pieces and scattered him all over town. They figured that would send a message to the rest of the bikers that in a war they were capable of anything. And if you read up on MS-13, you know they are. They've put contract hits out on federal agents. In Honduras, they machine-gunned twenty-eight people — mostly women and children — on a bus. They decapitate entire families just to warn off informants. And to think these guys are actually here in Grimstad — it blows my mind."

Kirkbride nodded. "So you think the motive behind Rufus's murder was retaliation?"

"Partly. But they also wanted to kill the king in the splashiest way possible so his guys would scatter."

"Did it work?"

Davis chuckled drily. "From what I can see, it did. The word is that Rufus's guys trailered their bikes and headed to Colorado and the mothership. I haven't seen any of them since yesterday. I drove by their clubhouse last night and the place is deserted."

"Interesting," Cassie said. "So MS-13 has a foothold here."

"More than that, I'd guess," Davis said. "I think they've taken over in one fell swoop."

"This Phillip Klein guy," Kirkbride said, "do you think he fits into any of this?"

Davis shrugged. "It doesn't make sense that he does, other than he disappeared at the same time all this was going down. It's possible, I guess, but I haven't heard a thing about him."

Cassie said, "Except Klein worked the man camp on the same night Rufus was murdered. Think about it. Grimstad isn't a normal town. There is absolutely no place to stay unless you've made arrangements well in advance, and there was no way the MS-13 guys could have known their meth would be intercepted ahead of time. So when that happened, maybe they'd already sent a couple of assassins up here to go after Rufus. But the practical question is, where would they stay?"

Kirkbride said, "If they didn't know the area — which I'm sure they don't — they might wind up at a man camp."

"And maybe they didn't like the rules there," Cassie said, "or the guy behind the desk."

Then she sat up with a start. "Or maybe, they didn't like the cameras. Didn't someone steal the server?"

Davis and Kirkbride exchanged looks.

Kirkbride nodded. "Which means they might still be here."

Then he turned to Davis. "What about Willie Dietrich? What do you think his role is in all of this?"

Davis shook his head in disgust. "Willie, yeah. He'll never go away. See, Willie is the middleman — the distributor. He doesn't cook, so he's no threat to either the bikers or MS-13. I'm guessing that if MS-13 showed up with more muscle and a better product, Willie would flip in a heartbeat. Rufus and Willie were supposedly real tight, but leaving pieces of Rufus all over town probably helped convince Willie to change sides and forget he'd ever even worked with those bikers. Willie's just switching wholesalers. Plus, it makes business sense to MS-13. Willie's guys fit in with all the old dopers and all the new dopers. If a bunch of tatted-up Salvadoran gangsters started walking around Walmart they'd be easy for us to spot."

"At least that used to be the case," Kirkbride added with a grim smile. "Have you been there lately?"

Both Cassie and Davis smiled at that. Davis said he'd read in the FBI reports that some of the more sophisticated MS-13 gang members were easing back on their facial and neck tattoos so they wouldn't be identified as easily.

"So tomorrow," Kirkbride said, bringing it back, "there's new product on the street."

"That's what I heard."

Davis hesitated, then said, "That's why I wondered why you shut me down today. Max thought it would be good for the guys to know so they could keep their eyes open. If they don't know it's coming, there might be trouble. And if the druggies don't get what they think they're getting, *they* could be trouble."

"I understand all that," Kirkbride said with a hint of irritation. "And the last thing I want to do is withhold intel from our team. But now I'm going to ask you a really tough question, Ian, and I want you to answer it honestly. There will be no hard feelings or repercussions based on your answer, but I trust you to be honest with me."

Davis sat back in his chair. Cassie noticed his face had gone white.

"What do you hear — are any of my guys dirty?"

The question hung there for thirty seconds.

Finally, Davis said, "I'm not the kind of cop who rats other cops out."

"I know that. But what you tell me doesn't go beyond this room. I'm not asking you your opinion or what you think. I'm asking you what you hear out there. Even if it's just a rumor with no foundation in truth."

Davis looked to Cassie for some kind of help. She didn't offer any, but she felt for him. She'd been in a similar situation once and the results had been disastrous.

"Well," Davis said, "there's a rumor that Willie has some protection at a higher level."

"Protection?"

"Someone who watches out for him."

"Which implies someone is getting a cut."

"It implies that I guess."

"Cam?"

Davis looked away so quickly it was just like saying yes, Cassie thought.

"People are always saying things," Davis said. "They all want to act like they're more inside than they are. I've never heard anything definitive at all. Never."

Kirkbride watched Davis carefully while he nodded his head. He said, "If Willie Dietrich switched sides so quick, I wonder if someone else did, too."

His words hung there.

Cassie broke the silence. "This is also speculation, but Cam Tollefsen was the first officer on the scene of that rollover — almost as if he were waiting for it. Like he was there to escort the driver into town. And although there's nothing at all in his report suggesting it, I think another car forced the gangster off the road. Why else would he have gone off it into that field? Maybe Cam saw it happen and decided to play both sides against the middle."

Davis looked over at her, his eyes wide.

"Are you suggesting Cam found the supply?" Kirkbride asked her.

"I don't think so," she said. "Otherwise, he wouldn't have shadowed me out in the field yesterday morning. There was no reason for him to be there except for the off chance I'd stumble over the missing meth and he wanted to be there if that happened. But he knows I didn't find anything except that tire track."

"What track?" Kirkbride asked.

She told Kirkbride and Davis about the missing cast.

She said, "There's nothing in Tollefsen's report about a witness, especially not someone on a motorbike or a bicycle. Lance Foster didn't mention it, either, but he wasn't the first on the scene. But Cam might have panicked when he found out I had Atnip go out there. He probably didn't know what I was after and I'm not sure I know myself. The track could be completely unrelated to the rollover and it could have been made hours before or after. I was just fishing around for something, but Cam didn't know that and he might have felt I was on to something and he thought he needed to derail my investigation."

"So you think he took the cast?" Davis

asked, incredulous.

"I don't know who took it," Cassie said. "But who else would have? Who else knew I was even out there in the field? And you," she said, turning to Kirkbride, "saw his reaction this morning. He was clearly confused when I showed up."

"Yeah," Kirkbride said wearily, "but proof of nothing."

Cassie nodded.

Kirkbride swiveled in his chair toward Davis again. "We've been all over that rollover. I had the guys cut the car apart with welding torches, just in case. We even opened up the tires and sawed the frame apart. No drugs. So if your theory is correct, where did they go?"

Davis shrugged. He said, "All I know is that they aren't on the market but they should be by tomorrow."

"So either MS-13 has them back and for some reason they're delaying distribution, or they're confident they'll have them by tomorrow."

"That makes sense," Davis said.

"So who in the hell has the shipment?" Kirkbride asked rhetorically. "If Cam had them or Willie had them the deal would be done, I'd think. We'd have meth-head central going on around here. So if you were to guess, each of you, what would you say? Where is the supply?"

Davis shook his head. He said, "Maybe no one knows for sure where it is yet. Or maybe a whole new shipment arrives tomorrow. Either way, MS-13 will want their first shipment back because it's probably worth millions."

Kirkbride shook his head, puzzled. "It makes no sense that someone would hold on to what they've got knowing they could be cut into little pieces and scattered around town. No one with any sense would mess with MS-13 — or Willie — like that."

Kirkbride nodded but was noncommittal. "Cassie?"

She said, "I don't think we're the only ones wondering where the shipment wound up. I think Willie and his contacts with MS-13 think they're close to getting it back so they put the word out it will be on the street tomorrow. But I don't think they have it yet."

Kirkbride leaned back in his chair and rested his elbows on his belly and steepled his fingers. He thought about it for a minute.

Then he said to Cassie and Davis, "Partner up. Start with Willie. I'll get some guys I trust to start making inquiries at all the man camps. If we've got a couple of Salvadorans staying here we should be able to identify them pretty quick. I'll reach out to Cam. I've known him for a hell of a long time and we've got a lot of history. If nothing else, I can talk with him and keep him off the street for a while. And who knows — maybe he'll fess up.

"But we've got to move quick," Kirkbride said. "I don't want that meth to hit the streets tomorrow and I don't want any more citizens butchered. I especially don't want a bunch of fucking gangsters in my county."

Davis nodded to Cassie and said, "You realize my cover will be blown if we work together in the open."

"It's already blown, right?" Kirkbride asked.

Davis put his head down. "Yeah."

"Go," Kirkbride said, shooing them out of the room.

Davis stood expectantly outside Cassie's office while she retrieved her parka. Lining the hallway was the delegation from China Kirkbride had mentioned earlier. They nodded at her respectfully as she passed and they looked just as Kirkbride had guessed: business suits, loafers, smart overcoats.

To Davis, she said, "Just a second," and stepped back inside Kirkbride's office.

The sheriff looked up. His eyes were red, and Cassie was taken aback.

"Yes?" he said.

Cassie said, "I still wonder about that tire cast."

"We'll worry about that later. Right now, I'm trying to get used to the fact that I might have a dirty cop right under my nose. I sure as hell don't like the feeling."

"The Chinese delegation is waiting outside."

Kirkbride's face fell. He said, "Don't invite them in."

Cassie nodded.

"Look," Kirkbride said, pushing back angrily from his desk, "the governor's office called and asked me to treat these Red Chinese like some kind of official delegation. I say, 'Fuck 'em.' This state produced Roger Maris, Phil Jackson, and Louis L'Amour. We're all-Americans here. Why should I divert resources to a dozen fucking Chicoms?"

She doubted his sudden anger had much to do with the Chinese.

CHAPTER TWENTY

Cam Tollefsen was parked on the north edge of Grimstad with his engine idling and the heat on against the cold. The sky was gray and dark snow clouds scudded high from the flat northern horizon to the southern horizon. He was perched on a small rise but it seemed as if he could see the curvature of the earth.

It wasn't silent like it had once been out here, when he used to sit and scope out the landscape and the only sound was the wind whistling through gaps in his pickup cab. Occasionally, he'd seen a small herd of pronghorn antelope or white-tailed deer picking their way across the fields toward the river. Sometimes, the fields were white with nesting snow geese. Now, though, the prairie roared with train after train. Empty tankers rolling into Grimstad, full tankers rolling out. Millions of barrels of oil bound for every corner of the country.

His cell phone burred on his lap and he checked the screen but didn't answer.

Two calls in a row from Jon Kirkbride. The sheriff rarely called him direct anymore, but he'd left a message after the second one.

Tollefsen had a pretty good idea of what the message would say. He grunted and bent forward and fished around under the seat with his fingers for his personal gear bag. He placed it next to him and unzipped it. Aspirin, a few energy bars, a .22 throw-down pistol he'd never had the need to use. And the pint of Jim Beam.

It had been years since he drank in the morning. Jon was known to do it on occasion, too, years ago. Back when they'd both been young and full of energy. Tollefsen remembered when the two of them would spotlight deer out on the prairie or ambush geese on the river, always a step ahead of the game warden. They'd drink beer and whiskey late into the night and show up for patrol the next morning with raging hangovers. Sometimes, after their shift Kirkbride would compete in local rodeos and Tollefsen would go along. Tollefsen couldn't care less about horses or rodeos but he liked the girls who did, and he liked Jon Kirkbride. Sometimes they'd convince a girl and her friend to go out dancing with them after the rodeo. That's how Jon met his wife, and how Tollefsen met that damned Tammy.

That was also before Jon started to pull away and to get political. That wasn't for Tollefsen, who preferred the ragged edges of law enforcement and not the white-hot center. He'd always thought Jon would come to his senses but he never did. Instead, his friend thrived in it. Tollefsen had grudgingly supported him in his run, of course, but he didn't raise money for him or campaign. When Jon got elected to the sheriff's job, Tollefsen expected to be rewarded by his old friend. But it hadn't exactly worked out that way.

Sure, he'd been named chief investigator and he finally got his own office. But that didn't mean Jon confided in him like he used to or let him make his own decisions. It almost seemed like Kirkbride wanted to pretend they'd never been close. Like those good times had never really happened.

Then they found oil by hydraulic fracturing out in the prairie and Tammy left. The whole damned world changed. Kirkbride was getting calls from television producers and *The New York Times.* Tollefsen started going out at night by himself. Lowlifes like Willie Dietrich bought him drinks and supplied women who were passing through.

People Tollefsen had grown up with got rich and moved away. A whole new class of people moved in. Money flowed, gushed, ran down the gullies like a flash flood. The department doubled, then tripled in size. Square heads from Minnesota, Wisconsin, and Michigan took over. It was all Tollefsen could do at times from his seat in the back of the room not to tell them all just to shut the hell up and calm down. That this job, like life, would disappoint them. That their friends would look out only for themselves.

He punched the voice mail key to retrieve the message.

Kirkbride sounded sad, weary. He said, "Cam, you need to come in. I need to talk with you. Bring your badge and gun."

Tollefsen had justified what he'd done by telling himself he was working with locals to supply a product to newcomers that they were already going to get one way or another. After all, shouldn't he get in on the action? Bachelor farmers without two nickels to rub together were becoming millionaires. Locals with no-account storefronts on Main Street were selling out for big money. Tammy had taken up with an executive from Baker Hughes and lived on a twelve-acre estate outside Houston.

■ ■ ■ ■

He finished the pint with a flourish and powered his passenger-side window down and threw away the empty. Who knew that new woman cop would react the way she did? What kind of person wouldn't be upset to find a decapitated head in their own home? Any normal person would have been freaked out. Hell, Tollefsen *himself* was freaked out just knowing it was in the plastic garbage bag after he'd found it mounted on top of a fence pole near the school. There was obviously something wrong with her and something hinky going on between her and the sheriff. Like they were in it together to bring him down. And now Jon was calling to close the trap.

Jon, of all people, would know what would happen to him if he was sent to the North Dakota State Penitentiary in Bismarck. It would be worse than a death sentence.

After all, how many inmates knew him? How many hated his guts? Tollefsen knew he wouldn't last long.

He put the Yukon into gear and drove down a rough two-track and parallel to the twelve-foot chain-link fence that kept vehicles away from the train tracks.

Twice, while lost in concentration, he let the SUV wander a bit and scrape along the fence itself. But he gathered his wits by the time he reached the edge of the massive new train yard.

Tollefsen put the transmission into park and hung out the window toward the security box. The little shack was unmanned but there was a closed-circuit camera and a speaker-box radio setup for those who didn't have authorized Burlington Northern keycards.

It was hard to hear the person on the other end of the speaker because of the noise of the trains.

He badged the camera lens and bellowed, "Bakken County Sheriff's Department. Let me the fuck in!"

He could hear some damned excuse, something about not having the authority to open the gate, but Tollefsen gestured again and again toward the camera with his badge to emphasize the gravity of the situation.

There was a high-pitched whir and the gate rolled open and Tollefsen was through it before there could be any more questions.

He roared his SUV through the yard, the tires popping on the cinder-gravel ballast. He drove right up on the tracks, his front wheels bouncing over the outside rail itself. Then he turned a sharp left so the train rails were between his tires.

"Here we go," he said. "If you're gonna take me down, Jon, I'm taking this whole fucking town with me."

The vibration inside the cab from the wild rhythm of the spaced wood ties beneath his wheels was intense. Every citation book and piece of paper he'd ever tucked under the visors or in the side compartments bounced out. The glove box opened and all its contents spilled to the floor. He could hardly see straight, but there was no doubt what was coming.

The single white high-tech halogen headlight hung out there straight ahead of him and the train engine was coming fast, a mile of tanker cars filled with Bakken crude right behind it.

He floored the accelerator.

CHAPTER TWENTY-ONE

Willie Dietrich heard a distant heavy *boom* from the direction of the rail hub as he climbed out of the Tundra in the Mc-Donald's parking lot. The sound caused a hitch in his step and he paused and looked to the north but there was nothing to see in the close gray sky.

He thought, Man, something blew up.

Willie looked back over his shoulder at Escobar and Argueta, who had remained inside the vehicle. Argueta motioned with an impatient "What's up with you?" gesture but Escobar stared icily ahead.

Willie shrugged and continued across the icy lot.

Of course, Willie knew Rachel Wester-gaard. They'd grown up together in Grimstad and they were two years apart in school. Willie was older but Rachel hung around the edges of his group, which was made up of stoners and football players.

She'd been a typical skank: stringy blond hair, skinny, with eyes so coal-dark with makeup she looked like a raccoon. But, he recalled, a decent ass and a feisty temper. He knew she'd had a thing for him — all the skanks did — but he couldn't remember if he'd put it to her or not. Probably had, he thought. He could vaguely remember her going down on him the night after they burned down that abandoned barn.

Silencio Argueta had made her. Throughout the morning, he'd gone into McDonald's three different times wearing three different hoodies. He ordered an Egg McMuffin from one counter worker on the first trip, a Sausage McGriddle from a second, and a Bacon, Cheese, and Egg Bagel from a third. He paid each time with a hundred-dollar bill and exited the restaurant with the food and a wad of change.

They hadn't worried about him looking suspicious. Willie had convinced the Salvadorans they had nothing to worry about. The McDonald's was jammed with customers like always and the McDonald's employees barely had the chance to look up, much less compare notes. Hundred-dollar bills weren't notable, either. There were so many men with so much cash these days.

It was the third order, the Bacon, Egg, and Cheese Bagel, that nailed it down.

While he ate, Willie scanned the currency with his ultraviolet light and it turned out to be awash with swoops and squiggles. When Argueta said the employee had a name tag on that said "Rachel," Willie whooped. That idiot Winkie had been onto something the night before.

Poor Winkie.

Blink.

Willie didn't really offer any assistance to Argueta and Escobar when they cut up Winkie's body that morning and put the pieces into a fifty-five-gallon industrial drum in an unoccupied oil field tool garage, but he marveled at their skill. Willie had just stood there hugging himself and glancing out the dirty windows to see if anyone was coming. It was colder than hell inside the unheated warehouse.

Willie didn't know who owned the warehouse or how the Salvadorans had found it, but it was obvious after a few minutes that they were familiar with it. He'd seen the notice taped on the front door by the Bakken County Sheriff's Department

— something about the facility being under investigation for "unlawful release of hazardous waste materials" — but he hadn't stopped to read it. All he knew was that the warehouse was empty and the Salvadorans seemed pretty confident that no one would show up to interfere with their project of cutting up Winkie.

Willie stood to the side, occasionally rising to his tiptoes to see what they were doing. Escobar and Argueta wore blood-spattered coveralls and thick rubber gloves they'd found in a storage room inside the warehouse. After a few minutes, it seemed to Willie no different than field dressing and butchering a deer, which he'd done a hundred times. In fact, Winkie was such a little squirt that his legs reminded Willie of deer haunches. Escobar was a surgeon with a blade, able to separate the knee and elbow joints with several quick cuts and strategic twists of his knife blade.

One by one, the pieces were dropped into the drum and dusted with a white powder. Willie asked what it was and Escobar smiled and said it was called posole, but the way he said it made Willie think it was some kind of sick Salvadoran joke because Argueta laughed and repeated posole aloud several times. Willie guessed it was lye. It smelled like lye and Willie had heard the cartels dissolved bodies that way.

When they were done, they sealed the top and wiped the steel of the drum clean and asked him to help roll it to a dark corner of the garage. There were a dozen other drums there, some with hazardous waste stickers, and they hid Winkie's drum in the back and surrounded it with the others. Willie noticed that Escobar had patted the top of a second drum with his gloved hand and said, *"Dulces sueños, labriego,"* but Willie had no idea what the hell that meant.

Winkie had been a big pain in the ass, Willie thought. Winkie made Willie ashamed to be a fellow Grimstad Viking, the way he kept crying and begging and passing out. Sure, his face hurt. *Of course* it hurt. But Willie thought Winkie should have sucked it up and shown a little dignity. A little North Dakota grit, as Willie liked to think of it. It took two hours to find out about T-Lock.

But where in the hell was that guy?

Now they knew where he lived in the crappy little rental, but where had he gone? There was no car parked at the house, which meant he was out and about, but where? Willie knew T-Lock had an uncle in Watson City, some old farmer who used to let football players hunt pheasants on his land, but when he called there the phone was disconnected. T-Lock's uncle, like so many of the old-timers, had moved on.

And everyone knew T-Lock didn't work in the winter.

But Winkie kept saying, "Rachel, Rachel," like the name meant something. Willie didn't put it together until the rental house was pointed out to them that morning. T-Lock lived with Rachel Westergaard. Rachel Westergaard worked at McDonald's.

And damn it if she wasn't in the process of laundering MS-13 cash in plain sight.

Willie had to kind of admire that one, although he doubted T-Lock was bright enough to have come up with it. Rachel, maybe. But not T-Lock.

He'd explained all this to Escobar and Argueta. Silencio lost interest halfway into it and looked out the window at the snow. Escobar listened carefully, though, and nodded silently while he drove.

He'd said simply, "We go to McDonald's and find her."

The restaurant had that familiar sweet grease and cleaning smell combo Willie had always liked. It was an odor that brought him back to his childhood when the old

317

man had him for weekends and a trip to the new Mickey D's was a big fucking deal. Plus it was warm inside. Three long lines snaked through the full tables from the back of the restaurant to the counter. The men in line studied the menu board above the counter like it was the Ten Commandments handed down from God, Willie thought with a smirk, like they'd never seen such a fascinating sight before. When an order was up, the customer in front would take it away and the line would shuffle a few feet forward.

Willie stood in the line on the far right. He didn't expect Rachel to recognize him, or even see him for that matter. She was working in a kind of controlled frenzy. Behind her, people of all ages in maroon smocks were frying meat patties, deep-frying fries, pouring drinks. It looked like hard work. Willie remembered working at the Dairy Barn when he was in high school. It was the most miserable day and a half of his life.

Until, that is, the Salvadorans arrived.

"Hey, good-lookin' — what's good on the menu today, Rachel? Any specials I should know about?"

Rachel snapped her head up, instantly annoyed. She was too busy and the lines were too long for playing around, for being on the receiving end of another guy flirting with her. She wasn't sure she'd squared up the cash in the register with the marked cash for the last transaction, and she knew she'd have to count it later to be sure. Even a one dollar mistake could cause her heartburn.

Her smock was roomy enough that no one could see the fanny pack strapped to her waist beneath it. The fanny pack was now nearly completely filled with unmarked cash from the register. There were only a few more marked bills behind a cardboard divider to transfer from her stash into the drawer and she'd be done for the day.

Then she recognized who knew her name and her entire body went suddenly cold.

"Remember me?" Willie Dietrich asked with that boxlike smile he'd always had. She hadn't seen him in line and she knew her reaction — freezing like a mouse caught in the corner of a kitchen — had given her away.

"Willie," she said with no enthusiasm. "What can I get you?" Her voice sounded scared and wooden even to her.

"I'm paying with a hundred-dollar bill," he said. "I wanted to make sure you still had enough change?"

She remembered the dark man in the

hoodie who had paid with a hundred not ten minutes before. She'd given him change with marked bills. This was Willie's way of saying he was on to her. Willie *knew.*

She thought, Damn you, T-Lock, you son of a bitch.

"So I guess you do have change," Willie said. Then he leaned back on his boot heels and studied the menu board. "Yeah, there are a lot of choices, you know that? I'd like something good. Is everything fried?"

She looked over Willie's shoulder. A man wearing oil-spattered coveralls rolled his eyes and sighed, not amused by Willie holding up the line. But he was also about fifty pounds smaller and six inches shorter. Further back, she could see a couple of men glaring at the back of Willie's head.

Willie wore a tight black DRIVE-BY TRUCKERS concert T-shirt with no coat. He'd never worn a coat in high school, she recalled, otherwise no one would be able to marvel at his biceps and thick forearms. Back then, he used to stop in the middle of the hallway between classes, flex both arms, and say, "Welcome to the gun show, ladies."

"Look," Willie said leaning toward her, "I know what's going on with you and T-Lock. You two have something that belongs to some friends of mine and we need it back,

320

like now."

Rachel knew he wouldn't get violent right there. He was probably aware of the security cameras trained on him. Which is why he spoke pleasantly and maintained the smile.

She said, "I don't know what you're talking about, Willie. Now will you please order? You're holding up the line."

Willie turned to the man behind him and said, "You don't mind, do you?"

The man obviously minded but he looked down at his steel-toed workboots.

"See?" Willie said. "Everything's cool. Now listen to me, Rachel. You and T-Lock are Grimstad Vikings, just like me. I don't want anything to happen to either of you and I know you somehow got involved in this because you didn't know what was going on. And believe me, you did the right thing not turning it in to anyone.

"But playtime's over. We need it back and you and I are going to figure out a way *right now* to return the property. When is your break?"

It was twenty minutes away, she thought, but she wasn't going to tell him that. Instead, she leaned forward and said, "I'll give you all the money. I have it on me right now. You buy something and I'll give you all the money in change and you can walk right out with it."

She could tell he was weighing her offer. Then the boxlike smile came back and he shrugged and said, "Naw, good try, but I'll wait around until you take your break and we can work out the arrangements. And in the meanwhile, I'd like a cup of coffee to go. I'll just hang around until your break, okay?"

The man in back of Willie lost his patience, and said, "All this for a god-dammed cup of coffee?"

Willie didn't even acknowledge him.

Rachel rang up a large coffee and turned to go get it from the bank of coffeemakers in the back. As she walked away from the counter, her legs felt stiff. She could feel his eyes on her back.

When she rounded the corner and was out of Willie's line of vision, she broke for the back door. As she did she pulled her cell phone out of her pocket to speed dial T-Lock, to warn him.

She pushed through the steel door into the cold white morning and before she could duck or scream the skinny dark man in the hoodie hit her hard in the face with his fist and she dropped like a rag doll. Hot blood filled her nose and mouth and spattered on the ice.

Rough hands grasped her under her arms from behind and lifted her into the backseat of a pickup. Her legs were limp and hanging outside the door and the skinny man shoved them inside and climbed into the back with her. He sat heavily on her legs and held her facedown into the seat cushions with his hand. She was afraid she'd choke to death on her own blood.

Her brain was scrambled and she couldn't think. She knew what was happening but she couldn't react. The pickup was moving for a moment and then it stopped again and she felt cold air as the front door opened.

She heard Willie say, "Damn it if she didn't try to run."

Then to her, "Rachel, we need to find your boyfriend. We know what he's got and we need it back. Nobody has to get hurt. All we want is our money and our product back before you two figure out a way to fuck this up even more."

She tried to speak but she couldn't draw breath. The idiot in the hoodie who was holding her down didn't seem to know he was smothering her. When she struggled he tightened his grip and pushed down harder, putting his shoulder into it.

She heard Willie say to the driver, "If she doesn't give us T-Lock there may be another way. I think she has a kid — some retard."

Then, as Rachel felt herself go limp, Willie said, "Hey, Silencio, don't fucking kill her before she even tells us anything."

His grip relaxed.

Rachel pushed herself up with strength she didn't know she had and coughed up a gout of blood that spattered on the back of the leather front seat and the side window. But at least her breathing passages were clear and she gulped for breath.

The driver said something calmly in Spanish to the man in the hoodie. The tone was threatening.

Before the man in the hoodie responded to whatever the driver said, she got a quick glimpse out of the backseat left window.

Kyle was twenty-five feet away, sitting on his bike. Their eyes locked. He had no expression on his face but he never did.

The man in the hoodie hit her again in the temple and she blacked out as the pickup drove away.

CHAPTER TWENTY-TWO

Cassie and Ian Davis had just cleared the town limits of Grimstad on their way to Willie Dietrich's place when they heard the hollow *boom* somewhere behind them in the distance.

"What was that?" Cassie asked.

Davis was driving Cassie's SUV, and she was grateful he was at the wheel. Finally, she thought, she'd have a few minutes to regroup and return the call to North Carolina. Her phone was out and on her lap.

Davis looked over his shoulder toward the direction of the sound and shook his head. "I don't know. It almost sounded like a sonic boom, you know? Maybe jets from Malmstrom or Minot?"

Cassie nodded. She was vaguely aware of the air force bases located in North Dakota.

The countryside outside of Grimstad to the east was bleak in the way that farm country in the winter was always bleak. There were endless miles of corn stubble with pockets of snow between each row. Every mile or so there was a farmhouse with outbuildings surrounded by gray, skeletal trees. Most of the houses looked unoccupied, but some had vehicles in the yards and farm equipment sitting idle. A few still had Halloween or Thanksgiving decorations hung outside that had been battered by the snow and wind. It was almost as if the oil boom had bypassed the residents, Cassie thought. But she knew that wasn't likely the case.

"Willie's been buying up some of these places out here," Davis said. "I don't know whether he thinks of them as investments or he uses them as a way to launder drug money or what. He sure as hell isn't a farmer, that's for sure. Farming's hard work."

"How far is his place?" Cassie asked.

"Another ten miles," Davis said, nodding at the straight dirt road ahead of them.

"Excuse me while I make a call," Cassie said.

County prosecutor Leslie Behaunek answered on the second ring and Cassie identified herself.

"I was wondering when you would call," Behaunek said.

Cassie could tell by the following beat of silence that Behaunek didn't have good news. She braced for it.

"Everything's gone pear-shaped," Behaunek said with a weary sigh.

Cassie closed her eyes and said, "What happened? Did something I say or do screw this up? Because if he gets out because of me —"

"It wasn't you," Behaunek said. She sounded disgusted. "You did everything right. Law enforcement gets all kinds of discretion when it comes to interviews. You can lie, promise the moon as long as you don't offer immunity or something legal like that. You can do pretty much anything you want. After all, he waived his right to an attorney. But despite all your good work and even setting yourself up so he'd attack you, he didn't confess to anything and you didn't cross the line into illegal coercion. The judge at the preliminary hearing said as much."

Cassie felt some relief, but before she could ask why the case had gone "pear-shaped" Behaunek shouted, "It was us! It was *my* guys who screwed this up. And I hate to say it, but right now I'd lay odds that monster will be back out on the road

327

within a week."

Cassie felt something cold form in her throat. "What'd they do? Couldn't they find any DNA evidence?"

"That's the worst part," Behaunek fumed. "They *found* some. The FBI hotshots found some in smears they did on the undercarriage of the trailer. He'd cleaned the inside with bleach or whatever, but there was some that had splashed up under the truck that he never thought about. We don't know who the victims were because we don't have any matches — yet. But there were two clearly identifiable victims and we've got the killer in custody. Not that it matters, though."

Cassie asked Behaunek to hold and said, "Please pull over," to Davis.

When the SUV ground to a stop on the shoulder, Cassie climbed out. She needed to have her feet on the ground, she thought. And she hoped the incredible cold would numb her from what she was about to hear.

As she stepped out into a shorn cornfield, Cassie said with barely controlled fury, "Why doesn't DNA evidence matter, Leslie?"

"Because Pergram finally wised up after you were here and hired the best criminal defense attorney in Charlotte. His name is Terry Mackey. Have you ever heard of him?"

"No."

"Well, he's kind of famous down here. Mackey took one look at the case and he went ballistic. He filed a motion to suppress evidence on the initial search of the truck itself where the sheriff found the secret room."

"What?"

"He said our guys had no probable cause for unloading it and searching inside."

Cassie felt as if she'd been punched.

Behaunek said, "The DNA doesn't matter, because that's what's considered 'fruit of a poisoned tree.' If that trailer had been stacked to the top with dead truck stop prostitutes it wouldn't have made any difference. We poisoned the tree by searching the truck without probable cause. I tried my damndest to make an argument about how the length of the trailer was suspicious and all. I tried to argue that when the Lizard King got belligerent with our officers that gave them cause to search his truck because they reasonably thought he might be hiding something. But Mackey pointed out that what was in the truck was never an issue because we *knew* what was in it: forty-eight feet of frozen food that was loaded a few hours before in front of witnesses. I argued that an inventory search was appropriate but Mackey said we should have gotten a warrant first. I even pointed to Pergram and said, 'Judge, there sits the Lizard King!' but the judge wouldn't go along. He was pissed that we'd held him without charging him, and he agreed with Mackey that the search was illegal and he suppressed all our evidence. Which means we've got nothing but the assault charge — Pergram going after you. Since Pergram or Spradley or whoever the hell he is doesn't have a rap sheet the judge will likely grant him bail for a first offense. We won't know for sure for a few days."

"I'm stunned," Cassie said. "The judge has to know what kind of monster you've got in your jail."

"He probably does," Behaunek said. "And it probably keeps him up at night. But he also knows that if he does the right thing he'll just get reversed on appeal. We didn't have a warrant, Cassie. We never should have even opened the back of that trailer."

Cassie gripped the phone tight and said, "You fucked up."

"We did."

"You know he'll just get back to what he does if he's on the highway again. More women will be tortured and killed."

"I know that. Believe me, I know that."

Cassie heard a hitch in her voice. Behaunek was fighting back tears.

Cassie heard a short beep on the SUV horn and turned around. Davis was waving at her frantically to come back.

"What are the odds that he'll be held until the assault trial?" Cassie asked.

"Maybe ten percent," Behaunek said. "No, less than that."

"I can't believe it."

"Welcome to my world," Behaunek said.

"I'll cling to that five percent," Cassie said.

"So will I."

"I wish I could say thank you for letting me know," Cassie said, approaching the SUV. Davis was talking excitedly into the mic of the radio.

"I understand," Behaunek said. "Believe me, I understand. It tears me up inside to think that the Lizard King will be back on the road and it's our fault."

She laughed a bitter laugh, then said, "The sheriff was right. We should have arranged some kind of accident while he was in jail. Now, though . . ."

Cassie was, in fact, numbed by the cold when she climbed back in the SUV. But her head was spinning. She barely comprehended the implications of what had happened in North Carolina when Davis said, "That boom we heard? It was from a train hitting a car on the tracks just outside of the rail hub. It's a Code Red."

Cassie shook her head, not understanding.

Davis said, "If that train catches on fire, it might blow up Grimstad and everybody in it."

Davis hit the lights and siren, executed a three-point turn, and sped back toward town.

Cassie sat fuming in silence.

"You all right?" Davis called out so he'd be heard over the siren.

"No, I'm not." Cassie said. She didn't want to explain. It was too painful to explain.

The radio was snapping with voices, dispatches, reports from the scene. She heard someone say, "It damn sure looks like a sheriff's department vehicle."

"Did you hear that?" Davis asked.

She nodded.

"It can't be," Davis said. "You can never trust the first reports of anything. That's something I learned on this job."

Empty fields flashed by their windows. Cassie looked out her passenger side and was briefly mesmerized by the rhythm of the corn rows that were zipping by.

"I don't see smoke," Davis said. "That's a good thing."

When she didn't respond, he said, "This is a big problem for us. Since nobody can build a pipeline anymore because of the environmentalists, oil goes out on trains. But trains can go off the tracks. Plus, they go right through the heart of population centers all over the damned country. You probably heard about that one up in Canada that blew up. Forty-seven dead. We had a big wreck here in North Dakota last year. They had to evacuate a little town of a thousand folks when the train exploded. We could see the smoke from here. Damn, let's hope this isn't as bad as that."

The dispatcher said, "All units, all units . . ."

"Here we come," Davis said.

Cars and trucks lined the shoulders of the roads in town to let the Yukon and other emergency vehicles through. Cassie caught glimpses of oil field workers on their cell phones in the cabs of their trucks as they shot by. A major explosion at the rail hub would impact *everyone*.

"How many cars are on each train?" Cassie asked.

"A hundred."

"How much oil is that?"

"Something like thirty thousand gallons," Davis said. "That's a big ole bomb."

They hit Main Street from the west and turned north. Vehicles were scattered on the shoulders and some were in the borrow ditches.

"Looks like the zombie apocalypse," Davis said.

"Look out!" Cassie screamed as a boy on a bike darted out onto the road from the side.

Davis jerked left on the wheel and managed to miss him.

"Jesus!" Davis said. "That was too close."

"It was," Cassie said. "And what's so weird is that I was in the sheriff's car the other night when we almost hit a kid who looked just like him."

Even down to the Grimstad *Tribune* canvas bags, she thought.

"In fact," Cassie said, "I'm pretty sure it was the same kid. Kyle Westinghouse or something like that. But more Norwegian."

She thought about the name for a moment and said, "Westergaard. Kyle Westergaard."

"Don't know him," Davis said. "But he better learn how to ride a bike in traffic or he'll be roadkill. Stupid kid."

Cassie looked over her shoulder and caught a final glimpse of Kyle. He was weaving in and out of the cars that had pulled over. He rode like his hair was on fire.

She said, "It's almost thirty below. What kind of kid rides his bike when it's thirty below?"

"Nobody," Davis said. "Maybe he's not all there."

"The sheriff says he's . . . challenged," Cassie responded. Then it hit her.

"Turn around," she said. "I need to talk to him."

Davis looked over, wide-eyed. "Are you out of your mind? We've got a train derailment inside the rail hub. *Inside city limits.* Kirkbride wants us all there now."

Cassie sat back and rubbed her eyes. "Of course," she said. "I don't know what I was thinking. But when we're clear we need to find that boy."

"Why?" Davis asked. "To chew him out about dangerous bike riding?"

"No. Because he might be the key to everything else that's happening around here."

Davis didn't respond, but gave her a skeptical sidelong glance.

"I'll explain later when we're clear," she said.

"I'm looking forward to it," Davis said with a bemused smile.

When they arrived at the rail hub it was a small sea of flashing lights of the entire Bakken County Sheriff's Department plus a half-dozen fire trucks, EMTs, and other emergency personnel. It was obvious what had happened: The engine of the train and the first fifty cars had derailed. To Cassie it looked almost surreal. The engine and the cars were huge but toylike.

"My son would love to see this," she said. "He loves trains."

"You have a son?" Davis asked.

"Yes."

"Does that mean there's a husband in the picture as well?"

"No." She didn't want to explain. But she found it intriguing he had asked.

Men in bulky fire suits climbed the sides of tanker cars and others swarmed the cab of the engine.

"No fire," Davis said with relief. "Yet."

Then he pointed and said, "Uh-oh."

Cassie followed his gesture. Wrapped around the front of the massive engine like a flattened aluminum beer can was what was left of a departmental Yukon. She could even see the logo on the side door.

"One of ours," Davis said.

There was a scrum of sheriff's department deputies huddled behind their units and Davis drove toward them. As he did, she saw Sheriff Kirkbride emerge from the gathering, shaking his head.

When Kirkbride saw them coming he signaled to Davis, who pulled alongside the sheriff and powered down his window. Kirkbride walked over and thrust his arms through the opening so he could rest his chin on them. He looked stricken.

Davis said, "We got here as soon as we could. Is it going to explode?"

Kirkbride shook his head. "The company troubleshooters say they don't think so. But for a few minutes there, we thought it would. And as long as there are no external sparks, we should be okay."

"Anybody hurt?" Davis asked.

"The train engineers got knocked around pretty good, but they looked okay. They're on the way to the hospital for evaluation."

"What about the driver?" Davis asked.

"It was Cam," Kirkbride said. "He's deader than dead. He got into the yard and drove head-on into that engine."

"Cam?" Davis asked. "Why would . . ."

Cassie didn't respond with the obvious answer and Kirkbride just glared at him.

"Oh," Davis said, going pale.

"I called him to come in and see me after our meeting," Kirkbride said. "He never picked up. But I'm thinking he knew what I wanted to talk to him about. Why the son of a bitch didn't eat his gun instead of going out in a blaze of glory shows you what kind of sick individual he was inside. If that train went up who knows how many people — our friends and neighbors — would have gone up with it?"

Davis threw his head back and moaned, "Oh, man."

As the three of them thought about what had happened in silence, another deputy rolled up.

Kirkbride noticed the late-arriving officer and his eyes narrowed in anger.

When Lance Foster climbed out of his Yukon, Kirkbride said, "Nice you could make it, Surfer Dude. Too bad the party's over."

Foster held up his hands, palms up, and shrugged before joining the rest of the deputies.

■ ■ ■ ■

Several hours later, the all-clear was given by the railroad emergency team. The engine had been decoupled and the full tanker cars were being towed back to the distant yard. Firemen and emergency personnel were monitoring the long process and company track engineers were assembling temporary rails at the front to remove the damaged engine.

Cassie watched as Sheriff Kirkbride was inundated with calls from county, state, and federal officials as well as the press. She felt sorry for him. Oil train derailments were obviously a hot-button issue, and the fact that it had apparently been caused by one of his employees made the explanation even more difficult. When asked what had motivated Cam Tollefsen to do what he did, Kirkbride said it was under investigation.

She said to Davis, "There's nothing we can do here. Let's go find that boy on the bike."

"I think we should go back to Willie's place first," Davis said, putting the SUV in gear.

Cassie said, "You've forgotten I'm the chief investigator here."

Davis blanched. He said, "You know what, I did. I'm sorry. I wasn't thinking."

"Happens a lot around here," Cassie snapped. Then said, "Okay, let's drive out and roust Willie first. We're pretty sure he's in the middle of this and if he isn't he might know who is. But on the way out there I want to run my theory by you and I want your honest take on it. Deal?"

Davis nodded. He said, "Really, I'm sorry. I was out of line."

"You were."

"I guess with all the shit that's been going on around here I —"

"Quit digging and drive," Cassie said, fighting back a smile. "And quit saying you're sorry."

CHAPTER TWENTY-THREE

Although he'd nearly been hit on Main Street by the sheriff's department SUV with its lights and sirens going as well as a company pickup truck that pulled off the road to let the emergency vehicles by, Kyle didn't slow down or look side to side as he weaved his bike in and out of traffic. The sirens and the scream of tires and air brakes couldn't penetrate his mission to catch up with the pickup truck with his mom inside.

He got glimpses of it in traffic ahead of him as he rode but it was still about a mile ahead. The pickup was hard to keep track of because of all the cop cars racing north on the road and all the trucks and other vehicles pulling to the side to let them pass.

The nightmare vision that hung out there ahead of him was of his mom's face appearing suddenly in the back window of a pickup and the splash of blood across the glass before her head was shoved back down out of view. It was like she spit the blood out on the glass. There was a look of pure terror in her eyes but also recognition: she'd seen him and he'd seen her and it was almost as if she'd cried out, *Kyle.*

His tears froze into rivulets on his face as he rode. Every time he saw that the pickup with his mom in it had pulled over again and he thought he could catch it, it moved again and rejoined the flow of traffic. The men inside didn't seem to realize he was trying to follow them. But despite the number of stops and starts, the pickup pulled too far ahead. The snow and ice on the shoulder of the road slowed him down, and twice he had to brake to a complete stop to let another car pull off the road as cars and trucks with flashers went by. He couldn't keep up with the pickup with his mom in it. Eventually, he saw it more than a mile ahead, topping the rise before vanishing down the other side.

He'd never seen her so scared before, and it was almost too much for him to even understand. She'd looked like a little girl, as young as him, a horrified little girl who happened to be his mom. He couldn't sort it out and he didn't know if he ever would or if that vision of her would stay in front of his face for the rest of his life.

When he thought that maybe that would be it, that he would never even see her again, ever, and that his last glimpse of her was of a scared little girl spitting blood on the glass . . .

Kyle opened his mouth and roared. His cry came out high-pitched and it cracked in the middle, but it sounded to him like he was a wounded animal.

Because he was.

Drenched in sweat, Kyle pulled out of the traffic on Main Street into the ditch and rode back toward town. He'd never catch the silver pickup and he didn't know where it had gone.

The thoughts racing through his head made him reckless and manic and he rode down the middle of the snow-packed streets and let cars and truck get out of *his* way. Someone yelled at him, called him a "peckerhead."

He rode through a gap in a chain-link fence that ran along the length of the service road, across the parking lot of the Work Wearhouse, down a snow-clogged alley made nearly impassable due to frozen ruts.

He decided to tell Grandma Lottie because he didn't know who else to tell. Maybe Raheem, he thought. Maybe Raheem's dad would know what to do.

When he roared a second time it sounded weaker. He couldn't feel his limbs, even though he could still move them. Kyle realized he'd worked up such a sweat and it was so cold that he was in the process of freezing to death. The only way to stay alive was to keep riding, keep his blood pumping, keep sweating.

And within a few minutes, he found himself back on his block.

The van he'd seen T-Lock driving was backing out of the driveway.

"Hey!" Kyle yelled.

Kyle saw a flash of brake lights in the street, and T-Lock drove away.

Kyle wondered what he'd been doing there, and if he had any idea what had happened to his mom.

He was so cold when he coasted to a stop on the side of the house that he couldn't work the hand brake and the front tire of his bike thumped into the washing machine. Kyle stiffly dismounted and trudged up the steps to the back door, praying it had been left unlocked because he didn't want to take the time to dig through his pockets beneath his coat for the key his mom had given him. It was locked.

Kyle moaned against the cold and fumbled with the key as it stuck to his frozen fingers, but he finally managed to slip it into the knob and turn it and he was inside.

Once inside he paced, flexing his fingers to get the blood flowing again. He tried to figure out what to do to save his mom. He wished T-Lock would come back but at the same time he didn't.

So Kyle plucked the telephone off the stand and dialed 911.

"Emergency operator," a woman's voice said. "If you're calling about the train accident we're well aware of it and we're in the process of sending emergency teams —"

Kyle said, "There's a lady — okay, she's my mom — well, she's being held prisoner in a pickup truck."

"Can you please slow down and *enunciate*?" the dispatcher said, drawing the last word out. She sounded annoyed.

"My mom," he croaked.

"Please identify yourself, sir."

"This is Kyle. Some guys — three guys — grabbed my mom and put her in a truck outside McDonald's and drove her away. Her face was bloody —"

"*Sir,*" she interrupted, "I'm sorry but I can't understand a word you're saying. Now maybe if you slowed down."

"My *mom*. Three men grabbed my *mom*." He hated that his voice cracked with emotion as he spoke.

"Sir, have you been drinking?"

"No!"

She must have understood, because she said, "Look, sir, I need you to do something for me right now. I need you to hang up and call back later when you sober up and can make some sense. The whole town is in an emergency right now, and we need to clear the lines."

"You aren't going to help me?" he asked.

Kyle stood there for a moment, gasping. Then he slammed the phone down on the counter so hard the 1 and the 7 keys popped off the receiver.

Kyle cried out loud in the hot shower. As his limbs and trunk warmed under the harsh stream of water, he ached all over as he thawed out. He sobbed and was grateful the hiss of the water drowned out the horrible sounds.

Why couldn't the 911 lady understand him? How could he save his mom?

He dressed in dry clothes — jeans, thick socks, T-shirt, hoodie — and walked through the house. He wondered what T-Lock had done and why he'd been there. He hoped T-Lock had left for good but the man's clothes were still in the closet in his mom's room, and there was a huge pile of them on the closet floor, along with his work boots and cowboy boots. T-Lock's razor and his hair products were still in the bathroom. So he was likely coming back, Kyle decided.

As he went through the kitchen back to his bedroom for his coat and boots, he saw a cop car cruise slowly down the alley and stop in back of his house. It was one of the SUVs like the one that had nearly hit him on the road a half hour before. The driver's door opened. Kyle stepped back from the window so he couldn't be seen by the cop who climbed out. The cop pulled on a pair of thick gloves and tugged on the bill of a green woolen hat with the sheriff's department logo on the front.

At first, Kyle thought the cop had arrived because of his 911 call. Then he recognized the cop as the one who had arrived second at the scene of the rollover car wreck — the younger one. He was by himself and he didn't march up to the back door like Kyle suspected he would. Instead, the cop was peering around, as if checking to see if anyone was looking out their window at him.

The cop approached the house cautiously with his right hand on the grip of his holstered pistol. Kyle thought maybe he was looking for T-Lock.

But instead of walking straight toward the back door, the cop hesitated when he saw something that interested him on the side of the house. Again, he paused and looked all around before changing his route. Then he walked out of Kyle's view.

Kyle padded into his mom's bedroom. The window that overlooked the side of the house was frosted with ice, but Kyle could make out the dark form of the cop as he passed by it and then came back. He was interested in something just below Kyle's view.

When the cop bent over, Kyle approached the window, ready to duck and run if the man looked up.

The cop was hunched over in front of Kyle's bike. Through a three-inch oval in the center of the window that was not obscured by frost, Kyle could see the man remove something blocky and white from his parka pocket and place it on the front tire of the bike. Whatever it was seemed to fit perfectly, and the cop nodded with some kind of inner knowledge and stood up and pocketed the white block. Kyle quickly stepped aside from the window as the cop turned toward it and leaned to the glass. Kyle flattened himself against the wall as the cop cupped his eyes with his hands and peered inside. His breath steamed the window.

And then he was gone.

Kyle went over to his mom's chest of drawers and pulled out the bottom-left drawer. Her small semiautomatic .25 Taurus was there beneath a heap of old sweaters. There was a box of .25 ammunition in there, too. He left the drawer open but didn't take the gun. If a cop saw him with a gun . . .

Kyle thought about the back door and was sure he hadn't locked it. He started to move that way when he heard the thump of boots on the back stairs.

Kyle doubled back and ran to his bedroom and rolled under his bed.

"Anybody home?" the cop called out from the kitchen.

It was dirty and cold under the bed. Kyle lay still on his belly in the dust motes, the shaft of the arrow in his right hand. There was an old balled-up sock under there and a pair of white briefs he hadn't seen for months. He clamped his jaws tight to try and prevent his teeth from chattering.

"Hey, is anyone home? T-Lock, are you here? Gig's up, man."

Kyle heard the cop clomp around. Into his mom's bedroom, into the bathroom, through the living room. The accordion doors of the laundry closet squeaked open and then shut.

In a moment he saw the bottom of his own door swing open. Kyle could see the lower half of a big pair of snow-covered boots.

"Anyone here?"

Kyle tried not to breathe in. The dust on the floor was thick and he didn't want to choke or sneeze.

The cop moved from the door to his closet. Kyle could hear the rustle of clothing as the man shoved his clothes aside. Then he waited for the cop to drop to his hands and knees and find him.

Kyle gripped so hard on the shaft of the arrow he could barely feel his fingers. He'd aim for an eye.

"Crap," the cop said, and turned on his heel and left the bedroom.

Kyle closed his eyes and breathed in slowly. He could feel his heart beat in his chest.

The cop strode through his house toward

the back door. Kyle heard the chirp of a cell phone and heard the cop say, "Nobody home," and continue on as he went out the back door.

He waited for he didn't know how long. It felt like an hour. Then Kyle slithered out from beneath his bed. He was covered in dust, the front of his clothing white from it. He wiped it off his face.

When he went into the kitchen he saw that the cop car was gone. But Kyle wondered about the white block the cop had pressed against his bike tire.

He pulled on his coat and went outside. The cold stung him immediately on his face and hands, but he retraced the steps of the cop to the side of his house.

His bike was fine, but there was a fine white powder on the black rubber of his tires and within the tread. It made no sense to Kyle and he shook his head.

Then he noticed something he hadn't noticed before. Apparently, the cop had missed it, too, or had not realized what it meant.

The snow was trampled down all around the washing machine, and the layer of snow on top had been disturbed. Someone had been there and had relocated the chain, although it was still locked tight with a heavy padlock.

T-Lock had told his mom a couple of days before that he'd moved the duffel bag out of the house so it couldn't be found there. But Kyle knew T-Lock. The man never did anything beyond the bare minimum.

"Out of the house" could mean "to the side of the house."

And T-Lock had been there when Kyle arrived, maybe checking on his stash. Maybe retrieving a little of it for personal use.

Kyle didn't have any idea where T-Lock kept his keys or if there was a spare key to the padlock somewhere inside the house. His mom might know, but . . .

Tears filled Kyle's eyes again when he thought of her face through the bloody window, and he stamped his foot out of frustration.

There were ways to cut through a chain, he knew. Raheem's dad had a bunch of tools in his garage. Maybe he could borrow some kind of cutter.

And with the duffel bag back, Kyle could save his mom. After all, he'd found it in the first place.

Kyle ran up the steps and was halfway through the kitchen when T-Lock reached out and grabbed his arm and said, "What in the *fuck* were you doing out there, you little shit?"

CHAPTER TWENTY-FOUR

T-lock looked bad, Kyle thought. His eyes were sunken and hollow, and his hair was matted on the side of his head. He sat on a chair near the table but maintained his firm grip on Kyle's arm. When he leaned in, Kyle could smell cigarette smoke and alcohol. His glassy eyes said something else was working in there, too.

T-Lock said, "Everything's gone to shit because I'm surrounded by fuckin' morons. Why is it everybody I know is a fuckin' moron? Why is it, Kyle?"

Kyle shook his head. T-Lock seemed dangerous.

"All I ask Winkie to do is set up a meeting. I tell him what to say and what to do. I make him repeat it back to me three times. Then he goes off and just fucking disappears."

T-Lock shook his head. "And your mom, man, I know she's your mom and all, but

all she had to do is make change at Mc-
Donald's. I wasn't asking her to do fucking
brain surgery. Just make change. So I go in
there a few minutes ago to see her and they
tell me she walked off the job. Just walked
away! And now *she's* gone. Fuck me."

T-Lock looked up and his eyes bored into
Kyle. He grasped Kyle's other arm and
pulled him closer. "Tell me where she is.
She's got my money, Kyle. I know you
know. I can see it in your damned face."

Kyle said, "Some men took her outside of
McDonald's. I saw them drive away with
her in a truck. Her face was bloody. I chased
it but I couldn't catch it."

"Jesus Christ," T-Lock said, grimacing.
"How many men?"

"I saw three."

"Three? Three? Who were they? Were they
cops?"

"No. It was that same truck that was
outside of the house this morning."

That struck a nerve in T-Lock and he
looked away and cursed.

Kyle tried to wriggle free of T-Lock's
hands but his grip was too tight.

"I saw those three guys," T-Lock said.
"Two greasers and someone in the back.
California plates. I kept going when I saw
them. Oh man, oh *shit*."

Kyle heard T-Lock's cell phone burr from his front jeans pocket.

"You just stay right here, Kyle. Don't you fucking move," T-Lock said as he released Kyle, leaned back, and fished in his pants for his phone. First he removed a ring of keys and tossed them on the top of the table, then came the phone.

T-Lock stared at the screen but didn't answer it.

"It's her phone," he said.

"Aren't you going to talk to her?" Kyle asked, upset. He thought of his mom holding her phone up to her bloody face. Was she somewhere warm?

"I gotta think," T-Lock said, running his free hand through his hair. "If they still have her they'll want to trade her for my stash. Then I'll end up with nothing."

Kyle felt his face and neck get hot. "What about my *mom*?" he screamed.

T-Lock stood and looked down at him with contempt. The phone in his hand burred two more times and stopped. He said, "Kyle, you're a fuckin' retard. You think they'll let her go after she's seen their faces? Get a clue, man. If I do what they want they'll get that product back and they'll kill her, and then they'll kill *me*."

Kyle stepped back.

The phone rang again. T-Lock glanced at the screen and said to it, "Leave me the fuck alone, greasers. Go back to California or Mexico or wherever the hell you're from."

Kyle said, "Let me talk to her."

T-Lock rolled his eyes and said, "Not a chance. We don't need any drama."

"But what if it's really her?" Kyle pleaded. "What if she got away or something? She needs our help."

"She didn't get away from three guys. I doubt that she's even breathing. They took her phone away from her and they want me to show up with the duffel bag so they can take it and cut my head off like they did to Rufus."

"You've got to do something," Kyle said, tears stinging his eyes again. "It's my *mom.*"

T-Lock took a deep breath. He said, "The best thing we can do for her right now is not answer this phone. If she's even alive, and I doubt that, they will have lost the only thing they have to bargain with. They'll keep trying to talk to me in the meantime. So get out of my face so I can *think.*"

"You're a liar," Kyle said. "You're gonna make it so they hurt her."

"Don't call me that, you little shit."

"Liar. You're a liar. You're going to get my mom killed because you're scared of them."

"I ain't scared of nobody," T-Lock said, and swung his right fist. Kyle tried to duck out of the way but the blow glanced off the side of his head and he dropped and saw stars. T-Lock kept coming.

Kyle dived under the table where he doubted T-Lock would follow. But T-Lock was really angry this time, and he'd dropped to his hands and knees while Kyle scrambled away. T-Lock reached for his foot between the chairs but Kyle was able to wrench it free.

He emerged on the other side of the table before T-Lock was back on his feet. Kyle plucked the set of keys from the top and ran, stepping over T-Lock's outstretched hand.

"Come back here with my keys, you little shit!"

Kyle ran into his room and slammed the door shut. He had no way to lock it. Instead, he got behind his bed and started pushing it with his full weight toward the door. The legs made a moaning sound as they scraped across the floor and the foot of the bed was nearly to the door when T-Lock threw it open.

The door slammed into the bed but wasn't fully open. There was about six inches of space and T-Lock shoved one of his arms through it. T-Lock's hand was balled into a fist. Kyle leaned into the bed and tried to shove it further. T-Lock cursed and pushed against the door. There wasn't enough of an opening for T-Lock to squeeze inside. Kyle could see T-Lock's red face.

"Kyle, I'm not kidding. I need those keys back and then I'm gonna whip your ass."

Kyle grunted and tried to set his feet so the door couldn't open any more.

"Goddamn it!" T-Lock shouted, then threw himself against the door and Kyle was knocked back. Before he could regain his balance and start shoving again, T-Lock slithered through the opening and stepped on top of the bed.

Kyle could hear the phone burring again in T-Lock's pocket. His mom. Then it stopped.

The look on T-Lock's face was murderous. Kyle had seen him mad before — many times — but never this mad.

"Where are my fucking *keys*?"

Kyle didn't see the boot coming, but it caught him hard under his arm and sent him sprawling. He slid across the dirty floor. He saw stars again and couldn't get his breath.

T-Lock stepped down from the bed and put his hands on his hips.

"I thought your mother was dumb but you're even dumber, if that's possible."

The phone chimed, which meant a text message.

Kyle rolled away moaning, trying to get air. He found his progress stopped by his River Box. It had remained in place while Kyle pushed the bed away. He turned to reach inside the box.

The next kick hit him hard in his butt, right on his tailbone. Kyle writhed and gasped, but reached inside the River Box and closed his hand around the shaft of the arrow.

When T-Lock bent over and reached down to pull him to his feet by his coat collar, Kyle drove the arrow deep into T-Lock's neck.

T-Lock was surprised. He let go of Kyle and stepped back and sat down on the bed. His eyes were wide with wonder, and he turned toward Kyle's bedroom mirror to look at himself and the arrow shaft sticking out of his neck. He reached up and gently touched the fletching as if to confirm to himself it was actually there.

He tried to speak but the only sounds to come out were guttural.

Kyle gathered himself up, panting for breath. His head throbbed and his right arm didn't want to respond. His backside was numb and cold.

He shoved T-Lock over on the bed so he was out of the way. T-Lock didn't fight back. He just flopped over to the side and lay there. Kyle reached into T-Lock's pants pocket and got the phone. Before he did, he put his fingers near T-Lock's nostrils. He was still breathing. Then he started to moan. It was a horrible, deep-inside-the-chest moan. Kyle felt bad for him but he knew if he had to do it all over again he would have done the same thing.

With the keys in one hand and the phone in the other, Kyle leapt onto the bed and jumped out the door.

He put the keys in his coat pocket and then looked at the message on T-Lock's phone screen.

It said it was from his mom. *PICK UP, YOU ASSHOLE.*

Kyle texted back. *MOM? THIS IS KYLE. U OK?*

Then Kyle punched 911 on the house phone again and set the receiver aside. That 911 lady would be able to hear the moans coming from the back bedroom. He sure didn't want to talk to her again.

As he trudged around to the side of the house toward his bike the phone chimed again. Another text.

It read: *WHERE R U, KYLE?*

CHAPTER TWENTY-FIVE

Cassie knocked on Willie Dietrich's farmhouse door while Ian Davis stood behind her. His hand was on the grip of his service weapon. It was still. The towering skeletal trees in the yard were dotted with starlings that looked double their actual size because they were so puffed up against the cold.

"That's his Range Rover in the garage," Davis said through chattering teeth. "So I'm guessing he's here."

Cassie knocked again, harder. It hurt her knuckles through her thin gloves.

Finally, she heard footfalls inside.

"Someone's coming," she said, and stepped slightly to the side to widen Davis's field of fire.

The front door cracked open an inch.

"Willie Dietrich?" Cassie asked.

"Not hardly." It was a woman's voice,

deep and slightly Southern. "Willie ain't here."

From somewhere inside, another female asked, "Who is it, LaDonna?"

"Couple of damn cops," LaDonna said over her shoulder.

"A couple of damn cops who are freezing to death on this porch," Cassie said with sarcasm. "Will you please let us in?"

"What do you want?"

"We need to talk to Willie."

"I told you — he's not here."

Cassie paused, trying not to get angry. She said, "I smell weed coming from in there. That's probable cause for my partner and me to enter. Now we can force our way in and start tossing the place and make some arrests, or you can invite us in and I'll pretend I don't smell what I smell. Your choice."

"That's bullshit," LaDonna said.

She was right, Cassie knew. Simply smelling marijuana wasn't just cause to enter a residence. But Cassie had no intention of arresting anyone for possession. She wanted answers.

Cassie turned to Davis. "Ian, go get that battering ram from the Yukon."

Davis tried not to grin. He said, "Tear gas, too?"

"Sure."

The door opened and LaDonna, a tall black woman wearing a tight fleece bodysuit and oversized pink slippers, stepped aside. "You don't have to be so damned harsh," she said to Cassie.

LaDonna Martin and Annie Bjorn, a pale blond woman with lank mousy hair, sat side by side on a couch in the dark front room. Cassie leaned back against a huge cable wooden spool that served as a kind of table, and Davis stood next to the roaring woodstove. The house did reek of stale marijuana smoke. Cassie had to push aside a baking dish of hash brownies on the spool top so she didn't sit on it.

After introducing herself and Davis and showing the two women her badge, Cassie said, "How long has Willie been gone?"

"Don't know," LaDonna said. "When I got up an hour ago he wasn't here. That's all I know." She looked to Annie Bjorn.

"I just got up," Bjorn said, yawning.

"You missed all the fun while you were sleeping," Davis said. "A train derailed at the hub and could have blown up the whole town."

"That'd be a damn blessing in disguise,"

LaDonna said with a deep laugh. Cassie smiled.

Cassie noticed that Bjorn was staring at Davis. She said, "Hey — I know you. You're a *cop*?"

"Afraid so," Davis said.

"Well, that kind of sucks," Bjorn said.

Davis said, "Sorry."

Bjorn turned to LaDonna. "I've seen him hang out at the clubs. He didn't seem like no cop."

LaDonna took a long look at Davis, and said, "Yes, he does. He's got that cop look of trying just a little too hard to be one of the people, you know? Like he's wearing a Halloween costume. I can tell."

Davis flushed.

"Anyway," Cassie said, "when was the last time you saw Willie?"

"Last night," LaDonna said.

"Was he alone?"

LaDonna and Bjorn exchanged looks. Then LaDonna said, "There were a couple of other guys here. There's always people around here coming and going. I don't pay that much attention to them."

"When you say a couple, do you mean two?"

"Uh, three."

"Did you know them?"

366

"I don't know anybody around here. I'm a working girl from Atlanta. I come here, do my work, and get out. I maintain my distance from these locals, you know?"

"What about you?" Cassie asked Bjorn.

"I didn't know them," Bjorn said quickly. "Well, one guy, but I don't even know his real name. I've heard him called Winkie on account of the really thick glasses he wears."

Cassie looked over to Davis. Davis nodded. He knew him.

"So Winkie was here," Cassie said. "Who else?"

"A couple of, you know, Hispanics," Bjorn said. "Real scary-looking dudes."

"I don't know," Cassie said. "What were the names of the Hispanics?"

Neither woman had heard their names, they said.

"What did they look like?"

"Mean," LaDonna said. "They looked small and mean. They were the types you just avoid if you see them across the bar. You know, shaved heads, big ears, dead eyes."

Cassie and Davis exchanged looks again.

"Did they have tattoos?" Davis asked.

"Not that I saw," LaDonna said. "But I didn't look that close and I sure as hell didn't see either one with his shirt off."

"Could they be Salvadoran?" Davis asked.

Bjorn shrugged and LaDonna said, "Mexican, Salvadoran, whatever. They just had a bad vibe."

"And Willie left with this Winkie and them?" Cassie asked.

Both women shrugged.

Davis said, "So the four of them left in another car. That's why Willie's Range Rover is still here." He asked the women, "What were they driving?"

"Don't know," LaDonna said. Annie shook her head as well.

"Do you know when Willie will be back?" Cassie asked.

"No," LaDonna said, "and I really don't care. I've got a shift tonight and I don't plan on coming back for the rest of my life. It's too damned cold here for me. I'm getting on that train tomorrow morning, for damn sure. I don't care if these johns up here have money. I'm freezing my ass off."

Bjorn didn't say anything. Obviously, she was staying around, Cassie thought.

LaDonna said to Cassie, "Seriously, lady, how can you stand it? You look like a nice woman. How can you stand this place?"

"I haven't figured out how to answer that yet," Cassie said.

"It's like thirty below zero out there. I

didn't even know that it was possible. Your spit freezes in your mouth if you go outside. That's just crazy."

Cassie said to Davis, "Please give these two ladies your card. I don't have mine yet. And, ladies, please give us a call when Willie Dietrich comes back. We just want to talk with him."

"They're never going to call," Davis said to Cassie once they were back in the SUV headed toward Grimstad.

"Of course not," Cassie agreed.

"But at least he'll know we're looking for him. That may force a move on his part, who knows?"

"So who is this Winkie guy?"

Davis shook his head. "He's a small-time user. Meth for sure, maybe heroin, too. I've run into him a couple of times. It's very distracting to talk to him because his eyes are all magnified by his glasses — he looks like some kind of bug. Maybe he does some sales for Willie, but I can't see him as a player any higher up than street level. Who knows why he was there last night?

"What I'm wondering is where the four of them went," Davis said. "Willie isn't a day person. I'm wondering if the two Salvadorans took him away, or what. Maybe we'll start finding pieces of Willie Dietrich all over Grimstad tomorrow. What do you think?"

Cassie was distracted and didn't respond. After a few miles, she said, "Think about it. Who would be outside in this weather at six in the morning? I mean, I know there are guys doing shift work out in the country any time of day, but who would be out and about at six?"

"I'm lost," Davis said. "I thought we were talking about Willie."

"A paperboy, that's who," Cassie said. "Maybe he saw the rollover. Maybe he rode down there where the crash took place. Maybe," she said, looking over at Davis, "he found the drugs."

"That's a leap," Davis said.

"It is. But whoever got it found it *before* the wrecker and all the emergency people got there. There were two officers on the scene the whole time between the crash and when the wrecker arrived. I think if anybody found the drugs they would have seen it — even if Tollefsen was dirty. He wouldn't dare tip his hand at that point. And I keep thinking about that single tire track I found. It was from a bike. It wasn't wide enough to be from a motorcycle."

Davis shook his head. "I'm not connecting the dots."

"Let's say the boy found the drugs and took them," she said. "Who knows what he did with them or who he might have told about it. The bad guys know the drugs are missing — obviously — but not where they went. They assume the bikers took them because the bikers are their only organized competition. So they send up a couple of thugs to take the bikers out of the picture and locate the drugs. Even though this place is booming, it's still a small town underneath and it doesn't take the MS-13 guys long to narrow down who might have their drugs."

"I think they all thought they'd have the drugs back by now. But for whatever reason, they don't."

"So if we find Willie," Davis said, "we might find the Salvadorans if that's what they are. And maybe we even find the stash."

"Maybe," Cassie said.

"Why maybe?"

"Because if they had the stash I think we'd know it. *You'd* know it. No, I think they're still looking for it but they're closing in. They think they're close enough to getting it back that Willie told his distribution chain to get ready by tomorrow."

She said, "Maybe if we find the paperboy

he'll lead us to the drugs."

"I still don't get it," Davis said. "I know you've seen this kid a couple of times, which is weird, and you had that tire track cast made. But don't you think maybe you're going at this with blinders on? If a paperboy took their drugs, why aren't they after him? You'd think he'd be easy to find. And if Cam Tollefsen was dirty like we think he was, why didn't he go after the kid? He must have seen him at the site of the rollover, right?"

Cassie said, "I think a kid like him is invisible."

They talked about Cassie's theory as they got closer to town. Cassie liked Davis, and he reminded her a little of her old mentor Cody when it came to discussing a case. He, like Cody, enjoyed building scenarios, making suppositions, and knocking down threads. He was good, too. He punched enough holes in her theories that she was starting to doubt them herself.

The big hole he punched was: If MS-13 thought they were close to getting their drugs on the street, why did they wait two days to go after a mentally challenged paperboy?

Cassie had no answer.

"I hate to even suggest this," Davis said to her, "but maybe the mom in you sees a twelve-year-old kid out riding his bike in thirty below weather and you want to, you know, *save* him. You can't get him out of your mind. So as we move forward on this case, you keep building it around that kid. Is that possible?"

Cassie said, "What a patronizing thing to say to me."

Davis clammed up.

"What I hate the most about it is you might have a point," she said.

Davis sighed in relief.

Cassie said, "I don't know what to think anymore about this. All we can do is good police work and hope things start to fall into place. Let's start with the newspaper office and Kyle. Someone there should know about Kyle's route and if he might have been around the rollover site that day. If we find him and he wasn't, well, then we can eliminate that possibility and we can proceed from there."

Davis agreed. He said, "With Tollefsen out of the picture, should we expand the inquiry now? Get more guys involved with looking for Kyle and Willie Dietrich and those Salvadorans?"

Cassie said, "Not quite yet. I'm not sure

why I say that, but it doesn't feel right to me to do that yet."

"You're the boss," Davis said. But it was clear he disagreed.

Cassie heard a dispatch on the radio as they entered Grimstad that caught her attention. She leaned forward and turned the radio up.

The dispatcher was requesting an officer drive-by at a house on Third Street. Someone had called 911 from the home but didn't make a report. The 911 operator said she thought she had heard sounds of distress inside.

There was no response. Cassie thought it strange until she realized all the other department personnel were still at the rail hub.

The operator read out the exact address as well as the name of the renter.

Cassie snatched the mic from the dashboard and said, "We're close and we'll respond."

"What unit is this?" the dispatcher asked.

"What unit are we?" Cassie asked Davis.

"BCS, zero-zero-four." Davis grinned.

Cassie repeated it.

"What are we doing?" Davis asked her.

"Didn't you hear the name? The house is

rented by someone named Rachel Wester-gaard. *Westergaard.*"

"Like Kyle Westergaard."

"Damn right — my paperboy again."

Chapter Twenty-Six

Davis drove up into the driveway of the Westergaard home on Third Street behind a minivan with dealer plates. Cassie recognized the small house in a block of small houses from her tour with Sheriff Kirkbride. The outside of the 1960s-style single family home needed a coat of white paint and there were broken shingles on the roof. It was a tired-looking house, she thought.

"Front or back?" Davis asked.

"I'll take the back. If no one answers in front, give me a count of ten after you knock before you go in."

"We're going in?" Davis asked, raising his eyebrows.

"The dispatcher said someone was injured. I'm *sure* we'll hear something or see a good reason," she said, opening her door. Then she added, "Even if we don't."

He smiled. "Is this the way they do it in

Montana?"

"It's the way I do it," she said.

The cold was stunning. It felt like a cup of acid had been thrown on her exposed skin. As she skirted around the side of the house toward the back she wondered if she'd ever get used to it. She could feel icy tendrils crawling down her collar and up her pant legs.

There was an old washing machine on the side of the house with a heavy chain and lock around it. The snow around the appliance was packed down by footprints. She paused for a moment when she recognized a distinctive bicycle tire track, but there was no bike.

Kyle, she thought, had been there recently. Where was he now?

Cassie hiked up the bottom of her parka to pull her weapon. It was a small-grip .40 Glock 27 with nine rounds in the magazine and one in the chamber. It fit well even in her gloved hand. She'd used it once to kill that trooper in Montana and had fired it only at the range since.

When she cleared the back corner of the house she was surprised to see they weren't the first police officers to respond. A sheriff's department SUV was idling in the alley, the front door still open as if the occupant had flown out without bothering to close it after him. There were tracks in the snow toward the porch — in fact, several sets of tracks both coming and going — but she had no idea who had made them or how long they'd been there.

She turned and rushed back around the house to the front to warn off Davis, but she heard him pound on the front door and identify himself.

When she appeared around the corner Davis spun toward her, his weapon out.

"Sorry," he said.

She said, "I think there's already a cop inside. There's a sheriff's unit in the back."

"What the hell?" Davis asked aloud. "I didn't hear anything over the radio about someone getting here first."

"Neither did I."

Davis furrowed his brow and poised to knock again. Cassie scrambled again to the back in time to see Deputy Lance Foster — the Surfer Dude — cock open the back storm door from inside. His head was turned in the direction of the pounding.

"Hello," she said.

Foster wheeled toward her, his hand on his weapon. When he recognized her he stepped out on the porch. He seemed flushed, Cassie thought.

"I found blood inside," Foster said quickly. "But no body."

She tried to read his face. She knew she surprised him by being there, but she couldn't tell if that was all it was.

"Where were you going?" she asked.

"To my unit," he said, pointing toward the idling Tahoe. "I was going to call it in."

"Why didn't you just open the front door? You must have heard Deputy Davis pounding on it."

Foster was at a loss for words for a moment. Then he said, "I didn't want to contaminate the scene any more by walking through the house. We always get yelled at by the evidence techs when we do that."

"So it's a crime scene?"

"I told you," Foster said with some heat, "I found what looks like blood inside."

At that moment, Davis came around the other corner of the house with his weapon up. He said to Foster, "Dude, what are you doing here?"

"Responding to the damned call," Foster said. "Isn't that what I'm supposed to do? What's with you two?"

Cassie nodded to Davis. "Let's search the house."

"It's in the back bedroom," Foster said,

leading Cassie and Davis through a small kitchen. He seemed to have calmed down, she thought. But still . . .

It was warm inside but the house had a lingering sour smell, she noticed. The linoleum floor in the kitchen was covered with muddy boot prints. Dirty dishes were stacked in the sink and on the counter. Someone had left the coffeemaker on until a ring of thick black tar was baked on the bottom of the pot.

Poor Kyle, she thought.

She glanced into a bedroom to her right as they entered a narrow hallway that led to the front room. There was an unmade queen-sized bed, clothes on the floor, and the smell of stale tobacco and something else. Weed, maybe. The bedroom was dark because the only window was covered in thick frost.

"This one," Foster said, stopping at the second doorway off the hall. He didn't enter the bedroom but stood in the opening, pointing inside. When Cassie approached Foster stepped aside so she could see.

It was a boy's room, no doubt. There were pictures of Plains Indians on the walls that looked torn out of magazines. A crooked shelf was crammed with boy's things: bones, toy cars, a baseball. The single bed was pushed haphazardly against the door so it would open only halfway. That bed was unmade also but there were several dark red blotches on the top of the worn coverlet.

"Have you been inside?" she asked.

"Not yet," Foster said. "I saw the blood and I was on my way to call it in when you two showed up."

Cassie nodded. "But you saw no reason to let Davis in the front door?"

"Look," he said, "I told you already."

"That you didn't want to disturb the crime scene. Right. Got it," Cassie said crisply. "So why didn't you respond on the radio that you were answering the call?"

"That's right," Davis said. "Why aren't you at the rail hub with everybody else?"

Foster's face went blank but the side of his mouth hitched up in an involuntary tic. He wouldn't meet her eye. Cassie thought he looked guilty of something. He said to Davis, "There was really nothing to do out there, Ian. I kind of sneaked away for lunch. I was a minute away from here on Second when the call came, so I just popped on in."

"On your own," Cassie said. "Without telling the dispatcher."

"Okay," Foster said, looking away from her. "Okay, okay. I screwed up the procedure. I mean, the dispatcher said she heard somebody moaning. It might have been a matter of life and death. You can write me up if you want to. If that's what floats your boat."

Cassie gestured toward the boy's room. She mouthed, "He's still in there."

Both Foster and Davis were obviously puzzled. Foster started to speak but she put a finger to her lips and glared at him.

"There's a car outside," she mouthed.

Then she pointed to the dirty carpet they were standing on and moved her open hand across the floor as if presenting it to them. There was no blood. Anyone bleeding as profusely as the splotches on the bedcover indicated would bleed on his way out as well.

She said out loud, "Well, I guess there's nobody here. I'll go out and call it in. Foster, we'll see you back at the department. I'll call the evidence techs to do an analysis of the blood."

They got it.

She gestured to Davis, you first.

Then to Foster, back him up.

And she moved aside.

Davis stepped up on the top of the bed and vaulted to the floor, with Foster right behind him. Davis spun and dropped to his haunches to check under the bed, his gun out in front of him. He shook his head.

"There he is," Foster said, aiming his weapon at the open closet. "Come out of there with your hands on your head."

There was a moan from the closet.

Cassie prayed it wasn't the boy, and it wasn't. Instead, a tall and gaunt man stepped out, knocking boy's clothes off hangers as he did. The man's face was paper white, and his eyes peered out from hollows. The shaft of an arrow stuck out of his neck.

"I'll call for an ambulance," she said, as Foster and Davis forced the man to his knees. He didn't fight back.

"He's known as T-Lock," Davis said to Cassie. "On a scale of one to ten for dirtbags, he's about a one point five."

T-Lock moaned again, this time in protest.

"Stay with him," Cassie told Foster. She gestured to Davis to come with her.

When Davis had stepped across the bed again and joined her in the hall, she whispered, "Let's search the house for the drugs. They might be in here. No Kyle, though."

Davis nodded, then said, "Is there something hinky with the Surfer Dude??"

"Maybe."

■ ■ ■ ■

It wouldn't take long for the ambulance to arrive, she thought. There were several on standby at the rail hub with EMTs in them so all they'd have to do was release one. Since there had been no explosions from the crash site, she didn't think it would be a problem.

Davis took the kitchen and bathroom. Cassie took the front room and the other bedroom. In Rachel Westergaard's bedroom, she went through the drawers and the closet, checked beneath the bed, and rifled through the nightstands. There was a half-empty box of .25 ammunition in one of the drawers but no weapon.

It was obvious Kyle's mother Rachel was living with a man, and Cassie guessed it was T-Lock. She confirmed it when she found a Walmart photo booth shot of the two of them together.

There was paraphernalia for shooting up between the box springs and the mattress: a syringe and needle, a spoon, a candle, and a couple of small baggies of black tar heroin. She didn't touch the syringe but she could see it was clouded with fingerprints. She hoped they didn't belong to Kyle's mother.

Suddenly, there was a thump and a cry from the boy's bedroom, then a deafening gunshot.

She drew her weapon and rushed to the boy's bedroom to find T-Lock sprawled on his back across the bed with a bullet hole in his forehead. His arms and legs twitched in death throes. Foster maintained his shooting stance in the middle of the room, his Sig Sauer gripped tight.

"Son of a bitch tried to kill me!" Foster shouted.

"How?"

"He pulled that arrow out of his own neck and came at me with it."

Cassie looked down. The arrow was in fact near T-Lock's twitching hand.

"My God," she said. "He pulled it out?"

"You're telling me," Foster said, taking a deep breath and holstering his gun. The room smelled of gunpowder and hot blood.

"What a fucking idiot," Foster said. "I had no choice."

Cassie looked from T-Lock's body to Foster and back again. Foster wasn't wearing gloves.

She said, "So when we check that arrow, only his fingerprints will be on it, right?"

Foster's face went slack, then he recovered quickly. He said, "Come on. You don't think

I pulled it out myself and then shot him, do you?"

She said, "We'll find out. But in the meantime I need you to come out of that room and hand me your weapon and badge. I'll keep both of them safe until we figure this out."

She felt more than saw Davis join her.

"You've got to be kidding me," Foster said. "Who in the hell do you think you are?"

He looked to Davis for support. "Ian, what is with this crazy lady?"

Davis said, "She's your boss."

Cassie asked, "Did he tell you where Kyle was before you shot him?"

There was a beat. There shouldn't have been a beat.

"Who?" Foster asked.

"The kid who rides a bike," Cassie said. She gestured to the white tire track cast that had fallen out of Foster's coat pocket during the struggle. It was on the floor next to his heavy boots.

"Oh shit," Davis whispered when he saw what Cassie had seen.

Cassie drew her Glock and raised it with both hands, aimed at Foster's big chest.

"Ian, take his weapon."

Foster was quiet for a moment, but his

386

eyes narrowed. She could tell he was weighing his options.

"I don't know how it got there," Foster said.

Cassie said, "Just like you don't know why you didn't respond to the dispatcher, right? So did you hook up with MS-13 while you were here or were you in their pocket before you moved here from California? I'd guess the latter. Am I right?"

"You're crazy," he said.

She kept her front sight on Foster's heart while Davis disarmed him. Davis also plucked a set of cuffs and a container of pepper spray from Foster's belt. Davis had a sympathetic look on his face while he did it. Obviously, she thought, he wasn't convinced she knew what she was doing.

"Do you know where the drugs are?" she asked.

"I want a lawyer."

"Do you know where Kyle is?"

"I said I wanted a lawyer. I want our rep here before I answer any questions."

"Step aside," Cassie said to Davis. "I'm going to shoot this son of a bitch."

Davis looked at her with horror. But there must have been something in her eyes, because he moved away from Foster.

Foster saw it, too.

He said, "Kyle's gone. I don't know where the hell he is. T-Lock didn't know either."

"So he *could* talk a little. What else?"

"Nothing else."

"Where is Willie Dietrich?"

"With MS-13. There's two of them."

"Names?"

He shrugged. "I only know them as La Matanza and Silencio."

"Where are the drugs?"

Foster hesitated for a moment, but when her finger whitened on the trigger he blurted, "Outside in that old washing machine."

"And where is Kyle's mother?" Cassie asked.

Foster lowered his eyes. He said, "MS-13 took her. I'm sure she's dead by now."

Davis said, "Jesus."

Foster was led by a stunned Sheriff Kirkbride to the Tahoe in handcuffs. Cassie stood with Davis and two other deputies while Undersheriff Max Maxfield went to his unit to retrieve a bolt cutter from the trunk.

Davis pulled Cassie aside and said softly, "I really thought you were going to kill him in there."

"I was," she said. "I hate guys like that."

"You really would have shot him?"

"I learned from the best."

Davis shook his head and laughed bitterly. He was shaken by what had happened. She was, too. His laughter was a sign of uncomfortable relief.

"That confession he made won't stand up, you know — given the circumstances. He asked for a lawyer and instead you kept your gun on him. What am I supposed to tell the sheriff?"

"I'll leave that up to you," Cassie said. "I won't ask you to lie for me. I'll tell the sheriff what happened later."

He nodded. She could tell he wasn't sure what he was going to say or do yet.

"Surfer Dude is probably going to walk," he said.

"I know. But he'll be out of the department and out of our sight and I doubt he'll ever get another job in law enforcement. That's not the worst outcome in the world."

"Man," Davis said, "two dirty cops. Who would have guessed it?"

"He did," Cassie said, nodding toward Kirkbride as the sheriff closed the back door on Foster. "Or at least he had his suspicions. That's why he wanted me to investigate on my own without involving any of his other officers."

"How did you know about Foster?" Davis asked.

"I didn't," she confessed. "I thought Cam was the only dirty cop."

Maxfield returned with the bolt cutter and fitted the chain between the sharp jaws and squeezed the long handles.

The link popped with a sharp *ping* and the chain fell away.

Maxfield opened the top of the washer and peered inside.

He looked up, confused. "There's nothing in here but some really old frozen clothes," he said.

After letting it sink in a few seconds, Cassie turned to Davis and said, "We've *got* to find Kyle."

CHAPTER TWENTY-SEVEN

The digital display on the bank clock in downtown Grimstad said it was thirty-two degrees below zero when Kyle heard T-Lock's phone chime in his parka pocket. The very air sparkled like sequins in the early evening light. The sun was ballooning and dropping behind the two-story buildings on the west side of the street, creating frigid pools of shadow. Kyle pedaled his bike like a wild man down the sidewalk toward the train depot with no real destination in mind. He didn't want to go to the train station. He was riding to keep warm because he had no place else to go.

He knew it hadn't been his mom who was asking him where he was, how he was. She always used real words when she texted — not something like *WHERE R U, KYLE?*

Someone was using his mom's phone just like he was using T-Lock's.

Kyle thought he would never forget the

look on T-Lock's face when he stuck the arrow in his neck. T-Lock's expression was a combination of horror, surprise, and grudging admiration. Kyle wondered if T-Lock recognized Winkie's arrow before it entered him. It was a weird thought.

He turned down an alley behind a coffee shop. He hated to stop because the minute he did the cold would come back, seeping through his coat and pants. But he had to see the message.

It read: *KYLE, ANSWER THE PHONE WHEN I CALL. LOVE U, MOM.*

"You're not my mom," Kyle said aloud.

But when it burred he looked at the display. Kyle had three numbers memorized, not counting 911. He knew his house phone, his mom's cell phone, and Grandma Lottie's phone number. The display showed the call came from Grandma Lottie's house. She didn't have a cell phone. He wondered why she would call T-Lock's phone.

He pressed the button and held it to his ear.

A man's voice said, "Is this Kyle?"

He was too stunned to respond.

"Kyle, is that you?"

"Yeah."

"Ah, good. Now don't hang up. You aren't

going to hang up, are you, Kyle?"

Kyle wasn't sure so he didn't answer.

"Kyle, why do you have T-Lock's phone? Is he there with you right now?"

"No."

"How do you have his phone, then?"

"I stole it."

"You talk funny, Kyle. But I think I heard you tell me you stole it. Is that right?"

"Yes."

"And T-Lock isn't with you?"

"No."

"No cops?"

"No."

"So far, so good. Now is anyone listening in on this call?"

"No."

"Do you know where T-Lock is right now?"

"He's hurt. He's in my house but he's hurt."

"That was a good answer, Kyle. That means you're telling me the truth. We know that's where he is — we know all about it. The cops have him. A friend of ours filled us in. So keep telling me the truth, Kyle, and we'll be all right."

"Okay," Kyle said. *The cops have him?*

"Good. Now listen carefully to me, Kyle. My name is Willie. I'm an old friend of your mom's. She's here with me now, Kyle. We're at your grandmother's house."

Kyle felt a bolt of ice shoot through his brain. He pressed the phone hard to his ear. *Willie was at Grandma Lottie's house.*

"Kyle, your mom told us everything. We know about how you found that duffel bag that belongs to us. We know that T-Lock, that bad friend of your mother's, took it from you and made real big plans that involved your mother and you and a guy named Winkie. Those big plans didn't work out because T-Lock is a moron. It's not your fault, Kyle. No one is angry with you. We know it was all T-Lock."

The man's voice was calm and soothing, but Kyle found him irritating. He was talking to Kyle as if he were stupid and five years old.

"Now listen to me, Kyle. You've done everything right. You took that duffel bag to an adult and you didn't involve the police. How were you to know the adult you trusted would turn out to make all this trouble we're in? You can keep doing the right thing. You want to know how?"

Kyle waited a few seconds, and asked, "How?"

"First, you need to answer a very important question as honestly as you can.

Here it is: Do you know where our property is?"

"Yes."

"Can you get to it?"

Kyle hesitated again. "Yes."

"So do you still want to know how you can fix everything and be the big hero?"

"Yes."

Willie kind of snorted a laugh. He said, "You're kind of hard to understand, Kyle. But I think I heard that you said yes."

"Let me talk to my mom," Kyle said angrily.

There was a beat, and Willie imitated Kyle's speech impediment. *"Leh me tog to mah mom.* You crack me up, Kyle. *You want to tog to yo mom?"*

"Yes."

The phone on the other end went quiet. Kyle envisioned Willie covering it up with his hand.

Then he heard, "I'm so sorry, little man."

It was his mom, but her voice was slurry and distant. It was the way she talked the night before when she came out of her bedroom. But it was her.

"There," Willie said. "Are you happy now, *little man?"*

"Is my grandma there?"

"Ish may granna they?" Willie taunted.

Kyle felt tears sting his eyes and instantly freeze on his cheeks.

"She's here, Kyle," Willie said, his voice more stern than before. "She's here because it's her damned house. Your mom told us about her and we thought maybe you were here. Turns out we were a few hours late. But back to what we were talking about.

"Kyle, you have something that belongs to us. It's ours, not T-Lock's, and it's not yours. You know that because you're a smart boy. All we want is our property back. That's all. You bring us our property and you can be with your mom again and your old granna. Bring it straight here right now. Don't tell anyone what you're doing and damn sure don't involve the police. If you tell anyone, Kyle, you'll never see either one of these special people ever again."

"Don't hurt them," Kyle said, crying.

"Don hut dem," Willie mocked. "No, Kyle, we won't hurt them as long as you bring us our property. Tell me, Kyle, did you hear about that guy who was cut into little pieces and scattered all around town? Did you hear about it? You wouldn't want that to happen to your mother or granna, now would you?"

Someone laughed in the background. Another man. So there were two of them.

"No."

"Are you *crying*, Kyle?" Willie asked with fake surprise. "Heroes don't cry. Man up, little man. You need to be a hero."

Kyle fought back a sob.

Willie said, "So that's the deal, Kyle. It's an easy deal. All you have to do is get our property and bring it to your granna's house. We'll be here for no longer than a half an hour. Can you do that, Kyle? Bring us our property and everybody will be happy. Especially you, Kyle, because you'll get your mom and your granna back."

"Okay."

"No tricks, Kyle. You understand?"

"Yes."

"Then we're all cool."

Willie's voice was distant when Kyle heard him say, "Hear that, Granna? Hear that, Rachel? Little man is going to come and save your sorry asses."

And the man in the background laughed again.

"See you soon, Kyle," Willie said, and punched off.

As he mounted his bike, Kyle remembered T-Lock saying, "I doubt that she's even breathing. They took her phone away from her and they want me to show up with the duffel bag so they can take it and cut my head off like they did to Rufus."

Which was why Kyle had his mom's .25 pistol in his parka pocket next to the keys he'd used to open the lock on the washing machine chain and reclaim his duffel bag.

At the end of the alley he took a left. His bike tires squeaked on the snow-packed street, and his breath billowed around his head.

As the sun dropped it felt even colder. He hoped he could get to Grandma Lottie's before Willie started cutting his mom and Grandma into pieces.

And before he froze to death.

Chapter Twenty-Eight

Before Cassie and Ian Davis left the Westergaard home, Sheriff Kirkbride walked stiffly toward their vehicle and motioned for them to hold up.

He climbed into the backseat and moaned, then shed his gloves and rubbed his face with his hands. He was red-faced and his mustache was frosty with mucus from his nose from the cold. Cassie handed him a Kleenex.

"All my joints seize up in this kind of cold," he said through gritted teeth. Then, "Talk to me."

Davis deferred to Cassie.

She said, "As you know, we think Foster was working with MS-13 at the same time Cam Tollefsen was working with Willie Dietrich. I don't think they knew about the other, but it explains why both of them were at the rollover so quickly. Cam was there to escort the gangbanger into town to Willie for distribution. Foster was there to make sure the gangbanger wasn't stopped or run off the road. They were doing it for the same purpose but from two different directions."

"That's a hard theory to prove," Kirkbride said.

"It is. Cam can't talk anymore and I don't think Foster will, either, unless he gets some kind of deal from the prosecutor. But he sure looks dirty. We went through his personal cell phone to find out who he's been calling. For the last three days, it's filled with calls to a 619 area code. That's the San Diego, El Cajon, Chula Vista area in Southern California, so the phone comes from there. It's probably where our MS-13 boys came from."

The sheriff nodded, then said, "Two corrupt cops in my department. I still can't get over that. I know we expanded pretty fast, but still. I worked with Cam for years and I personally hired Surfer Dude."

"So there was nothing in his background to suggest he was in with MS-13?" Cassie asked.

"No. No priors, nothing in his work history in SoCal. And he sure as hell didn't volunteer anything like that when I interviewed him."

Kirkbride blew his nose and wiped his

mustache clean. "What you got him to say in there won't pass muster with the county prosecutor, you know."

Cassie nodded.

Kirkbride said, "But I guess you kind of have to wonder why a Southern Cal type would want to work here," he said, gesturing outside the window. "He's probably never been anywhere where it gets this cold."

"But it makes some sense," Cassie said. "The MS-13 are looking to establish new territory. This oil boom is perfect for them and the competition wasn't up to their level. If they had their hooks into Foster they could convince him to apply for the opening. It's no secret you're desperate for deputies. That way, he could come out here in advance and provide them with intel and cover while they made their move."

Kirkbride said, "Yeah, I can sort of buy it. But right now it's a matter of time before the DA hears why we grabbed him and cuts him loose. The only way I can keep him off the streets is to suspend him with pay while we call in the state boys to investigate an officer-involved shooting."

Cassie said, "We've got his phone. At least he won't be able to communicate with the bad guys and tell them all our moves. That could give us an advantage."

Kirkbride leveled his eyes on her. "So you really threatened to shoot him?"

Davis looked away, suddenly interested in something down the street.

"I did," Cassie said.

"I ought to take *your* badge and gun away," the sheriff said without enthusiasm.

"You could," Cassie said. "But let Ian and me finish this job. I'll come in tonight and turn them over in person. Let us have the chance to find Kyle Westergaard and the drugs."

Kirkbride cocked his head to the side. "Kyle?"

She explained her theory to Kirkbride and he listened closely.

He said, "So if we find the kid before they get to him we might save his life."

"Yes."

"It sounds almost personal, Cassie," Kirkbride said.

She took a deep breath. "Sheriff, we've got a mentally challenged kid riding around on his bike in thirty below weather. It's going to get dark soon, and even colder. Plus, if we find him we might find the drugs before they get sold all over Bakken County."

Kirkbride grumbled his approval.

"One more thing," she said. "I think our troubles are over in the dirty cop department."

When she said it, he winced. He was taking the unveiling of corruption in his department hard.

She continued, "We could use some help. In fact, we could use a lot of help. Willie Dietrich wasn't home, which means he's out and about. We don't have a location on the two Salvadorans if that's what they are. There's supposedly another local with them and it might be Willie. They have to be somewhere in the county because they wouldn't leave without their drugs. We need to *find* them."

Kirkbride thought about it for a second, then pulled out his cell phone and speed-dialed the dispatcher.

While he waited to be connected, he said, "Keep me in the loop with updates."

When the dispatcher was on the line he said, "Judy, We need to put out a department-wide BOLO for an individual named Kyle Westergaard. He's ten or twelve years old but small for his age. He was last seen riding a bicycle on Main Street. . . ."

He went on to ask that a second and third "Be On The Lookout" be issued for Willie Dietrich and two unnamed male Hispanics who might have tattoos indicating they were MS-13 or *Mara Salvatrucha.* He spelled it out for the dispatcher.

While Cassie and Davis cruised the residential streets in the old section of Grimstad looking for Kyle and listening to the back and forth on the radio, Deputies Jim Klug and Fred Walker called in.

"We're at the *Home Away from Home* man camp," Klug said. "The desk guy says two Hispanic individuals matching the description and driving a new model Toyota Tundra pickup with California plates checked in here a couple of nights ago. They paid cash for a Jack and Jill unit and they haven't checked out. Their truck isn't in the lot, but the manager agreed to go with us to knock on the door. I'd like to request backup."

"Could be them," Davis said.

Kirkbride came on the radio. "Proceed with extreme caution, Jim. You should assume these guys are armed and dangerous."

The dispatcher asked, "Are there units in the vicinity?"

Deputy Tom Melvin called in to say that he and Deputy Shaun McKnight were a minute and a half away from the man camp.

Cassie said, "I'd be shocked if they were in."

"Still," Davis said, "if we know where they're staying . . ."

"Right. That could be helpful — if it's them."

They listened to the cross talk over the radio while the four officers and the manager entered the unit. It was empty except for a pile of clothes, a box of 9mm ammunition, and a couple of votive candles.

The call came from Deputy Bryan Gregson. "I'm at the corner of Pine and Main and I just saw a kid on a bike matching the description."

Cassie bolted up straight in her seat and increased the volume on the radio.

Gregson said, "I hit my lights and siren and followed him when he ducked down an alley. But there's a bunch of crap in the alley — Dumpsters and stuff — and my unit can't get through. I lost him."

Cassie grabbed the mic. "Deputy Gregson, what direction was he going?"

"I thought I saw him turn southeast."

She turned to Davis, wishing she was more familiar with the layout of the town to know where they could head Kyle off.

"Sounds like he's headed toward the park," Davis said.

"Then go!" she shouted to Davis. *"Go, go, go!"*

Davis took the corner fast and accelerated down a snow-packed street. He lost traction on the ice but fought to regain control. Parked pickups sizzled by through the passenger window.

"Don't hit the siren or lights," she said. "I don't want to scare him."

"Just calm down," Davis said, sliding into a sharp left turn. The Tahoe fishtailed again on the slick road and when Davis recovered they clipped off the side mirror of a parked oil field utility truck.

"Shit," Davis muttered.

"Don't *ever* tell a woman to calm down," Cassie said with heat.

"Sorry," he said as they cleared the block and the park opened up in front of them.

"There he is," Davis said urgently.

Cassie peered ahead. A small figure on a bike was racing through the park toward an empty playground located in the center. She recognized the park as the same one where the trunk of Rufus Whitely was found impaled the day before.

The park was one block square, surrounded by chain-link fence. There were openings wide enough to drive a vehicle through on all four sides.

"He's in the park," Cassie said into the radio mic. "All units in the vicinity — we need you here *now*. Cut off all the exits."

At that moment, Kyle turned his head and saw them. He was about a hundred yards away, approaching the playground. Then he leaned forward and powered the bike faster through the snow.

Two or three sheriff's department deputies said they were on their way and called out their present locations. Cassie didn't know if they were minutes or seconds away from the descriptions.

"He saw us," Davis said. "We can only block one entrance. He has three more to escape from."

"Where are the other cars?" Cassie asked. "We need them to block the other openings."

"They're coming," Davis reassured her as he pumped the brakes to slow down. The Tahoe skidded on the ice but came to a stop inches away from the north opening of the fence.

Inside, Kyle looked at them again over his shoulder and turned straight away toward the south exit from the park.

Cassie felt desperate. If Kyle shot through the south opening he would cross the street and vanish in a big bank of Russian olive bushes. By the time they backed the Tahoe out and drove around the park, Kyle could be gone for good.

But Kyle suddenly turned an abrupt left as a sheriff's department vehicle appeared from the direction of downtown and blocked the south gate.

"No need for lights or sirens," Cassie said over the radio. "But we need units on the east and west sides of the park and we need them now."

Kyle powered toward the eastside fence. Cassie thought he looked winded by the way his bike swayed from side to side as he pedaled. He turned when another unit appeared and nosed through the east gate and stopped. She felt for Kyle. There was no adrenaline rush as if she were boring in on a suspect. This was a twelve-year-old kid and they were trapping him like an animal.

When a fourth unit plugged up the westside gate, Kyle desperately rode away from it toward the playground again in the middle of the park. The bike swayed dangerously from side to side.

Cassie grabbed a handheld radio and turned it up as she stepped out of her vehicle.

Davis opened his door to get out and Cassie held up her hand. "Stay inside, Ian. Let me do this. We don't want to spook him.

"Everybody stay put and watch him so he doesn't figure a way out," she said into the radio, walking past the grille of the Tahoe. "I'm going to approach him on foot when he stops. Remember, he's just a kid. We don't know what he's going to do, but be careful not to hurt him if he tries to get away. We just want to question him."

Kyle stopped near an empty jungle gym on the side of a silent swing set. She watched him drop his bike and clamber up a ladder to a kind of crow's nest. The metal structure of the jungle gym was covered with frost that looked like thick white felt.

She fitted an earpiece into her ear, keyed the mic open on the handheld, and dropped it into her parka pocket so the other units could hear what would take place. She guessed Kirkbride would listen in as well.

"Can you hear me?" she said softly.

"Roger that," Davis said. The other officers surrounding the park checked in as well.

"Okay. I'm going to talk to him."

"Don't tell him to calm down," Davis said.

"This isn't the time," Cassie said, taking a deep breath that instantly froze the hairs inside her nose.

■ ■ ■ ■

Kyle was hunched in a squat hugging his knees as she approached. He watched her closely like a feral cat. She could see his face was red from all the pedaling, and his exhaled breath hung around his head like a thought balloon.

"Kyle Westergaard?" she said.

He didn't move. He looked scared. His eyes were moist and small.

"Kyle, I'm Cassie. You have nothing to be afraid of. I'm here to help you."

Nothing.

"I don't think you trust the police," she said. "I understand. You've had some bad experiences with them, or at least with a couple of bad cops you might have seen recently. But, Kyle, they're not here. One man is dead and the other is in jail. They can't hurt anyone now."

Kyle grunted and hugged himself tighter. Cassie could see that his cheeks were glazed with frozen tears. Involuntarily, her eyes teared up as well.

She said, "Kyle, I have a son of my own. His name is Ben. When I see you up there I can't help but think of him in the same situation. I would hope that if he's ever scared or in trouble someone would try to help him. I think that would happen because most people are good. I'm good, and you are, too. Will you let me help you?"

Kyle croaked, "They have my mom."

Cassie wasn't sure she understood.

He said it again, but this time his voice broke on the last word.

"They have your mom?"

"And my Grandma Lottie." It was almost a shout.

"I stabbed T-Lock in the neck. Are you going to arrest me?"

Cassie felt terrible asking him to repeat it. When he did she understood the words "stabbed," "T-Lock," and "arrest me."

She said, "Kyle, it sounds like you were defending yourself. You have a right to protect yourself in a situation like that."

"Really?"

Her heart was breaking. She fought back tears and said, "Kyle, please come down. We can go over to that warm car and you can tell me everything. And then we'll figure out a way to keep your mom and grandma safe."

"How are you going to do that?" he asked.

She didn't quite understand what he said, but she got the meaning through his inflection.

Cassie said, "We're going to do it because we're the good guys." And she smiled.

Kyle nodded and climbed stiffly down the ladder.

Chapter Twenty-Nine

Fidel Escobar disconnected the call he'd placed from his cell phone when it went — once again — straight to voice mail. The cop, Foster, for whatever reason, wasn't picking up.

Escobar, along with Diego "Silencio" Argueta, Dietrich, and the woman they had taken from McDonald's, were all in the home of the old lady. It was warm in there, which Escobar appreciated, and he'd sent Silencio outside twice already for more wood to feed into the stove.

Outside, the last shafts of sunlight poured through the branches of the old trees on the west side of the road to the old lady's house. The indoor-outdoor thermometer on the kitchen counter said it was seventy-six degrees inside and minus thirty-four degrees outside. Escobar parted the vinyl miniblinds over the front window with two fingers and peered out. The road to the house — the *only* road to the house — was white and empty.

To the old lady, who they had bound with silver duct tape to her straight-back kitchen chair, Escobar said, "That's a hundred and ten degree swing, old lady."

The old woman's eyes flashed at him. She couldn't talk because of the tape over her mouth. But she wanted to sass him again, he could tell. She reminded him of Auntie Beatriz. Auntie Beatriz would not be shut up by anybody and she felt it was her right and her duty to speak her mind. She could use some tape, Escobar thought. But he'd never smack Auntie Beatriz the way he did the old lady when she ordered them out of her house. He'd broken her glasses with the blow and her left cheek was bruised and swollen. But she was still feisty.

Escobar's toolbox sat by the back door. He'd had no reason to use it except to retrieve the roll of tape. His machete was on the table in full view of the old woman, who looked at it often. He had a 9mm semi-auto in the waistband of his pants.

Silencio was slumped in an old overstuffed chair in the living room with his feet up and his 9mm on his lap. He was watching a station with nothing on it but cartoons. Silencio had been upset there was no Univision in North Dakota. Escobar could tell just by looking at him that Silencio, who had kicked his boots off, welcomed the warmth as well and was getting comfortable in the chair.

Escobar gently patted the old woman on the top of her silver head — she didn't like it and tried to jerk her head away — and went into the front room.

Dietrich was on the couch with the woman, Rachel. At first, she'd been scared and crazy until Dietrich shot her up with a hit of black tar heroin. Silencio had to hold her down on the backseat floor of the pickup while Dietrich found a vein. It wasn't long after that the woman calmed down and moaned. Escobar had seen enough junkies to know this Rachel liked heroin and was no stranger to it. The drug gave her peace and soon she told them about T-Lock, about her son Kyle, about her mother's house just outside of town.

They believed her when she said she didn't know where T-Lock had hidden the duffel bag of product. There was no reason not to believe her because she told them everything else they wanted to know.

"I think Kyle knows where the duffel bag is," she'd said, making her eyes big. "I *know* T-Lock does."

"So call him," Escobar had said to Dietrich. "Call him from her phone."

They'd parked the Toyota Tundra behind the old lady's house so no one could see it from the access road. Rachel was more than willing to knock on the back door. Escobar, Silencio, and Dietrich flattened themselves against the back of the house so they couldn't be detected by the occupant inside.

When the old lady realized that it was her daughter outside, the door opened and the old lady said through the storm door, "What are you doing out in these conditions, Rachel? And where is Kyle? I was hoping you'd have him with you."

Then she said, "What's wrong with your eyes? You aren't using again, are you?"

Rachel stepped aside and Silencio bull-rushed the door, sending the old lady sprawling across the kitchen floor.

And they were in.

Escobar had tried to eat a sheet of what Dietrich called lefse from the refrigerator but he didn't like it. He thought it tasted pasty and bland. Dietrich liked it, though, after buttering the sheets and sprinkling them with brown sugar. He rolled one up for Silencio, who seemed to like it, too.

The old lady sat in her chair watching

416

them eat. If her eyes could kill, they'd all be dead, Escobar thought.

He wondered why these people lived in such a cold place and preferred food with no taste. It was a mystery to him.

This whole place was a mystery to him.

When he entered the front room, Escobar looked at all the family photos on the wall. There were some black-and-white ones of a young woman in a long dress standing next to a stern-faced farmer. Newer photos revealed this Rachel to have been quite a looker in high school, but even then there was a wild glint in her eye. There were several framed photos of a small boy who looked straight into the camera but didn't smile. He must be Kyle, Escobar thought.

Escobar said to Dietrich, "My man won't answer his phone."

"Maybe he's in the middle of something," Dietrich said. "If he's with a bunch of other cops, I can understand him not picking up."

"I've called five times."

"Yeah," Dietrich said, "that's a lot. But I wouldn't get excited yet."

"I don't get excited."

Dietrich shut up. He wasn't a man who shut up often, Escobar thought, but he was smart enough to shut up now.

The woman lay on her back on the couch, her feet curled up against Dietrich's thigh. Her eyes were closed and she looked peaceful.

"She is sleeping?" Escobar asked, surprised.

"I shot her up again," Dietrich said.

"Was that a good idea?" Escobar asked, raising his eyebrows.

"She wanted it."

"Of course. Addicts always want it. She loves her son but her real love is inside her veins right now."

"I don't know if she can walk," Dietrich said. "I can always carry her out over my shoulder if we have to clear out of here. She's pretty light."

"So is *la abuela.*"

Dietrich looked up and cocked his head to the side, confused.

Escobar nodded toward the old lady at the kitchen table, then at Rachel. "They've seen us. They die."

"That's what I thought," Dietrich said. "You guys don't leave witnesses. Do you have enough barrels at the shop? You wouldn't want to run out of barrels."

"We won't."

Dietrich nodded. "Then what — you load the barrels in your pickup and drive 'em to

SoCal?"

Escobar nodded his head, almost with sadness. *"Silencio!"*

The man bolted upright from the chair, his gun in his hand.

"You were sleeping," Escobar said calmly. "No sleeping."

Silencio started to argue but thought better of it. He had obviously drifted off.

"Go outside and get more wood," Escobar said. "That will wake you up."

He told both Dietrich and Silencio about the one hundred and ten degree difference between inside and outside.

"Yeah?" Dietrich asked, puzzled.

Silencio shrugged dully.

"Maybe you are both too simple to understand the significance of it," Escobar said with a sniff. "It's like we're astronauts in space. Warm inside, cold outside."

While Silencio pulled on his heavy coat to go get more wood, Escobar said to Dietrich, "I think she's dead."

Rachel's eyes were partially open and her mouth gaped. A still bubble had formed on one nostril. Her arm was splayed out from the couch in midair.

Dietrich frowned and touched his fingertips to her neck beneath her jaw. Then he pressed the back of his hand to her nose and mouth.

"*Shit,*" he said.

"You shouldn't have given her that second hit," Escobar said. "You gave her too much."

They both looked over at the old lady. She'd been watching everything. She closed her eyes and her head dropped forward. It took them a moment to realize she was crying.

"Poor old lady," Escobar said.

"Does that mean —" Dietrich started to ask.

"It doesn't change anything."

Escobar checked the clock on the face of his cell phone as Silencio struggled through the storm door with an armful of frozen wood. Then he pried the blinds open again and looked up the road. Nothing. It was getting dark.

He said to Dietrich, "Ten more minutes, then we go."

"He said he'd be here."

"You trust a ten-year-old boy." It was a statement, an indictment, not a question.

Dietrich said again, "He's twelve, I think. You want me to call him again?"

Escobar shook his head.

He turned to the old lady, who raised her

head. Her eyes were red and puffy. He said, "We'll be gone soon, *Abuela.*"

Seven minutes later, Willie Dietrich untangled himself from Rachel's stiffening legs and approached the front window. Escobar watched him from the kitchen. Silencio watched him from the reclining chair. Unlike before, Silencio hadn't taken off his boots and coat. He knew they would likely be leaving soon.

Dietrich made a snorting sound. Escobar squinted his eyes at the sound.

"Son of a bitch," Dietrich said with relief. "That little shit is coming up the road on his bike."

"Does he have our property?"

"There are a couple of bags hanging from the handlebars. So yeah, it looks like he does."

Escobar nodded. Then he retrieved the Condor El Salvador machete from the table and handed it to Silencio. Silencio understood.

The old woman pleaded with him with her eyes. He refused to look at her.

CHAPTER THIRTY

By the order of Sheriff Kirkbride, Cassie, Davis, and the other deputies hung their optics outside their vehicles by the straps as they converged on Lottie Westergaard's home outside of town. The reason for hanging the binoculars and spotting scopes outside was so the lenses wouldn't fog up when used in the extreme cold.

With lights off, Davis had nosed their SUV into the trees on the left side of the entrance road. He pulled a few feet ahead so Cassie could get an unobstructed view through the trees of the front door and portico of the little house. It was dark enough that the three distant squares of light from the blinded front-facing windows could be clearly seen.

Kirkbride and another unit, also with their lights off, were across the road in the trees as well. If it weren't for a reflection of the moon on Kirkbride's windshield, Cassie would not have known they were there at all.

"I hate this," she said to Davis.

"I know you do," Davis said softly.

The radio was squelched down but she could clearly hear Kirkbride checking in with his force. Three units with two deputies each had been sent along an old two-track road that paralleled the river so they could get behind the property. Six heavily armed men — the Bakken County SWAT Team — were now on foot making their way through the trees toward the rear of the house. Four other deputies were approaching the home from each side, two from each direction.

"Let me know when you're in position," Kirkbride asked over the radio.

There were three vehicles — Kirkbride's, Klug's, and Cassie's — on the side of the road leading to Lottie Westergaard's house. Two other units were on standby. So were two EMT vans.

"We have a visual of the house," one of the SWAT deputies whispered. "There's a late-model pickup parked in back."

"California plates," another deputy said.

"Roger that," Kirkbride said. "That'll be our friends from MS-13. Get into position and get ready. When you get the signal from me and no one else, you know what to do."

There was a round of "Roger that" from all the deputies in place.

"Be safe," Kirkbride said. "Don't fire unless you double-check your target — if you have to fire at all. Remember, we've got deputies all over these woods. I don't want anybody getting hurt because of friendly fire, boys."

Cassie's mouth was dry when she turned in her seat and said to Kyle, "Are you sure you're ready for this?"

Kyle nodded that he was.

"You don't have to do it," she said. "Remember, we talked about it earlier. You absolutely don't have to do this."

"I know."

"Are you sure you want to go?"

"Yes. My mom and grandma are in there."

"Remember," Cassie said, speaking slowly and clearly and reaching back for his hand, "you'll ride up to the front of the house and drop the duffel bag in the snow so they can see it. Nothing more. Then you'll turn your bike around and ride back here like hell. If anything happens, you ride into the trees on the side of the road. Got it?"

Kyle nodded.

"Tell me, Kyle. Assure me you've got it."

"Got it," Kyle said.

She squeezed his hand. He squeezed back, but he didn't seem scared enough.

"You're brave," she said.

He nodded that he was.

"I'll get the bike out," Davis said, careful to toggle the kill switch so the interior light wouldn't go on when he opened the door.

The strategy was simple and aggressive as outlined by Kirkbride. Everyone knew their roles. Cassie could see how gung ho his deputies were when Kirkbride outlined the plan.

For the first time Cassie had seen since she met him, Kyle grinned as he listened.

He had said there were three — and possibly four — bad guys inside the house. The idea was to isolate them, confuse them, then engage them with overwhelming force. It was the only way, Kirkbride said, they could possibly save the lives of Rachel and Lottie. Otherwise, they'd be looking at a hostage situation at best, a double homicide at worst.

But they'd need Kyle's help. Kyle had readily agreed, despite Cassie's misgivings.

The idea was to surround Lottie Westergaard's home before Kyle arrived and the exchange was made. Kirkbride knew the terrain intimately, and he positioned his deputies using old roads and game trails through the trees from the river.

When the intruders exited the house to get the duffel bag, they'd be apprehended by the four deputies hiding in the front. Simultaneously, Kirkbride would give the order and the SWAT team behind the house would throw flash-bang grenades and tear gas canisters through the windows before storming it and rescuing Rachel and Lottie. By putting the most pressure on the back side of the house, Kirkbride said, it would force the remaining bad guys to flee out the front where they'd be in the open.

Cassie climbed out of the Tahoe and helped Davis get Kyle's bike out of the back. They filled the left newspaper pannier with the duffel bag and balanced the right pannier with several heavy rocks. Kyle stood to the side pulling on his gloves, fitting his stocking cap to his head, rocking from side to side in anticipation and fear.

She approached him and slid her handheld radio into his parka pocket.

"This is on," she said. "But it's set to transmit only. You won't hear anyone talking. But this way we can hear what is said.

"If you get into trouble," she told him, leaning down so their faces were inches apart, "start yelling for help. We'll be there in seconds. Do you understand, Kyle?"

He nodded that he did.

"Are you ready, then?"

"Yes."

"Remember — just deliver the bag and get back here."

She leaned forward and hugged him. He felt small, even through her parka and his heavy coat.

As Cassie watched Kyle mount his bike and ride away through the snow toward the house, she had trouble breathing.

So much could go wrong.

"I don't like involving the boy," she said.

"I know you don't," Davis said. "But none of us could ride up there on a bike in his place. They've got to see that it's him."

"If something happens to him I'll never forgive myself."

"I know," Davis said. "I feel the same way. But he's a willing participant and we've got every deputy in Bakken County here to protect him. He could have said no."

"He's twelve years old, Ian."

Davis had no answer for that.

Kirkbride talked to his team, keeping them apprised.

"Kyle is on his way to the house," the

sheriff said in a whisper. "Pray for the little guy."

Through the radio, Cassie could hear Kyle's muffled breathing as he pedaled. She raised the binoculars.

"Can you see him?" Davis asked.

"Yes."

Cassie kept her field of vision on Kyle as he progressed down the snow-packed road. The light from the stars and moon had turned the road aquamarine. He looked so small.

"He's stopping," she said as Kyle reached the house. She watched him fumble for the kickstand with his heavy right boot. Finally, he found it.

"He's going to take the duffel bag out," she said.

"I hope they know he's there," Davis said.

Cassie shifted the binoculars up over Kyle's head and the front of the house came into view. Someone had parted the blinds to see out the front window. Then they snapped shut.

"They see him," Cassie said.

When she shifted back to Kyle, he was still standing on the side of his bike. The duffel bag was still in the panniers.

"Get ready," Kirkbride said to his deputies over the radio.

Cassie could feel her own heart beat, and it made the binoculars vibrate. She tried to steady them by resting the barrels on the top of the half-opened passenger window.

The front door opened and two figures came out on the portico. The first man was Caucasian and heavily muscled. She couldn't believe he was wearing only a tight black T-shirt. The second was thin and dark and bundled up in an oversized coat. Their breath fused with the glow from the porch light.

"Take the bag out and drop it," Cassie whispered as if Kyle could hear her.

"I've got a visual on Willie Dietrich and an unknown male on the front porch," one of the hidden deputies reported.

"Roger that," Kirkbride responded in a whisper. "We see him too. The other guy must be one of the MS-13 peckerheads."

"Take the bag out, drop it, and turn around and come back now, Kyle," Cassie said aloud. "Ride the hell away from them like we talked about."

Cassie saw the blinds in the front window pull up. Another man, short with protruding ears, watched what was going on outside in front of him with his hands on his hips. He was so still it was eerie, she thought.

Over the radio, they heard Dietrich say,

"Well, you must be Kyle. Did you bring our property?"

"Yes," Kyle said.

"Kyle, damn it, get the hell out of there," Cassie said, nearly shouting.

"What's he *doing*?" Kirkbride asked, sounding as exasperated as Cassie felt. "He's supposed to clear the scene."

To his team, Kirkbride said, "Nobody take any action until the boy is clear."

"Kyle," Cassie said aloud, *"run away."*

"So where is it, Kyle?" Dietrich asked. "Is it there in that bag?"

"Yes."

"Well, you need to take it out and give it to my friend Silencio here. He's got to check that everything is there like we expect. We know your old pal T-Lock and your mom sampled the product, but the rest of it better be in there."

"Where's my mom?"

"She's inside, Kyle. She misses you."

Cassie couldn't believe Kyle was confronting them. She couldn't breathe.

"Where's Grandma Lottie?" Kyle asked.

"Mare's granna?" Dietrich mocked. Then, with a laugh: "Why, she's in the kitchen making some of that good lefse for me and the boys."

Silencio had moved down from the porch

430

and was descending the steps and walking toward Kyle and his bike. There was a flash of steel in the moonlight.

Before she could scream that Silencio had a blade, Kyle extended his arm and a pistol flashed.

Pop-pop-pop-pop.

Silencio crumpled to the snow.

"Kyle has a gun!" Cassie shouted. As she said it she flashed back on the box of .25 ammunition in Rachel's drawer.

Pop-pop-pop.

Willie Dietrich staggered back until he hit the house. Then he slid down the siding until Cassie couldn't see him through the binoculars.

"Now!" Kirkbride shouted into the radio, "Go *now.*"

Cassie saw the figure at the front window vanish to the side as three loud concussions flashed from inside the house. The explosions were so bright that for a moment all she could see was an afterimage imprint in the dark.

She was jerked forward as Davis reversed the SUV out of the trees, and when her vision came back she realized they were speeding down the road toward the house behind Sheriff Kirkbride's unit.

Thick yellow smoke rolled from the open

door and vents of the house. Heavily armed cops in tactical vests, helmets, and gas masks were swarming the house. All three units approaching the house from the front access road hit their lights and sirens within seconds of one another, and suddenly the night turned from cold and dark to cold and throbbing.

"Where's Kyle?" she asked Davis.

"I lost him," Davis said.

Cassie was frantic when she finally saw Kyle being escorted out the front door of the house by Deputy Klug. The boy was hunched over, stumbling, his gloved hands covering his face.

She ran up the steps and took over, leading Kyle into the front lawn toward her vehicle.

"I can't breathe!" Kyle cried.

"It's the gas," she said. "It stings your eyes and lungs for a while. But don't worry, it will get better now that you're out of it."

She could tell by the way his back was heaving that he was crying. She didn't know whether it was because of the gas or something he saw inside the house.

"Give me your gun," she said, opening the door of her unit.

With his eyes clamped tight and fluids

streaming out of his nose, Kyle fished through his coat like a blind man and handed the .25 pistol to her without argument. She dropped the gun in the pocket of her parka while kicking herself for not even considering that he might have taken it from his mother's drawer and hidden it in his bulky coat.

Cassie climbed into the backseat of the Tahoe next to Kyle and shut the door.

She said, "Stay here and keep warm."

He didn't argue. He seemed spent, and he collapsed onto her. She held him while watching out the windshield and listening to the radio.

She clearly heard one of the deputies say, "There's a body here."

Kyle's body racked with silent sobbing. He tensed as Kirkbride said, "We might have as many as four victims."

Cassie knew of the two outside. Who was inside?

Although there was too much excited chatter and cross talk, Cassie discerned that the officers inside had found two females. One was alive but injured and the other was dead. The woman found alive was described as "elderly." She covered Kyle's ears with her arms, and he burrowed into her.

She realized Kyle had seen his mother's

body through the smoke and gas. He was in shock.

Her eyes watered because she'd gotten a whiff of the gas as well. At least that's what she told herself.

Then a deputy cried, "Shit! There he goes!"

Cassie looked up in time to see a man hurl himself through the glass of a side window and land on all fours in the snow. It was the man who'd been standing at the picture window in front. The man scrambled to his feet and turned her way. There was a snarl on his face but his eyes were calm.

"Stay down!" Cassie shouted to Kyle and pushed him flat on the seat. She drew her weapon and opened the back door and braced behind it.

For a brief second, her eyes locked with the MS-13 gangbanger and he started toward her. There was a gun in his hand and he raised it and she saw the muzzle flash and felt the bullet hit the door.

Cassie aimed through the opening between the body of the SUV and the open door and fired four shots as fast as she could pull the trigger.

The man stopped, wheeled, and vanished in the dark brush on the side of the house.

A second later, a deputy appeared at the

broken window, pointing outside.

"He's on the run," someone said.

"Which direction?"

"West toward the river. He's on foot."

Jim Klug appeared at the front door and saw Cassie, who still had her weapon pointed.

"Did you hit him?"

The target may have jerked to the side when she fired, but she wasn't sure.

"I don't know. I think so."

"Are you hurt?"

She looked down at her parka. "No."

Kirkbride came on the radio and said, "Find that son of a bitch."

CHAPTER THIRTY-ONE

The farther Fidel Escobar ran from the house, the more quiet it got. He crashed through wicked brush that pulled at his clothing and cut his hands. It was so cold his face felt as if it were on fire. His boots crunched in the snow.

When he pushed through a thick bank of scrub into an opening, he paused to look back. He could see blue and red strobes of light on the tops of the trees, and he could hear shouting. But no pursuers.

Yet.

The cop bitch had hit him twice. One through his left shoulder and the other in his guts. That one burned like a blowtorch.

There had to be a house or a car ahead, he thought. He wasn't that far out of town. If he got to a road he'd stand in the middle of it and stop a car and throw the driver out into the snow. Or take a hostage to bargain with. If he found a house, he'd force himself inside.

Anything to get warm and stop the bleeding.

He felt the cold grip him even as he stood there catching his breath. But as long as he kept moving, as long as he kept his blood pumping, he had a chance.

He knew how bad a gutshot could be, but he knew guys who had survived them. He didn't plan to die here in this place, this unnatural setting. He was La Matanza.

Vehicles were moving out back at the house. Would they try to cut him off?

If he could get to one of the sheriff's department SUVs he'd shoot the driver in the head and take it.

A spotlight swept through the trees right behind him, and he started to run again. There was a shout, and as he ran he ducked forward covering his head with his hands, waiting for a gunshot that didn't come.

There were all kinds of trails and openings in the brush, he found. Animals had probably made them. As long as he stayed low he could keep going forward. A few times he dropped to his hands and knees and crawled through holes in the thick brush. There was no way they'd try to follow him through this stuff in the dark, he thought, even though his tracks wouldn't be hard to find.

He looked behind him. There were a few specks of blood but he wasn't bleeding heavily. Escobar knew that happened sometimes with gutshots. They bled inside, not outside.

And then the brush gave way and he was suddenly in the open beneath the slice of moon and the cruel hard stars. He staggered forward, crossing a two-track road that had been driven on recently by several vehicles.

He realized why the brush had abated when he saw the big frozen river across the road. It was wide and still, the ice on top of it reflecting the stars. He could see the lights of a house across the river on the side of an embankment. Although it was more than a quarter of a mile away, he could even make out the blue square of a television screen through a window.

He heard a vehicle coming from his left. A wall of dense brush on the side of the road was suddenly lit up by headlights.

Escobar crossed himself with a hand he could no longer feel and stepped down the embankment to the edge of the river. Shards of ice had been pushed into the bank and had frozen in place there, and he scrambled over them. He looked out and saw that the ice in the middle of the river was smooth as glass, and he thought he could be halfway across it before the men in the vehicle saw him, if they saw him at all.

He didn't step so much as slide one foot in front of the other so he could keep going forward. He held his arms out to the side for balance. He had to look over to make sure his 9mm was still in his hand. It was, but he couldn't feel it. He wondered if he'd even be able to pull the trigger if he had to.

Through the window across the river, a fat woman got up from a chair and looked out. No doubt, she saw the cop lights in the distance. But Escobar didn't think the woman could see him.

Somewhere upriver, the ice moaned and Escobar stopped, terrified. But nothing happened. He didn't know ice moaned, just like he'd never walked across a frozen river in his life.

Behind him, he heard a squeal of brakes and a shout.

He shuffled faster, his arms pumping at his sides. His shoulder was starting to hurt now, and his belly screamed red at him. His wounds were holding him back.

The texture of the ice changed. It was grittier now, and he could actually get traction to walk. He was a lucky man!

Escobar started to run, even as the white light from a spotlight hit him in the back. Twenty more feet to the other side . . .

When the ice cracked open beneath his feet and he dropped through.

For a moment everything was unbelievably quiet. He was underwater. He saw streams of white specks floating upward looking like pearls on a necklace. He realized they were bubbles.

Escobar's boots softly hit the bed of the river. *So it wasn't deep.* He bent his knees and pushed off.

His head came out of the water and he reached for a handhold on the lip of the hole in the ice and found one. There was a small ridge of ice he grabbed on to. His wet head and shoulders were exposed to the frigid air.

It was so still he could hear one of the deputies talk on his radio.

"Sheriff, we found him. He tried to cross the river down around the bend and he fell through the ice. We can see him out there trying to crawl back up on top."

"He fell through?"

"Roger that."

"Must be right where that thermal springs

comes up. The ice there is always unstable. If it wasn't so damned cold that spot would be open and there would be a bunch of geese sitting on it."

Escobar could no longer feel his body or his legs. The bullet in his guts no longer hurt. But he didn't think he could kick himself up onto the ice. Was the ice ridge stout enough to support his weight if he tried to crawl out? Then he realized the ridge of ice had already snapped off. He was being held up because his hands and arms had frozen solid to the surface of the river.

He cried, "I need some help!"

This was no way to die, he thought. There was no dignity in it, nothing for his compadres to talk about. This was a bad dream. He'd always assumed he'd be shot down after killing three or four men who'd come after him. Not by a doughy woman from behind a car door. Not like *this.*

The deputy said, "He's calling for help, Sheriff."

There was a long pause. Then the sheriff said, "Tell him to hold on. We'll send somebody out first thing in the morning."

"Come again?"

"You heard me."

"Loud and clear."

So did Escobar. He closed his eyes and found when he tried to reopen them his eyelashes had frozen to his cheekbones. Seeing out was like looking through jail bars.

That was the last thought he ever had.

■ ■ ■ ■

PART FOUR:
THREE WEEKS
LATER

■ ■ ■ ■

CHAPTER THIRTY-TWO

Cassie was washing the dishes from dinner when her alternative cell phone rang on the kitchen counter. She'd set a different ringtone than her primary phone.

She quickly dried her hands on a towel and snatched up the phone. It was from an unknown caller.

"Excuse me," she said to her mother, "I need to take this outside in the hall."

Isabel looked up suspiciously. She was reading *The New Republic* in her overstuffed chair while Ben, Kyle, and Raheem were engrossed in a project that had taken over the entire front room of her apartment. The project involved card tables, blankets, and ropes.

"Outside?" Isabel asked, arching her eyebrows.

Cassie nodded, then stepped around the boys' project and went into the hallway, closing the door behind her.

She punched the button. "Yes?"

The call was like all the others thus far in that she could hear distant motors idling, background chatter, and sometimes wind.

"Hey, I'm callin' about the LTL you've got up on the board. I'm in Billings and headed your way with a reefer. How many pallets we talkin' about?"

The voice was thin, reedy, and Southern. It was not familiar.

She said, "I'm sorry, but we just made a deal with another carrier."

"But it's still up on the board?" he said. He sounded put out.

"They haven't had a chance to take it off yet," she lied. "This just happened."

"Well," he said, drawing out the word until it had two syllables, "I guess I'm a day late and a dollar short."

"Sorry," she said, and disconnected the call. She dropped the phone into the left pocket of her sweater and went back inside.

Willie Dietrich had survived the shooting. He credited his "thick chest." In exchange for dropping some of he charges against him — conspiracy, kidnapping, and being an accessory to the murder of Simon Bierstadt, aka Winkie — Dietrich started talking. He held court for a week from his bed in Bakken County Memorial Hospital.

Yes, he said, Cam Tollefsen was dirty and he'd provided protection and inside-the-department intel to Willie for the past few years.

Yes, the two Salvadorans were MS-13 and had been sent to Grimstad from Los Angeles to take out the competing biker operation.

Yes, Fidel "La Matanza" Escobar and Diego "Silencio" Argueta had murdered and dismembered Rufus Whitely, Phillip Klein, and Simon "Winkie" Bierstadt. Willie gave the sheriff's department directions to the warehouse and told them which barrels to open.

Yes, Lance Foster, aka Surfer Dude, was the inside man for MS-13. In addition to Dietrich's testimony, Foster's and Escobar's cell phone records proved that they'd been in contact for weeks and in constant communication during the seminal week in December.

Yes, Dietrich said, Rachel Westergaard had died of her own hand from a heroin overdose. Right in front of him. Dietrich's account was disputed by Lottie Westergaard, who was still in the hospital recovering from a broken hip and shoulder from being thrown around. She said she saw Dietrich administer the fatal overdose himself.

And yes, even though the MS-13 drug pipeline had been temporarily disrupted and the Sons of Freedom were regrouping in Colorado, Dietrich said with confidence there would be new product on the streets of Grimstad within a week.

"You can throw me in prison in Bismarck and let all the gangbangers freeze to death in the Missouri River," Willie said, "but you can't do nothin' about demand. When there's demand, there'll be supply."

He was right.

Cassie skirted around the boys' project and went back to the kitchen, where she observed the three boys. They'd been so wrapped up in whatever it was they were doing they hadn't so much as looked up at her when she passed by.

Ben liked Kyle the moment he met him, and Kyle seemed to take Ben under his wing. Ben had no trouble understanding Kyle when he spoke, which was something Cassie found intriguing. Even when Kyle got excited about something — fishing, for instance — Ben hung on to every word and translated later.

Having a couple of older friends — especially one with a newfound reputation for danger — suited Ben perfectly, and Kyle treated Ben like the younger brother he'd never had. Kyle took Ben to school on the front handlebars of his bike — something Cassie didn't approve of and Isabel refused to watch. Kyle was easy to have around, and Cassie already knew she would miss him deeply when Lottie had recovered and Kyle could move back in with her.

The therapist seeing Kyle said the boy showed few signs of trauma, despite what had happened with T-Lock, his mother, and at his grandmother's house.

In fact, the therapist told Cassie, Kyle came across as remarkably composed.

"His life has been one trauma after the other," he said. "Maybe he's used to chaos and he welcomes the respite from it. One thing for sure: the kid is resilient. He doesn't let his special needs or his circumstances get him down. What I do know is that he likes you and considers you a kind of mother figure, maybe because his was so unstable."

Cassie was speechless. Inside, she was thrilled.

For Kyle, it was now a matter of months before the ice broke up on the river and he and Raheem could begin their great adventure. His River Box was under the bed at Grandma Lottie's, and he'd crossed out several more must-have items.

Although sometimes he wanted to shout about the boat trip he would take across America, he knew not to say anything about it except to Raheem. Otherwise, he knew, they'd try to stop him.

Of course, one thing he'd learned about himself was that he couldn't be stopped if he was determined to do something. It was a remarkable thing to find out about himself.

He thought of his mother often. He tried not to think of her face through the pickup window, or how she'd looked on that couch when he knew she was already gone. She looked peaceful, and that made him happy. The things that had happened in those last few days made him miss her almost as if she were a little girl, not his mother. He didn't tell the therapist that.

Kyle never thought about her life with T-Lock or the times she was so depressed he had to feed himself because she couldn't get out of bed. What he remembered were the small kindnesses — how she'd cup his face in her hands and bend over to kiss him, how she'd sing him to sleep sometimes, how she'd call him "her little man." How she'd taken his side when T-Lock called him a retard.

Because he wasn't.

Even the kids in school who used to tease him or ignore him looked at him differently now. The girls looked at him with sympathy: he had lost his mother.

The boys looked at him with awe and even respect. He had shot two gangbangers and stuck an arrow in the neck of a third man.

Teachers and counselors looked at him carefully, weighed his every word and gesture to note changes in his behavior. They tried to understand how a boy could go through what he had and not be changed by it.

What they didn't understand was that Kyle wasn't damaged.

He was *improved.*

Isabel put down her magazine and got up clumsily from the chair. She was wearing a large flowing dress covered with tropical flowers she'd had for years. She said she liked the apartment very much but she didn't know how long she could take Grimstad, even though a man had actually winked at her in the grocery store a couple of days ago.

She padded over to Cassie in her old moccasins and nodded toward the second cell phone Cassie had placed on the counter.

"How many phones do you have?" Isabel asked. Isabel was offended, Cassie knew, because she believed that cell phones caused brain cancer. She'd read it somewhere.

"Two."

"Why do you need more than one?"

"I just do."

"Why does that one play that awful song?"

"So I can tell them apart."

"Is it *him*?" Isabel asked.

Cassie was confused and shook her head.

"You know," Isabel said, pointing to the flowers Ian Davis had sent Cassie on her birthday the week before. *"Him."*

"No, he didn't call. And if he did he'd call my regular cell phone."

Davis was divorced, no kids. They had gone out twice. For Cassie, it was supremely uncomfortable and she drank too much each time. She liked Davis but couldn't wrap her mind around the concept of dating again after all these years. They'd gone to a movie — she was one of two women in the theater — and to dinner. Same ratio.

Although Davis was pleasant and polite to her, she couldn't stop thinking of the fact that at her apartment both Ben and Isabel were waiting for her to come home. She felt selfish. Sex was out of the question, and a deeper relationship would need to involve Ben.

At work they acknowledged each other but kept the fledgling relationship a secret.

Cassie knew it probably wouldn't end well. Still, though, she appreciated the flowers and Davis's attention.

Cassie's primary phone vibrated and she saw it was from Leslie Behaunek in North Carolina.

This time, Cassie went into her bedroom and shut the door. As she connected the call, she tossed two pillows from her bed toward the door and kicked them into place at the base of it. She didn't want Isabel to overhear.

"Leslie, hello."

"Hi, Cassie, sorry to call so late."

"It's late for you, not me. So what's up?"

Behaunek asked if Cassie had been getting any calls on what they both referred to as her "trucker phone."

"One or two a day," Cassie said. "No hits yet."

"Damn it."

They'd hatched the plan together after the Lizard King was released from jail. In the preliminary hearing, the judge had thrown out all the charges because of the illegal search. He'd also dismissed the assault charge on Cassie due to "insufficient evidence of the requisite degree of injury." In effect, the judge said that he thought the police, including Cassie, had been engaged in misconduct throughout the case.

Under a fake name, Leslie had joined several Internet-based trucking industry load board enterprises. Each day, she posted a new listing requiring a refrigerated truck for an LTL — "less than a load" — pickup in Grimstad, North Dakota. The destination for the LTL varied from day to day as well, so it wouldn't stand out as similar to the listing the day before. The phone number for an enterprising trucker to call was for Cassie's alternate cell phone.

"He'll call you eventually," Behaunek said. "That's his specialty — always keeping his trailer filled so he can get maximum income. He'll eventually work his way up there."

"Where is he now?" Cassie asked. Behaunek had told her the sheriff had illegally installed a GPS tracking device under Dale Spradley-Ronald Pergram's truck.

"He's off the grid." Behaunek sighed. "He must have found the device. All we know is his last known location was Savannah, but that was over a week ago. He could be all the way across the country by now."

Cassie said, "I told the sheriff."

There was a long pause. Cassie could hear Behaunek take a sip and set down a wineglass. "You must trust him," she said.

"I do. He knows all about the Lizard King and he'd love to help shut him down."

"Do you have a plan yet for when he actually shows up?"

Cassie said, "I'm working on it."

"So how are things going? Are they calmer now?"

"A little," Cassie said. "But like I was told, this is the new Wild West."

"I'd like to see it someday."

"Come in the summer." Cassie laughed.

Isabel was giving her the eye when she came out of the bedroom and Cassie ignored her.

She paused and looked over the project in her living room with her hands on her hips. The boys had upended three card tables — they had to borrow two of them from other cops down the hall — and had placed them end to end on the carpet. A rope had been strung from leg to leg and blankets had been draped over the ropes. Ben was in back, Raheem in the middle, and Kyle up front. Kyle was speaking so quickly Cassie couldn't understand what he was saying.

"What is this?" she asked Ben.

Ben didn't even look up. He was too enraptured in the project.

"We're building a boat," he said.

Cassie thought it charming.

After he'd gone back to school, Kyle had asked Cassie to take him back to the Badlands on the weekend. Kyle wanted to see the photo of Theodore Roosevelt arresting the boat thieves again.

She'd agreed and they made a family outing of it, bringing along her mother, Ben, and Raheem. While they were in the museum, Kyle wandered away from the others and noticed a display about Roosevelt called "Early Tragedy." He stood at the display for a long time, struggling with reading the placards. But he found himself glued in place when he learned that Roosevelt had lost his mother, too. Not only that, but his wife and mother died hours apart in the same house.

Kyle was stunned. Theodore Roosevelt lost his mother and his wife before he went west to the Badlands. Before he pursued the boat thieves on the icy river, became a colonel and charged up San Juan Hill. Before he became president of the United

States and got his face on Mount Rush-
more.

He thought about that all the way back to
Grimstad in Cassie's car. He and Theodore
Roosevelt had something in common. Kyle
found himself smiling at that.

Colonel Theodore Roosevelt.

Captain Kyle.

ACKNOWLEDGMENTS

The author would like to sincerely thank Sheriff Scott Busching of Williams County, North Dakota, for his assistance, experience, wisdom, and expertise. Thanks also to Barb Peterson and Fred Walker for their sharp North Dakota insight.

Special thanks to Attorney Becky Reif for her excellent legal assistance.

My invaluable first readers were Laurie Box, Molly Donnell, and Roxanne Woods. Thanks again.

Kudos to Don Hajicek for cjbox.net and Jennifer Fonnesbeck for social media expertise and merchandise sales.

It's a sincere pleasure to work with the professionals at St. Martin's Minotaur, including the fantastic Jennifer Enderlin, Andy Martin, Hector DeJean, and the incomparable Sally Richardson.

Ann Rittenberg, you know you're the greatest.

ABOUT THE AUTHOR

C.J. Box is the author of twenty novels including the award-winning Joe Pickett series. He's the winner of the Anthony Award, Prix Calibre 38 (France), the Macavity Award, the Gumshoe Award, the Barry Award, and an Edgar Award. His most recent novel, *Endangered*, debuted at #2 on the *New York Times* bestseller list. The novels have been translated into 27 languages and have sold over three million copies in the U.S. alone. *Open Season, Blue Heaven, Nowhere To Run,* and *The Highway* have been optioned for film and television. Box lives with his family outside of Cheyenne, Wyoming.